Sawford turned to
dispassionate. I lifted m
His expression shifted, a
depths of his pupils, radi
nearer, his eyes on me cc
felt the stone wall agair
step for step until his body touched mine. A slight smile
curled on his lips as he placed his hands on the wall
either side of my shoulders, pinning me in place.

He dipped his head toward mine. His warm breath
caressed my mouth, and I inhaled the aroma of spices
and masculinity. I had only to lift my head a fraction to
meet his lips. He brushed his mouth against mine, and
my skin tightened in response. He drew back, and I
whimpered in frustration. I was a woman starved, my
tormentor denying me what my body craved. I tipped
my head up, unable to think of anything save those lips.
He smiled triumphantly, holding his mouth
tantalizingly close.

"I will only kiss you if you ask."

Her Dark Seduction

by

Emily Royal

This is a work of fiction. Names, characters, places, and incidents are either the product of the author's imagination or are used fictitiously, and any resemblance to actual persons living or dead, business establishments, events, or locales, is entirely coincidental.

Her Dark Seduction

Cover Art by *The Wild Rose Press, Inc.*

The Wild Rose Press, Inc.
PO Box 708
Adams Basin, NY 14410-0708
Visit us at www.thewildrosepress.com

Publishing History
First Edition, 2021
Trade Paperback ISBN 978-1-5092-3391-5
Digital ISBN 978-1-5092-3392-2

Published in the United States of America

Dedication

For Sarah.
No explanation necessary.
Thank you
xxx

Acknowledgments

This book was a labor of love and will always hold a special place in my heart because I achieved so many firsts with it, with the help and support of so many.

Firstly to Margaret, for being kind, but also brutally honest with the first manuscript critique I ever had. It was your encouragement which first made me believe in my writing. To my fabulous beta buddies, thank you for being my first and best tribe of fellow writers. Thank you to Roger, my Kentish inspiration, and to Colm & Des for your support and advice when I was wondering what to do with this book I'd just drafted. And, as always, to Neil, Jasmine, and Frankie, thank you for being there!

Prologue

The metallic smell of blood—my blood—faded, but the screams remained, seeping from the stones in the wall and echoing around me. They were the cries of my fellow inmates, both those who'd preceded me and the ones who would follow. The darkness in my cell mirrored the black void in my heart, which had long ago swallowed up any hope.

As the screams gave way to low moans, a faint scuffling sound grew louder until its source moved in front of my eyes. I was not alone. I took a breath, wheezing against the stone floor. The shape turned. Two silver pinpricks flashed, then sharp, yellow teeth. I bared my own teeth, hissing until the shape drew back. One animal against another.

How had I come to this? For my entire life, five and twenty years, I'd built a fortress around my heart and mind, protecting the soul within. Yet over the course of one short year, that fortress had been destroyed by nobody's hands but my own.

As a woman, I was the property of others since birth, a commodity to be used to suit their purposes. But my mind had been free, nurtured and encouraged by my beloved Maman. She schooled me to protect my maidenhead and my heart. Dearest Maman, who'd had so much love to give. Her one weakness had been her desperate need to be loved in return, and she'd paid for it with her life.

Lying on the cold, damp floor, separated from my own child, only now did I truly understand her despair. Her lover was dead. The sweet delivery from torment that death gave her had been made bitter by the knowledge she was abandoning her only child—me—to a traitor and madman. My father.

Now my own life had come full circle, my fate identical to hers, except for one thing.

The man I loved still lived.

A hoarse cry echoed from deep within the dungeons, and I shifted, the cold air contrasting with the white hot shards of pain in my shattered arm. My body was lost. Twisted and broken, it lay on the floor of my cell as my mind drifted above it and looked down at the pathetic creature I had become.

It would be all too easy to let myself slip away, to surrender to the pain.

Yet I had to fight for them.

For him.

My husband.

What would they do to him? These men who, with cold detachment, had told me of their ability to keep a man alive, screaming for days. Would his screams join my own—and those of the long-dead victims who haunted me?

Tomorrow they would destroy me, but I would fight them—take their blows and field their questions. I would never see the sun again, but my death would bring about life—the life of my beloved.

Spots of gray stained the walls as the light bled from the first rays of the sun, picking out the shadows of the pock-marked texture of the stone. With a squeal, my companion turned, claws scraping, a blur of a tail disappearing into the shadows.

An echo of footsteps whispered in the distance before growing louder, the rhythm of a man with a purpose.

Dawn had broken.

They were coming for me.

Chapter 1

"Wife, remove your clothes."

Standing in the center of the solar, the cold of the stone floor seeped into the soles of my bare feet. The voice coming from the figure propped up in the bed by the far wall was harsh and showed far greater strength than the hand which had gripped mine when the priest had placed the wedding ring on my finger that morning.

From his bed, my new husband watched me. Clad in a white nightshirt, he looked like a ghostly apparition. His eyes gleamed like two fetid yellow orbs sunken into aging flesh. At that moment he reminded me of an emaciated wolf, hungry and vicious and relishing the anticipation of sinking its teeth into the warm, pulsating throat of a frightened rabbit in its path.

I was that rabbit.

He licked his lips as if to savor my terror, and I curled my hands into fists, fingers tightening against my slickened palms. I focused on the sharp sensation as I dug my nails in, and the effort caused a slight tremor in my arms but achieved its aim by preventing the rest of my body from shaking. I closed my eyes, wanting to hide within the darkness, which had terrified me as a child.

The loss of one of my senses heightened childhood memories. For a moment I was transported, and the smell of burning wood and oil, the sound of flames crackling in the air, enveloped me as I heard the whimpers, cries, and screams that had echoed around my father's courtyard on that long ago, terrible day.

Coarse and grating, my husband's voice brought me back to the present. "You will do as I bid, madam, or Monsieur Sawford will do it for you."

"My Lord."

A different voice spoke, softly, and I caught a slight movement to my left. A tall shape stepped forward, and in spite of myself, I turned my head.

It was Sawford, my husband's manservant. He had been standing beside Lord Mortlock when I'd arrived at Mortlock Fort that morning. I had kept my head down as Papa helped me out of the carriage, and then focused on the ground as we followed the steward into the main hall. I'd looked up only once, when we'd approached two pairs of feet.

Two men had bowed to me—one, my betrothed, the other his manservant. I'd held out my hand to the younger man, to Sawford, thinking him to be the one I'd be marrying. But Papa had corrected me by steering me toward the outstretched hand of the older man. "Lisetta, would you humiliate me in front of your new husband?" he'd hissed.

The older man smiled then, curling his lip up and revealing his rotting yellow teeth. "No matter, Baron Shoreton. She will learn respect. She is young yet."

I was hardly that. At four and twenty summers, I was considered by many as beyond marriageable age. Papa had refused many petitions for my hand, and I'd begun to prepare myself for retirement to the convent near Shoreton, until the news of Lady Mortlock's death ignited his interest in opening betrothal negotiations. As

Lord Mortlock looked older even than Papa, I doubted if my age would matter much to him.

The color rushed to my cheeks then as I kept my eyes downcast and studied the younger hand I had initially reached for. It was large, with long, slim fingers and it bore the tell-tale scars of a warrior, despite the man being a clerk.

Sawford had known I was staring for he flexed his fingers and let out a heavy breath, almost a sigh. I lifted my gaze to his face, but had been unable to meet his eyes. He was tall—considerably taller than I, with thick dark hair that almost reached his shoulders. A faint scar curled across his chin, giving him an air of brutality, and a slight growth of beard surrounded his mouth. His lips were full and sensual, yet exuded masculinity.

I unconsciously parted my own lips as I studied his mouth, running my tongue across my top lip to ease the sudden dryness. For a moment, the ghost of a smile flickered across his features, then slowly turned into a sneer. Lord save me, he'd known my mind. I forced my expression back into the mask I wore, which in the years since my mother's death had begun to feel like my own skin. It was the mask of indifference and disdain, hiding my true feelings beneath. I'd learned that to harbor any sense of emotion, let alone love, led to one's downfall. As a girl, I was the property of my Papa—as a bride, the property of my husband. To have feelings for any man and display them, would lead to ruination and death. I would not willingly share my mother's fate.

"Sawford."

I cringed at the rise of that ancient, sinister voice. Having successfully disposed of his daughter to secure his alliance with Mortlock, Papa had already left for Shoreton. I was on my own.

I sensed the man standing behind me before light fingertips touched my upper arm. I stepped away from him and, uncurling my fists, took my nightshift in both hands, pulled it over my head, then dropped the garment onto the floor. My skin tightened with a combination of chill and revulsion, but I lifted my head and looked my husband in the eye, swallowing any shame at my nudity. I forced myself to remain calm, despite the fact my stomach churned and threatened to expel what little I'd managed to force down during the wedding feast.

From a distance, my new husband inspected me. The bruises on my stomach from Papa's last beating were fading but the bridegroom showed no sign of seeing them.

I stood there, naked, expecting to be summoned to join him in the bed, but the order did not come. Instead, I watched as he slipped his hand under the bed fur near his waist. For a moment he gazed at me, then he closed his eyes and gave out a strangled grunt. His hand then reappeared and he wiped it on the fur.

My wedding night.

Papa had told me a wife's sole purpose was to serve her husband's needs and yet, the scraps of conversations I'd overheard when the servants at Shoreton gossiped about their lovers told a different story—a story of pleasure.

However, looking at my new husband, it became all too clear Papa was right. There would be no pleasure.

"Come closer." At my husband's bidding, I moved

toward the bed until he raised his hand.

"Far enough, woman. Sawford, you know what to do."

From behind me, I heard the sound of material tearing. I looked around in fear, not knowing what horrors my husband had in store for me, and I suppressed a cry as my gaze met the manservant's for the first time. His eyes were a brilliant, icy blue, radiating a sharp intelligence. I saw a flash of a flame in them before it was extinguished, and he regarded me coldly. My skin tightened at his searching expression, which began to strip away my calm exterior and plunder the depths of my mind until I had nowhere to hide. I could withstand the physical nudity of having my body on display for my husband's pleasure, but Sawford's gaze had the power to expose my mind and render me completely naked. I took a step back, unwittingly into the candlelight, widening my eyes at the glint of a knife in his hand, yet he was the one who stopped and murmured under his breath as he looked at me.

A low chuckle came from the bed. "My wife has eyes to drown in, does she not, Sawford?"

The servant said nothing as he held up my shift and continued to tear it into pieces.

My husband laughed again, then changed the subject. He spoke to his servant conversationally, almost casually, as if I was no longer in the room.

"You did well in brokering the purchase of the mare. I trust you'll have no difficulty finding a stallion to stud her for me. There ought to be plenty among the stables, but you need to find one with an acceptable bloodline, who will not whinny too loudly over the

8

deed."

"Aye, my lord. I shall visit the stables directly."

Sawford's voice was low, a deep rumble that reverberated from his chest, and it made me shiver. The knife caught the candlelight again and to my horror, he drew the blade along his arm, keeping his eyes trained on me as he cut. I heard him curse as he looked down. A deep gash ran along his forearm and the blood was already running down in rivulets. He held out his arm and scarlet droplets scattered onto the tattered remnants of my gown. He picked up the pieces of fabric, rubbed them along his arm and stained the shreds of silk. My husband drew back the fur and Sawford walked to the bed, then held his arm over it, letting the drips fall onto the white linen.

"Good, very good." My husband's voice was thick and hoarse as he nodded his approval. "And now deal with my wife."

The servant moved to stand behind me once more. The fingers which only moments ago had brushed against me almost in a caress now curled painfully around my arm as he pulled my naked form toward him. I lost my balance and fell against his muscular body. Drawing me to him, he bent his head, pressing his face against my hair. The heat from his breath seeped through to my skin, heightening the sensitive spot at the base of my neck. Then a fur was placed round my shoulders with a gentle touch before he gripped my arm again and forced me out into the passageway. The fall in temperature was unexpected. I pinched my lips together but could not control my body's reaction and started to tremble.

"Draw the fur close around you. 'Tis a cold night.

Do you wish for another?" His voice was a whisper, his breath forming a faint mist. His closeness was unsettling, and I said nothing.

"I would have an answer."

I kept my voice firm and steady to disguise my discomfort. "I am not answerable to a serf."

At that, he increased his pace and the sound of his boots clomping echoed through the passageway as he dragged me along with him. Eventually, we came to a dark wooden door, and he opened it. It was the room where my maid Harwyn had prepared me for my wedding night before leading me to the solar; my bridal gown was still folded over the chair where she had left it.

Sawford pushed me through the door, then turned me to face him. Standing tall, dressed almost completely in black, he was an imposing figure who was obviously trying to intimidate me as punishment for my earlier words.

I set my jaw into a hard line and tipped my head up to look at him, determined not to give him the satisfaction of witnessing his success. His eyes met mine, the blue as sharp as a winter's sky, and he continued to stare at me as if trying to read my soul. I stuck my chin out and used my well-rehearsed tone of contempt before stepping back and waving a dismissive hand at him as if attempting to swat a fly.

"A servant has no business in a lady's room."

The flicker of anger in his eyes disappeared almost as soon as I saw it forming and without warning, he pulled me to him and crushed my mouth with his own. He grasped my hair with his free hand, forcing my head back to receive his kiss while his lips moved over mine.

He splayed his hand across my back and moved it lower to caress and squeeze my buttocks. I let out a cry at the shock of his touch, and he thrust his tongue through my parted lips. He invaded my mouth, running his tongue along my teeth and curling it around my own, a velvety soft weapon teasing, probing, and assaulting my senses. He leaned forward, supporting my weight as I was bent backward, and I became aware of his hardness against my belly.

The fur slipped from my shoulders and fell to the floor ,and he gave a low growl and moved his free hand to my chest. I felt my nipples tighten, as he brushed across them to lightly cup my breast, and a wetness began to pool between my thighs. He teased my nipple with his fingers while he continued to kiss me; then he moved his hand away. With a whimper, I pressed myself back against him, not wanting his touch to end.

He lifted his hand to my face, caressing my mouth with his thumb as he had done earlier with his lips, but this time his touch was tender. I closed my eyes and parted my lips, and he ran his thumb across my bottom lip before pushing it gently inside my mouth. Instinctively, I drew it in and began curling my tongue around, feeling the edge of his fingernail. He tasted of the honeyed figs I adored, which I'd been too unsettled to eat at the wedding feast. I relished that taste now and gave a little sigh as I found more sweetness.

Abruptly, he pulled away, his lips curling into the sneer he'd worn that morning. I flushed with shame at my wanton reaction, which had angered him so much. I wanted to chastise him for dishonoring me but did not trust myself to speak.

As if he knew my thoughts, he gave a dark laugh.

"Scratch the surface of any woman and you find the whore within."

"I am no whore," I retorted. "I am your mistress and you have no right to—"

He silenced me again with his mouth, sending a fresh assault of sensations to my center as he palmed my breast. I pulled away, but not before my chest tightened with that same exquisite feeling.

"Your body betrays you, *cherie*. Mayhap the goods are not as unsullied as your father would have us believe."

His words made no sense, but I flushed at my reaction to his closeness. The silence hung between us until I lifted my head and gave him a look of contempt.

Sawford made no move to kiss me again, but released me from his embrace and merely gave a small sound of derision before stepping from the room and slamming the door in my face. His quick, heavy footsteps faded into the distance.

I stepped back until I felt the bed against the back of my legs and sank down on the mattress, the bed ropes creaking. I was free from Papa, but my new cage harbored new horrors. Unobserved I was able to let the mask slip, unlocking the tears which slid down my cheeks in silence.

Chapter 2

The next morning, after we broke our fast, my husband lined up the men of his household to swear fealty to me, Lady Mortlock.

I had never met the previous Lady Mortlock, yet her death had sealed my fate. With no mother to prepare me for my role as a wife, I had listened to Papa's instructions on how to be dutiful to my husband and show due reverence and gratitude for the honor of being Lady Mortlock. Papa had been a close friend and ally of the old King Stephen and an active participant in Stephen's campaigns to thwart his sister, the Empress Matilda, when she attempted to claim the throne of England. He'd strongly objected to any suitor who fell outside his circle of close associates and fellow supporters of Stephen. Though Stephen had been dead three years, his successor, the current King Henry, still faced much objection.

I had long suspected Papa of being a traitor to Henry. Might my new husband be one also? He had a small army of men now lined up to swear fealty to me. But what of their loyalty to the king?

Each man approached me in turn, bowed and kissed my hand. The knights were first and I kept my face impassive as they swore to protect me, only inclining my head slightly to the left and nodding in response. Sawford was next. Clad in black, he wore the clothes of a clerk rather than a knight's *hauberk*. He walked toward me with a casual, easy grace.

My hand trembled.

He bowed and took my hand, his grip a little tighter than that of those who had gone before him, his lips lingering on my hand a little longer. Before straightening, he tipped his head and met my eyes with his piercing gaze, a curl of dry amusement on his lips.

The squires came after him, followed by the steward and, finally, the senior servants. The last squire was a young man by the name of Percy. He smiled after kissing my hand, a gentle blush spreading over his face. He was a mere boy—barely six and ten—and clearly nervous. For a moment, the mask slipped and I squeezed his hand in reassurance, returning his smile.

A cough brought me to my senses. Sawford watched me with narrowed eyes. I pulled my hand away from Percy's.

"I fear my wife finds our gallantry tedious. Come." My husband dismissed his men before holding his arm out to Sawford for support. My heart sank when Percy turned to smile at me before following the squires out.

****

For the next few days, I saw little of my husband during the day, but after the evening meal he would send for me. Sawford accompanied me to the solar where, each night, my husband ordered me to remove my nightshift and stand before him while he pleasured himself. Staring straight ahead, I let my mind drift. Harwyn had taught me to concentrate on each beat: one, two, three, all the way to one hundred, before starting again. It was a technique I used to disassociate myself from the horrific events around me. Afterward, Sawford helped me back into my nightshift before returning me to my room. Other than his hand on my arm, he barely touched me.

On my second night at Mortlock, I had tipped my head toward him, expecting a kiss like that he gave the first night. But he merely curled his mouth into a smile and pushed me back before closing the door in my face.

The Mortlock servants were wary, unfriendly even, yet efficient in their duties, and I had little to do. The chatelaine, a woman of over two score years, had run the household for many years. My husband's previous wives had not involved themselves in her activities, and she did not expect my arrival to change that. I should have been disappointed, but I wasn't. Having been schooled by Maman in the customs and traditions of a lady, I had a right to expect to fulfill that role here. The atmosphere in the building, however, was so oppressive I was glad to remove myself from it and chose instead to spend much of my time outdoors in the grounds.

I re-established my authority over the chatelaine when I discovered there was nobody to tend to healing in the household. The injured or sick either had to make do or travel. I had some skill at healing and had often helped Maman at Shoreton when she tended to our servants. Of all the duties of the mistress of the castle, this was the one I took most fulfillment from, and Maman had encouraged me. She'd pointed out the different herbs, flowers and berries, explaining their healing properties and showing me which ones could be used to sustain life and warning me of the dangers of those which invited death. A similar occupation here at Mortlock would give me a much-needed purpose. That same morning, I told the chatelaine what I wanted, and she arranged for a room to be cleaned and prepared for me and began to accumulate the list of supplies I had given her. She stiffened her body in dislike at my haughty demeanor but obeyed my instructions flawlessly.

A maidservant was cleaning the room when I arrived to inspect it. Nodding unsmilingly when she curtsied, I immediately dismissed her. She was an old woman and looked harmless enough, but I knew not who to trust and had no desire to form any attachments, however slight. The one person I could trust was Harwyn. Papa had permitted me to bring her with me, not out of compassion, but for the benefit of having one less mouth to feed at Shoreton. Nevertheless, I was grateful. During the dark winter mornings at Shoreton, when I would rise before daybreak, she'd light a candle in my room so I would not wake in the dark. Often she woke me herself. Aware of the nightmares that plagued me, she would take me in her arms, stroking my head as she had done ever since my mother died. She alone knew the feelings running deep within me and understood my fears.

I was constantly watched, often sensing someone following me—an echo of a step in a corridor, the twitch of a wall-hanging as I walked past. Only outdoors did I feel safe from prying eyes. Away from the ostentatious main garden, a wilder, unkempt garden ran along the outer edge of the bailey wall. It was beautiful and natural, sloping down toward a copse, through which a small stream ran into a lake. Wildflowers and grasses grew all over and, on exploring it, I discovered a seat beside a tree. In this garden, I found peace.

The garden brought back memories of my home at Shoreton—distant memories of another life, a small child, happy in the loving care of her Maman, who would walk with her in the sunshine and relate tales of knights and chivalry. Maman would speak of her hopes for my future—the joy of having a home of my own to manage, the love I would have from my children and the comfort I would take from the occupation and duties of a lady. I heard her words but never truly listened, missing the undertones of her voice. The unspoken notes of despair in her voice were brought about by her marriage to a cruel man and her unfulfilled yearning for love. That yearning had taken her from me. Now, I had none to care for me except Harwyn.

****

Shortly after I arrived at Mortlock Fort, I asked my husband for permission to explore the estate on horseback. By making such a direct request, I wanted to show I was not afraid of him.

I found him in the solar, deep in conversation with Sawford, bent over a desk covered in papers. At my request, he cocked his head to one side, blinking to clear the film over his eyes.

His mannerisms were easy to read, unlike the body language of the taller man who stood silently beside him. His yellowed eyes showed surprise at my boldness, followed by mild irritation. Before he blinked again, a twitch in his lips implied he would grant my request.

"Very well, your behavior has been exemplary; but you must take an escort."

"My lord, if I might—" the manservant said.

"No, Sawford. I need you here. Take her ladyship

to the stables and send for Wyatt to accompany her."

I recognized Wyatt as he approached the stables. Thick set and gap-toothed, he had little to recommend him other than being the youngest son of a baron. He had been recently knighted, and his golden spurs glinted in the sunlight as he mounted his horse. Like all men, he desired power. The lust for it exuded from his voice, his arrogant stance in the saddle and curl of his lip as he dismissed Sawford.

Ignoring him, Sawford held his hand out to help me to mount. Lifting me onto the saddle, he issued a quiet warning.

"Do nothing foolish, woman."

Were it not for the dark expression in his eyes, I would have believed I'd imagined his words. He cast a quick glance in Wyatt's direction before he gave me a slight nod and returned to the main building. I followed him with my gaze before Wyatt's voice pulled me back.

"I hear you are eager for company, my lady."

"I merely wish to ride," I snapped. "I have no wish to engage in conversation with you."

Spurring the mare on, I rode out of the stable yard, ignoring the servants bowing before their mistress.

The spring air almost banished my melancholy. Riding through the forest, seeing the leaf buds beginning to form, I could almost believe I was living the blessed life of a noblewoman—one with a purpose and a loving family. A life filled with fulfillment from tending to the people that depended on me.

Urging my horse into a gallop, I closed my eyes and tipped my head skyward, relishing the warmth of the sun on my face, safe in the knowledge that my horse and I rode together as one. The soft rush of the breeze danced in a melodic rhythm with the mare's hoof beats, though they were soon drowned out by the staccato footfall of another horse.

Looking behind, I saw Wyatt approaching. Though I slowed to a canter, he continued to bear down on me until he drew level and steered his horse against my own, forcing me to stop.

"You are not to leave my side, lady."

"For what purpose?"

"For your safety. Come, 'tis time we returned. Your husband has never taken kindly to any of his wives running about unfettered."

"How dare you speak to me so!" I cried.

Grinning, he reached out, his hand moving too quickly for me to pull back, and he took my wrist, squeezing it with his thick, fleshy fingers.

"Let me go," I said.

His smile widened, showing the gaps between his teeth as he thrust his face close. I wrinkled my nostrils at his sour breath, and he chuckled.

"Who is it? Has he been chosen yet?"

"I do not understand."

"Come, come, my lady. You've been here for three whole days. Are you telling me the deed has not yet been done?"

I shook my head and tried to pull free, but his grip only tightened.

"My bloodline should suffice," he said, the stench of his breath intensifying. "My lord Mortlock values me highly. Mayhap he'll reward me now I have earned my spurs—and what a tasty reward it would be."

His grin disappeared and his eyes narrowed.

Swallowing my fear, I smiled back at him, my free

hand trembling only slightly where I held a knife against his wrist, pressing into the flesh where his vein lay. Too often, I had fended off unwelcome advances from Papa's men. From an early age I always concealed a small knife about my person for defense.

"Perhaps we should ask my husband who he values more," I said, "a baron's younger son, a landless lackey who lives in servitude, or his wife—the only child of a baron, with all the estates and titles bestowed on her."

His fingers twitched, and I increased the pressure on the knife.

"The blade is sharp, Monsieur Wyatt. I would advise you to loosen your hold."

"I could snap your neck, woman, whether your blade cuts me or no."

I gripped the knife tighter, steadying my hand.

"How might you explain a dead wife to your master when she has been placed in your care?" I challenged. "Try it—if you dare."

He withdrew his hand. Tucking my knife into my kirtle, I reined my horse, turning her in a tight circle, and spurred her into a canter, aware Wyatt was following. As soon as I spotted the outbuildings surrounding Mortlock Fort, I called out to the stable hands to assist me, my voice almost breaking with relief as they came into view. Dismounting, I turned my back on Wyatt and crossed the yard, but not before he called out to me.

"You will soon learn your true value, woman. Then I shall take my due and make you pay for your insult today."

Chapter 3

Helping me dress for the evening meal, Harwyn touched my stomach with her fingertips. It had been seven days since my marriage.

"The bruises are almost gone, lady."

"Aye." I smiled at her. "They no longer hurt."

"Perhaps a husband does not beat his wife as often as a father beats his daughter."

"I know not yet, Harwyn."

"I wager Lord Mortlock would not administer a beating over a spilled flagon of wine or bowl of potage."

Papa had once beaten me so severely for tipping over his wine that I was unable to eat for two days. His methods of education were deliberate, the blows aimed at the center of my body where they could be concealed. All for my benefit. Visible marks on a woman's body were evidence of disobedience. No man would want such a woman for a wife.

With Papa, years of observation had taught me what to expect from him. As for my husband, I spent little time with him. Yet, even in a few short days, I noticed a sly furtiveness in his behavior. His men would act differently around him, as if they anticipated something.

Sighing, I shook my head. "I would rather my husband discipline me as Papa did. At least I would know what he expected of me. But, I do not understand him. Something seems afoot. The very air here is thick with it, and it centers on him. Do the servants speak to you of it?"

"No, lady. They say little and cease all conversation when I approach them."

"I am sorry for that, Harwyn. I had hoped you'd find some companionship here."

"I have you, my lady."

"And I you."

I lifted my arms as Harwyn helped me into my overgown, pulling it over my head, and smoothing it down. The pale gray silk matched the color of my eyes and provided a deep contrast to my black hair.

"Harwyn, do you know aught of his manservant?"

"Lady?"

"The one who accompanies him everywhere."

"Ah, Monsieur Vane."

"Vane?"

"Vane Sawford." Harwyn rolled her eyes. "From what little I hear, he has bedded most of the maidservants, who regularly vie for his attention. Rumor has it, he seduced one of the Lord's previous wives, though I also hear she threw herself at him like a wanton."

"Idle gossip, nothing more."

"Nay, my lady. Lord Mortlock had her put to death for adultery…"

Her voice trailed off as I gasped.

"Oh, my lady, forgive me!"

I shook my head. "There's nothing wrong in telling me, Harwyn. I must know where the danger lies."

Harwyn sat me down and began brushing my hair

before braiding it. She secured a veil over my hair, and placed a light hand on my shoulders to indicate she had finished.

"Be careful of him."

"Harwyn?"

"Monsieur Vane. He moves about too quietly for my liking and always appears when you least expect it. Do not secure his notice. He has a way of seeing right inside a person."

"Nonsense!" I said. "How could you form an opinion of him so readily?"

"Out of necessity for your welfare."

I thought of my first encounter with Vane Sawford, the strange sensations I had experienced and my suspicions of being watched. I took Harwyn's hand.

"I know," I whispered. "I am grateful for your caution. Rest assured, I do not intend to spend any more time in his company than is absolutely necessary."

I stood up and Harwyn moved to open the door.

"What is this?"

She bent down and picked up a folded piece of parchment and handed it to me. Written in a clear, bold hand was a brief message in French.

Have a care, Lady Lisetta. You are in danger, but you have a friend here who watches over you.

"What can it mean?" Harwyn sounded worried. "Someone knows you can read."

"Not necessarily," I replied, "but it may be a trick. We must be ever watchful."

"Is there any truth in those words?"

I laughed mirthlessly. "The danger, aye. I am merely the latest in a long line of disposable wives. But as to having a friend, I trust none but you."

"Wise words."

My smile faded. "I will never forget Maman, of that you can be certain."

****

That night, after the usual ritual in the solar, my husband spoke to me.

"I will be leaving tomorrow, wife, and expect no trouble from you in my absence. Sawford will tend to my affairs in my stead, and I'm certain he will take care of you."

As Sawford took my arm, my husband called out after us.

"I expect that mare to be in foal when I return, Sawford."

Sawford bowed before returning me to my room. His closeness compared to previous nights was unsettling. We reached the threshold of my room. To my shame, my heartbeat increased and the heat rose in my face. I was growing afraid of him. He simultaneously thrilled and terrified me. His heavy, powerful silence was overwhelming, but also compelling.

"You are to be in charge of the stables as well as the estate?" I couldn't help asking. My curiosity was piqued and I wanted desperately to break the silence.

He let out a sharp breath through his nose.

"After a fashion."

His jaw tightened. Was he angry at my curiosity, a trait which in a woman was more likely to yield punishment than praise? Lord save me. Would he tell my husband? The mask slipped back into place, and I kept my voice low and cold.

"A rather strange occupation for a mere serf."

He snorted. "You know very well, madam, that you hold me in considerably more interest than you would a *mere serf.*"

Shocked at his perception, I did not trust myself to speak further. I should have heeded Harwyn's words. He released his grip, and I ran across the threshold, shutting the door in his face. I leaned against the thick piece of oak separating us, terrified he might force his way through; but, part of me wished he would, hoping he would touch me once more, as gently as he had caressed my mouth with his thumb. I clung to that moment of tenderness.

That cursed note. It affected me more than I cared to admit. The hope that someone watched over me in friendship had shattered, not comforted me. Though I loved Harwyn, I desperately wanted a friend here. But I had no desire to risk trusting a stranger. In all likelihood, my husband had asked someone to spy on me. Perhaps this was how he removed his wives. I served little purpose for him other than to perform a nightly ritual in the solar. He would soon tire of me, and then I would suffer the same fate of my predecessors. Was the note the first step in this process?

I bit my lip, letting out a cry when I drew blood. A noise made me fall silent. I held my breath and pressed my ear against the door, straining to listen. The door handle moved and I backed away. Dear Lord; Sawford was still there. After a moment, I heard the telltale sound of his boots clicking on the floor, growing fainter.

Sawford was gone, but he had heard my cry. I felt horribly vulnerable. While my husband was away, I would be entirely at his mercy.

****

Over the next few days, the oppressive atmosphere lifted, and I spent the daylight hours tending to the various injuries and ailments of the household staff. I engaged in little conversation with those I treated, tying bandages, applying poultices, and administering healing herbs in silence. I studied each visitor carefully for signs they were the author of the note, but with no success. Harwyn kept watch when she spent time with the other servants, but after a sennight we almost gave up on the idea of ever finding out who had composed it.

So it was much to my surprise when, one morning, I walked into the treatment room to find a folded piece of parchment on the table beside a jar of dried rosemary. I opened it to reveal the most beautiful love poem I had ever read.

The words were written in the same hand which had penned the first note. They spoke of the beauty of my eyes, likening them to the moonlit reflection of the lake. Anywhere else, those words would be enchanting, but here they only heightened my sense of danger. Someone was either deliberately trying to entrap me or I had an admirer. Both possibilities could be fatal. I closed my eyes, trying to calm my fluttering heartbeat but opened them almost immediately, as I was overpowered by a specific memory: the smell of burning oil, the sound of wood crackling, and my mother's screams…

A knock on the door brought me to my senses. Composing myself, I tucked the parchment into the front of my gown and called out. The maidservant who walked in, showing me a minor burn to her hand, was totally unaware of what I felt inside.

Occupation was the best cure for my inner turmoil. I busied myself with setting the room into order, cataloguing the various items, and treating the handful of servants who visited me that morning.

After I had dismissed my last visitor, I pulled out the poem and read it again. How cruel fate could be! On second reading, the words were even more passionate, describing me as if the author knew me intimately. Below the poem was a brief note saying that the author watched over me from afar and would fight to his last breath to keep me from harm. Did I have a protector? If so, he was surely doomed, for I was constantly watched. Though my husband was away, his men stared at me with their lustful gazes. I would hurry past them, always fearing they would force themselves on me.

But not Sawford. His gaze held no lust. He regarded me dispassionately, calculatingly, as if sizing me up to determine my worth as a commodity.

Percy was the only man in Mortlock's employ I felt I could come close to liking. His youthful exuberance for swordplay and potential knighthood had yet to be tempered by the harsh realities of life. Whenever he saw me, he nodded and smiled, and I struggled not to respond, desperately wanting to discourage him. My fear was that his partiality, if noticed, risked both our heads. Was he the author of the note?

My cheeks burned with shame at the small spark of desire those words of love ignited. I thought of Eve, who had given into sinful temptation, condemning every woman to a similar fate. Was it so sinful to wish for love? My mother had longed for it and had paid the greatest price of all. In her last words to me, she'd begged me not to give in to temptation, not only of the flesh but, also, of the heart. My flesh had reacted too swiftly and easily to Vane Sawford's touch. Now my heart showed the same weakness for a few marks on a piece of parchment. I was a fool, weaker than my poor mother had been and destined to fail as she had.

Desperate for sanctuary, I scrunched up the parchment in my hand and left the room, running up the spiral staircase to my bedchamber. On reaching the top, I gave a small cry of fright. The tall silhouette of Vane Sawford stood on the top step. Had I not stopped so abruptly, I would have run straight into him.

The only acknowledgement he gave me was a slight lift of his eyebrows. He stepped closer, and I froze, panting. I squeezed my fist against the note, concealing it behind me, praying he'd not heard the sound of the parchment crackling. His cold blue gaze bore into mine, and I quailed under his scrutiny. He knew.

He lifted his hand to my face, and I stared back, clenching my jaw while fighting the urge to run. My skin tightened as he ran his fingers across my cheek. I parted my lips and took in a sharp breath. He kept his gaze locked on mine until he removed his hand. He looked down, his eyes widening. Following his gaze, to see what had fascinated him, I noticed a bead of moisture on the tip of his forefinger. It was a solitary tear.

I straightened my shoulders and spoke coldly.

"Let me pass."

I expected a sneering response, but he merely complied, standing aside while I passed him. Only when I was inside my chamber, with the door closed behind me, did I lift my hands to my face. My cheeks were wet with tears. The mask of the lady had dissolved. Vane Sawford had seen the desperate creature beneath. Before my wedding, Papa had told me he would instruct my husband to keep me on a tight rein. Sawford now held those reins, and I feared he was waiting for an opportunity to use them.

Chapter 4

Dressing for dinner that evening, I told Harwyn about the poem. She was more suspicious than I.

"Oh, dear lady, please take care!"

"But the words, Harwyn. They're so full of feeling. I cannot believe it's a trap. I would be surprised if any of the men in my husband's employ can read or write, let alone compose this."

"Please, lady, I know you wish for an ally but compelling though the words may be, Mortlock may have employed a bard to write them."

I shook my head, unwilling to believe her but she persisted.

"Remember your Maman. Trust none but yourself."

Maman's counsel had always been to take precaution. The day she died she gave me one last warning. I would be watched—every action and word noted, to be used against me, however my husband deemed appropriate. Papa had married Maman, despite her lineage, for her dowry. As a distant cousin of the Empress Matilda's husband, Geoffrey D'Anjou, Maman was an enemy in Papa's eyes. Before Stephen named Henry his successor to the throne, the civil war between Stephen's and Matilda's supporters had divided the country—pitching Englishmen against each other in bloody battles. Though Maman openly supported Papa, her true loyalty, and thus my own, lay with Matilda and with King Henry.

Even after Stephen publicly named Henry his heir, thus effectively ending the war, there were many barons who remained opposed to Henry taking the throne. They argued that he had poisoned Stephen's oldest son, Eustace, and was not fit to rule. My own father was one such baron, as was my husband's cousin, Wulfric Baron de Tourrard. Might my husband also be in opposition to the king? Was that why Papa had accepted his offer for me? To ally himself with another traitor?

On returning with Papa from the coronation of Henry and his wife Eleanor of Aquitaine at Westminster, Maman had been confined to her chamber, her face darkened with bruising. In less than a year, she was dead. A word, or look, out of place, was enough to secure Papa's anger and punishment. If my husband knew of my loyalties then Harwyn was right. I was in as much danger here as Maman had been at Shoreton.

I remained silent, wishing that Harwyn was wrong. I dismissed her with a wave when she finished dressing my hair.

"Oh no—not again."

I looked up to see her picking up a note from under the doorframe. She handed it to me and I read it in silence.

Your friend will be waiting for you tonight as the moon rises over the lake.

"What does it say, lady?"

I crushed the note in my hand and threw it on the fire. "Nothing of importance."

During dinner, I watched the other diners for signs

of recognition but saw none. Careful to avoid arousing suspicion, I hid my observations behind the haughty expression a lady would bestow on her subjects. After the meal, I excused myself quickly, eager to retire for the night. Watching the flickering light of the candle, I lay in my bed, reminding myself of the folly in heeding the note. Though my eyelids grew heavy, I could not sleep. When all sounds of activity ceased, except for the pacing of the night guard, I finally admitted to myself that I was going to the lake.

I pulled on the rough woolen gown I wore when tending to the herb garden, and my cloak. Opening my door a little, I checked to see if the passage was clear before slipping out. Unbolting the gate, which led through the bailey wall, I followed the path leading to the wild garden and, beyond it, the lake.

The night was clear and cold, the moon almost full, casting shadows across the path. The moon's reflection was perfectly mirrored in the still waters of the lake, reminding me of the poem.

I waited, hidden in the shadows, until my hands and feet were numb. A sharp cry made me jump, but it was merely the sound of an animal—a mouse or some other creature caught by an owl. Poor thing—trapped in the talons of a predator.

Trapped…

The folly of my actions struck me. Had I lost my mind? Not only was I wandering about at night on my own, surrounded by all manner of predators, human and animal, but the bailey gate bolted from the inside. If the night guard discovered the bolt was not drawn and secured it, I would be trapped in the talons of darkness outside the bailey wall.

Another shriek, this time much closer. I panicked and ran, each breath sending clouds of terror into the night air. On reaching the gate, I almost sobbed with relief to find it unlocked. I had to stop to catch my breath, to ease both the ache in my side and the pounding in my ears. I cursed my rashness. Barely a month into my marriage and I was already betraying my mother's memory by letting my emotions rule my actions.

I took a few deep breaths, counting each one until I reached ten. The exercise worked and, with a lighter heart and a resolve to act rationally in future, I picked my way back toward the main building.

A sound from behind made me freeze. My skin tightened, and the hair prickled on the back of my neck. Lord save me—I was being followed. I stopped, my ears straining, but could hear nothing. I took a few tentative paces forward, stopping after each one to listen. Rationality over rashness again. My imagination must be playing tricks on me. With these words in my mind I slipped back inside the building.

After a minute, I once again had that uneasy feeling of being followed. A breathy sound came from behind, but I dismissed it. With luck, I would soon be warm and in my own bed.

I approached the passageway to my room and my luck ran out.

The night guard was walking toward me. He had not yet seen me and I turned back down the staircase, careful to keep to the outside of the spiral, painfully aware of my slippers slapping against the stone steps. The passage on the floor below gave an alternative route to my room. Though it ran past the men's quarters, I had to take the risk.

Each gust of wind sent the candles flickering, casting menacing shadows across the floor. A door ahead of me was flung open with a crash and I almost screamed. From the room, loud, raucous laughter erupted. Retreat was impossible; discovery was certain.

Behind me, I heard that sound again, like a soft whisper of a sigh. Before I could move a large hand clamped over my mouth, and a voice whispered in my ear.

"Make no sound if you wish to live."

An arm coiled round my waist, pulled me back against a large body and dragged me to one side into an alcove. My captor's body was unyielding and my struggles only made his grip tighten.

"Do as I say, you fool. What do you think those men will do to you? They have little regard for a woman wandering about at night on her own, be she servant, whore, or their Lord's latest wife. If you continue to resist, I shall hand you over to them. Do I make myself clear?"

I nodded. The authority of the lady of the castle had little weight against drunken, lust-fueled men. Upon my marriage, I had ceased to exist in the eyes of the world as anything other than the replaceable property of Lord Mortlock.

We waited until the footsteps passed by. The shouts of laughter increased. Had they discovered me, I would not have been escorted back to my room. My husband's men were a murderous and crude lot.

The door slammed shut, muffling the voices. My assailant let me go, and turned me to face him. Vane Sawford. He held a finger to his lips, but I needed no instruction. Muffled laughter and cheering came from behind one of the doors, mingled with the excited shrieks of a woman. A man, giddy with lust after the services of a whore, would not stop to question whether the next woman in his path were willing or not.

He took my arm and led me back to the staircase, turning not up, to my chamber, but down, to a small room on the floor below. He pushed me inside, before releasing my arm and closing the door behind him. The light of a single candle revealed sparse furnishings—a small cot in the corner, two chairs and a desk. I was in Sawford's bedchamber.

He turned to face me, his eyes cold and dispassionate. I lifted my head, staring back defiantly. His expression shifted, and a spark of fire flashed in the depths of his pupils, radiating outward. He drew slowly nearer, his eyes on me constantly. I backed away until I felt the stone wall against my back. He matched me step for step until his body touched mine. A slight smile curled on his lips as he placed his hands on the wall either side of my shoulders, pinning me in place.

He dipped his head toward mine. His warm breath caressed my mouth, and I inhaled the aroma of spices and masculinity. I had only to lift my head a fraction to meet his lips. He brushed his mouth against mine, and my skin tightened in response. He drew back, and I whimpered in frustration. I was a woman starved, my tormentor denying me what my body craved. I tipped my head up, unable to think of anything save those lips. He smiled triumphantly, holding his mouth tantalizingly close.

"I will only kiss you if you ask." His voice was thick and intoxicating.

I shook my head but, as he drew closer again, I parted my lips to receive him. In the battle between my mind and body, the balance of power was shifting.

"Ask." His voice became more insistent. I shook my head again, trying to ignore the sensation threatening to control my body. I felt weightless, as if the world was melting around me. My surroundings began to disappear. The cold air, the hard stone wall, the sounds of laughter in the distance slipped away until only one thing remained. Him.

"Then take me, lady" he whispered. His gentle voice broke through my mental defenses, and my bodily desires triumphed. With a small sound of defeat, I reached up, curling my fingers in his hair, pulling him closer to me. I pressed my lips against his and waited to feel him push me away. I needed a connection with someone—anyone—in this oppressive, lonely place.

A low, primal sound rumbled in his chest, and he pulled me hard against his body, forcing my mouth open with his tongue, ignoring my cries. I tried to move, but he was too strong. He pushed me until I fell on the cot, his weight crushing me. Unable to fight with my limbs, I used the only weapon I had and forced my own tongue into his mouth, relishing the taste of him— of spiced wine. I wanted him, wanted to give myself to him, though I belonged to Mortlock. Lord save me.

I felt the cold air against my legs before a burning, stinging sensation ripped between my thighs. I tore my mouth away from his and cried out. He gripped the hair at the back of my neck, forcing my head back toward him and silenced my cries with his mouth. His kisses grew gentler as I surrendered to him, my body willing. The pain faded and was replaced by another, lighter sensation. He was stroking my forehead much like my mother, and later Harwyn, had done to calm me. It was such odd behavior, for any man, that for a moment, I forgot my fears, until the candle in the room hissed, plunging us into darkness.

"The candle!" I cried out, panic swelling in my throat.

"Shhh, you're safe."

I might have imagined the words; they were spoken so softly. Reassured by his strength I clung to him as the darkness thickened around me.

He kissed me again, almost reverently, whispering incoherently. Then he moved. The pain increased with each movement of his body. I squeezed my eyes shut, holding on to his arms. His muscles rippled beneath my fingers, and his breathing grew harsher until he released a deep groan and fell on to me. He wrapped his arms around me, and I held on to him, vaguely aware of a warm sensation spreading between my thighs.

I lay still in his arms, listening to his breathing growing steadier. Eventually, he moved away. I heard the sound of a flint being struck then saw the flickering light of a candle.

"Get up." His voice was cold. I sat up and pulled my skirts down, overcome with shame. My thighs were smeared with blood, as was the bed sheet.

I controlled my voice and spoke equally as coldly. "You are in no position to give orders after what you have done to me."

He gave a low, mirthless laugh. "You asked me to, remember?"

"I did no such thing." The indignation in my voice could not disguise the lie on my lips and he knew it.

"Aye, madam, you did, with your body as assuredly as you would have done with your voice. My stained sheets will make a fine keepsake."

"How dare you!" I cried. "Lord Mortlock…"

"My lord will listen to the counsel of a trusted employee over the tattle of a woman. 'Tis better he knows not you are now soiled goods. I'm sure I do not have to remind you of the penalty for adultery."

Death by fire.

In a fit of madness and desire, I had reached out to Sawford and, in doing so, had thrown my worth away. As a bride, my maidenhead was the only value, other than my dowry, which the world placed on me. Years of schooling and Maman's nurturing had taught me to protect my virtue and never succumb to my desires. Yet, in a fleeting moment I had destroyed it all. He had only to tell my husband of my sin and I would share Maman's fate.

"Maman," I whispered. My throat tightened and I struggled to breathe, bending over in physical pain. At that moment, I hated him more than I thought it possible to hate another living soul.

"What did you say?" he demanded.

"Nothing."

He remained silent for a while before I thought I heard him sigh. I jumped as he laid a hand on my shoulder.

"Come, I will take you to your room."

"I can manage by myself."

I stood up to leave, but his hand snaked round my wrist.

"Nevertheless, I insist. You would not want to meet Mortlock's men."

"I fail to see why not," I replied bitterly. "What can they do to me that you have not already done?"

His hand tightened its grip and he bowed his head, staying still for a moment. He then led me out of the room and back to my chamber.

Before we approached my door, he stopped, his senses alert to something. After a while I heard it too. Hoof beats, the sound of a carriage, and voices echoing outside could only mean one thing.

"Your husband has returned. I will greet him but, before I go, a kiss, my lady, for your lover."

I turned my face away, but he took my chin and planted a light kiss on my lips. I opened my door and recoiled at the darkness inside. He gave me his candle before disappearing into the darkness of the passageway. I stripped off my cloak and gown, and crept into my bed, curling myself up into a ball. Loud voices approached, my husband's among them. Had Sawford told him of my adultery? Was I to die tonight?

Much later a noise woke me. It was still nighttime and the candle had not yet burned out. Footsteps echoed outside my door, and I sat up, sick with fear. A faint rustling came from the door and something appeared at the bottom. Another note. The footsteps receded. I ran to the door and opened it, but there was no one in sight. Wearily, I picked up the note. Written in the same hand as before were two words.

Pardonnez-moi.

Forgive me.

Chapter 5

The next day my husband sent for me.

As Harwyn helped me dress, my hands shook so badly I struggled with my garments. I tried to appear calm, but she knew me too well. Her soft touch and natural kindness overwhelmed me. I choked back a cry as she took me in her arms.

Unable to look her in the eyes, I told her everything that had happened the previous night, my voice thickening with shame as I uttered Sawford's name. Holding me close, she stroked my forehead until my sobs subsided. Then she combed my hair in silence. The rhythmic motion of the comb pulling through my scalp was comforting. Counting in rhythm with each stroke, I began to control my breathing. By the time she started braiding my hair, I was calm again.

When Harwyn finished I stood, my body no longer shaking. She took my hand and drew me to her.

"Courage."

"Aye, Harwyn. I'll not give him the satisfaction of seeing me distressed, and will face my fate as bravely as Maman would have done."

She gave me a light kiss on the cheek before opening my door. I knew not whether I would see her again or whether I was walking to my death.

Lord Mortlock waited for me in the main hall, Sawford by his side. Focusing my attention on my husband, I ignored the tall man in black, repressing a shudder of revulsion as Mortlock's claw-like fingers curled round my own.

"Welcome home, husband." I spoke blandly. He nodded and looked greedily at me with his milky eyes. This close, I could see they were bloodshot. The smell of sour wine on his breath mingled with another smell, the stench of decay.

"A kiss for your husband." His voice rattled in his chest before erupting into a hacking cough, which sent out droplets of spittle. I flinched, and he grinned, drawing me toward him and crushing his lips against mine. I stiffened at his touch.

"What say you, Sawford? Is my wife pleased to see her husband return?"

Sawford's silence formed a void, and I waited for the words that would condemn me. Eventually he answered, his voice quiet and cold.

"Who can tell, my Lord?"

My husband chuckled. "That's right, Sawford, your tastes run to different livestock do they not? I hear you have no fondness for thoroughbreds. Come, wife, we shall take the air together."

He smiled nastily at Sawford. "A noblewoman cares not for one who is bastard born."

My husband's words and demeanor exuded his hatred for others and his hunger for power. But Sawford was impossible to read, remaining hidden behind an impassive expression. Only a slight tic in his jaw gave any sign he had heard. My husband held out his other arm.

"Sawford."

Sawford took Mortlock's arm, supporting his

weight. I was once again unnerved by how silently Sawford moved. The three of us shuffled out into the main garden.

The sun cast its heat into the spring air. I inhaled deeply, wanting to erase the stench of my husband's breath.

"Sawford has been telling me of your behavior during my absence."

My stomach lurched, and I almost stopped walking. Were we, even now, on our way to the dungeons, or worse, the courtyard? I strained my senses, trying to detect the smell of oil and wood in the air.

"Husband?" I croaked, my throat constricting.

"Aye," he replied. "I am pleased with you, but I expect you to continue to behave."

We took a silent turn about the garden. The only sounds were the rushing of the wind through the trees, the voices of the men training in the courtyard, and the occasional bellow of an animal carried over the air from the farms surrounding the estate.

At length, my husband spoke. "Wulfric tells me that devil spawn of Matilda who would call himself king…"

"My Lord," Sawford interrupted, his voice strained. I looked up quickly to see him staring directly at me.

"How foolish of me, Sawford." My husband let go of my hand and waved me away.

"Leave us, my dear. I will send for you tonight after I have retired."

I was so thankful to be released, I almost ran back to the building. Reaching the door, I glanced over my shoulder. My husband and Sawford were talking in earnest. For a brief moment, Sawford turned his head in my direction.

Harwyn had been right. Something was afoot and my husband was involved. "That devil spawn of Matilda" could only mean King Henry, Wulfric, my husband's cousin. Were the two cousins plotting treason? Was Papa involved?

I thought of my poor Maman, having to conceal her loyalty to Henry. My love for her would always ensure my loyalties were aligned with hers. My chest constricted with grief for her. I missed her so much. She had taught me to read and write, encouraging my inquisitiveness. She'd also warned me never to reveal my inner thoughts to anyone. As women, our lives were not our own. Our lives belonged to Papa, and if he was revealed to be a traitor to the crown, then by association, so would we.

Papa would regularly hold meetings with his associates who opposed Henry. At one such meeting, shortly after Maman died, I'd hidden myself in the solar at Shoreton. The loss of my beloved Maman had driven my recklessness and my childish belief that I might unearth a plot against King Henry.

Papa spotted me hiding under the bed and gave me a beating in front of his guests. Among them was my husband's cousin Wulfric, a strikingly handsome man about ten years older than I, who'd watched while I howled and struggled, a smile playing on his lips. At one time, Papa had thought him a suitable match, but he'd married another woman before I reached a marriageable age.

God help me. I was in enough danger merely living

in this hideous castle. If my husband were plotting treason, then as his wife, I would also be branded a traitor. I shivered at the thought of Sawford's eyes on me, watching as I went back inside the building. He was silent and observant, taking note of my reactions to my husband's careless words.

How might Sawford react if he were aware of my suspicions? I had grown used to Papa's discipline and could withstand physical beatings. However, Sawford would be an expert in infinitely subtler forms of torture. The air hummed with the power he exuded. I could still feel the thrill my body had felt with his hands on me. There existed a bone-deep need in me which I could not conquer when he was near—the need to surrender myself completely to him. My fear was not of the man himself, but of my body's reaction to him and what he had the power to make me do. Yet, I was drawn to him. Something dark, nestling at the very core of my being, whispered to me that nothing mattered except him.

Safe in my chamber, I read the anonymous notes again. Did the author know of a conspiracy against the king? Was he as loyal to Henry as I? Perhaps that was why he wrote to me in secret. I dared not speak of this to Harwyn. She would dismiss it as the foolish fancy of a woman desperate for an ally. But that little flash of hope, which began upon first reading that note, continued to grow.

Who was he? The squire Percy seemed so young, but he was the only one, save Harwyn, who gave any sign of friendship. Perhaps he was a spy for a baron loyal to Henry. Or perhaps Baldwin, the knight he served? Surely an opportunity would arise to speak with Percy. Some casual enquiry about his origins and family might bring something to light without arousing suspicion. Now my husband was back, Sawford would be relieved of his task to follow me, and I would have my chance.

****

That evening, a sharp knock on my door made me jump. One of the maidservants stood in the doorway. Not curtseying, she eyed me insolently.

"The master awaits you in the solar, milady."

I closed my eyes, swallowing the tight knot of fear in my throat. If he was to bed me now, my husband would know I was no longer a maiden.

"Lady?"

Stiffening my body, I opened my eyes, lifted my chin, and glared at her.

"How dare you show such disrespect to your mistress."

Fixing my stare at her, I waited until she dipped into a curtsey. She lowered her eyes, but not before I caught a flash of hatred.

I swept past her, in the direction of the solar, taking care to nudge her aside with my shoulder. When we arrived, the door was closed. I stood at the threshold, glaring until she curtseyed once more and stepped in front of me to knock. The door swung inward to reveal Sawford, filling the doorway with his tall frame. Almost instantly, her demeanor changed from insolent to inviting. She pushed her shoulders back to reveal her ample bosom and smiled seductively.

"Monsieur Sawford, I had not expected to see you here," she purred, tipping her face up to kiss him. Pushing her away, Sawford took my arm and pulled me through the doorway. She scowled before turning her smile on him once more.

"Shall I visit you tonight, Monsieur?"

"No."

He shut the door in her face and led me to the bed where my husband sat waiting.

****

As soon as Sawford returned me to my chamber, I turned my back on him. The door banged shut behind me but another noise made me look around. Sawford had followed me in. It unnerved me at how quietly he could move. He took my shoulders and turned me to face him. He then pushed me back until we reached my bed, where I fell back and lay looking up at him. He leaned over me and held me down by the arms.

"Get out," I ordered.

"I will leave if you truly wish it, *cherie*, but I know you want your lover here tonight."

"You know nothing of love," I spat.

He released my arms and lifted up my nightshift, his fingers brushing against my thigh.

"You impugn my skills, if you think I cannot have you willingly. There is only pain your first time. Now there will be only pleasure."

His cold words brought me to my senses. "You flatter yourself, unless you speak of your own pleasure."

"Nay, *cherie*. 'Twill not be long before you open your thighs and beg me to take you, as countless others have done."

"Never."

The low laugh vibrated through his chest. He moved against me and once more claimed me as his own.

He was right in that there was no pain this time. Yet, I felt no pleasure, only a burning need that intensified but was never satisfied, followed by a sense of loss when he withdrew. He turned his back to adjust his clothes and stood to leave.

"Where are you going, Monsieur?"

"Are you hungry for more pleasure?"

I pulled my nightshift down, mortified at my unwillingness to fight for my honor.

"You know nothing of pleasure except perhaps your own. Nothing of love…"

He laughed coldly. "I know all there is to know about pleasure. As for love—I love no woman."

I turned my head away and jumped when he touched my chin. He ran a thumb across my lips, bruised and swollen from his kisses.

"And what of you? Are you foolish enough to know aught of love, my lady?"

"I have seen enough of the consequences of love to know it will bring me nothing but death."

"Bitter words for one in such a privileged position."

"Privileged?" I cried. "What if you get me with child?"

He shrugged. "Mortlock wants an heir. You merely need to convince everyone that he is the sire. As 'tis known you visit him nightly, it will be an easy task."

"Why does he not take me himself?"

His body stiffened and he withdrew his hand. "Do you wish him to?"

"No!" I cried, shaking my head, trying to forget the image of my husband's shriveled body, his wrinkled yellowing flesh against my skin.

"Lady, I would never..." Sawford spoke softly, reaching his hand out to me before his eyes hardened, his voice growing cold once more.

"My lord seldom takes pleasure from lying with a woman," he said. "His first wives rarely quickened with child, and those who did were never able to carry them to full term. His body is diseased. The whores he took would sicken and die, and some of his wives met a similar fate. Others—well—they met their ends in other ways. He is not long for this world and wants a healthy heir before he leaves it. Rarely is his desire for an heir overshadowed by his wish to lie with a woman. It happens when...when he is in a particular frame of mind."

"Then I must pray that never happens," I whispered to myself but Sawford heard me.

"Prayer will not help you, woman, though foolish behavior will be your downfall."

"Such as quickening with another's child?" I cried. "Surely he'll know the babe would not be his?"

"He merely wants an heir."

So this was my purpose—and Sawford's. To provide Mortlock with a son.

"Does he know 'tis you?" I asked.

Sawford shook his head. "He cares not for the sire. With such a mare in his possession, he does not concern himself with the stallion that mounts her."

"What will become of me"—I spoke in a horrified whisper—"when I have fulfilled my purpose?"

"I know not. Once you have borne my lord a male heir, I will have my reward."

"And what is that?"

"It concerns you not, woman."

"Once he has no more use for me, will I share the fate of my predecessors?"

His lips curled into a sneer. "There are more important things, madam, than one insignificant, adulterous woman, naïve enough to expect happiness in marriage."

"I never expected it in this marriage—or indeed any marriage," I said, choking down a sob. "I expected sorrow, but not degradation and death." I closed my eyes, attempting to stop treacherous tears from rolling down my cheeks. Moments later, I heard the door close and I was alone again.

At last, I understood my worth to my husband. He cared nothing for my lineage, mind or ability to tend to the people of his estate. I was nothing more than a vessel, akin to a farm animal intended to breed and then be discarded. I was no different from the servants Papa had taken, only I would be disposed of after a child was born—or earlier, if I did not quicken with child soon.

I had feared the destruction of my maidenhead would bring about my downfall, but Mortlock must have planned it from the day Papa offered me to him. I was trapped. Having engineered my adultery at the hands of another, my husband had not only secured the means to beget an heir but, also, the justification to rid himself of his new wife, however he saw fit.

Was this the fate Mortlock's previous wives shared? If so, I would be lucky to be alive this time next year. Given the kind of life I would be leading here, I might welcome death when it came.

Chapter 6

Spring turned to summer and my life fell into a routine. Leaving me alone during the day, my husband would send for me at night, before Sawford led me back to my room to take me for himself. I found comfort in Harwyn's company and in treating the various ailments and injuries of the household. My favorite part of the day was early afternoon when I could peacefully sit alone in the wild garden. I would close my eyes, listening both to the wind in the trees and the nearby stream, and imagine I lived somewhere else.

Had I never married, I would have retired to a convent near Shoreton. The abbess was a relative of Maman's and would have given me sanctuary. I could have taken Harwyn with me to live a life of duty and contemplation. But now, as the property of Lord Mortlock, such a life could never happen.

I received another poem, together with a note urging me to be strong and promising the author would keep me safe. Might he take me away if I asked?

What would it be like to live the life of a nobody? Possibly the wife of a villager? She would have little to concern herself with, except the welfare of her husband and children and the mundane activities of village life. She would neither be surrounded by evil nor be under constant scrutiny.

In the solitude of the garden, I fancied myself a young maiden waiting by the woods to meet her sweetheart. I had yet to visit the village surrounding the Fort. I dared not ask permission for fear my husband would insist Wyatt accompany me. But I often saw the villagers from my window, going about their business, tending to cattle in a field, trading at the market. Once, I saw a young couple stealing a precious moment together. The boy placed a tender kiss on the girl's hand before they ran out of sight, hand in hand. How I envied them!

I rarely saw Sawford during the day. Whenever I did he inclined his head slightly to acknowledge me before continuing on his way. I maintained a mask of cold disdain though my heart tumbled inside my chest. I was not alone in my reaction—I saw how the female servants acted around him. My hatred rose every time one of them approached him, exaggerating a loose-hipped gait to attract his attention, touching his arm or leaning against him.

At night, in my room, I saw glimpses of the man beneath—a sigh as he took me, a tender touch on my forehead afterward. His kisses were mostly savage and demanding, but occasionally his lips brushed mine softly, reminding me of the young lovers I had seen. Though I yearned for those tender moments, my weak soul could better withstand his cold brutality.

****

While I finished bandaging the finger of a stable boy, who'd been bitten by a horse, the door to the treatment room opened.

"Leave us."

The boy scrambled to his feet at Sawford's

command. Murmuring his thanks he ran out of the room.

I stood as Sawford moved closer. My stomach flipped as he bent his head toward me, bringing his face close. I gripped the table for support, but could not stop myself from tipping my face up to receive his kiss. He sat down with a sneer.

"So eager for me, but I am not here for your pleasure."

"You have no business here," I said, as steadily as I could. "Leave me to get on with my work. No doubt you have duties of your own to attend to."

He smiled knowingly. "As you well know, *cherie*, I undertake all my duties thoroughly."

"What do you want of me?"

For a moment his eyes widened, understanding what I was really asking him. Did he see me as nothing but a body intended to both quench his lust and serve as a means to his reward? Afraid of what he might say, I waved my hand at the scraps of bandages on the table.

"In this room you can only find succor for injuries and ailments of the flesh. For sicknesses of the mind and soul, I suggest you try the chapel."

He rolled up his sleeve and I let out a gasp. A long gash ran along his forearm. The flesh surrounding it was red, swollen and seeping with an ugly, yellow liquid. I wrinkled my nose at the faint sickly sweet odor. For such an extensive infection this could not be a recent wound.

The horror in my face must have shown.

"Is it too much for my mistress' delicate eyes?"

"Not at all." I composed myself. "I was merely wondering how you sustained such an injury."

"The night of my lord's wedding."

I remembered. It had been two months yet I saw it as if it were yesterday: Sawford's eyes trained on me as he'd drawn the knife along his arm, to produce evidence of my virgin's blood. His look had turned to irritation when he'd cut deeper than intended.

I reached for his wrist, ignoring the sensation I felt down my spine at the touch of his skin against mine.

"The wound has festered. I'll need to take out the infection and bind it, but it will hurt."

"Then get on with it."

I gathered what I needed, checking the pot of water I always had over the fireplace. Satisfied it was hot enough, I brought it to the table along with the healing herbs I would need. His gaze was on me all the time, but I tried my best to ignore him. I picked up cloths and bandages and lit a candle. As I drew out a knife and held it in the flame, I heard him sigh.

"Do you need something to bite down on?" I asked, looking up at him. His eyes narrowed, and he shook his head.

"Hold out your arm."

He did so, laying it on the table with the wound facing upward. I took his hand and curled my fingers between his.

"I'll be as quick as I can."

Making a swift, deep cut down his forearm I traced the wound to re-open it. His arm muscles tensed, and he curled his fingers round my own, but he made no sound. Using the edge of the blade, I scraped away the infected flesh and thick, yellow liquid. Dropping the knife, I dipped a cloth into the hot water then held it against the wound, letting the heat draw out the infection. I was able to work calmly and efficiently, taking satisfaction in my abilities. Sawford's earlier comment about my delicate tastes had pricked my pride, and I was determined to show him I was no faint-hearted creature. I stopped as my train of thought caught up with me. Why should I care for the opinion of a soulless creature like Sawford?

"Is it too much for you?" he asked.

I wondered at the lack of emotion in his voice. The pain must be unendurable.

"Not at all. I've treated worse. Keep still," I admonished him as he moved his arm. "I need to dress the wound. You're a fool for not coming to me earlier."

"Surely you would not have wanted the wound—or its purpose—to become widely known."

I shrugged my shoulders. "I care not, Monsieur. 'Tis your own pride that prevented you from seeking help. The pride of men is the bane of society and of the lives of women. But, I would expect nothing else from a base born servant."

He gripped my hand and I winced. "Better to be base born and earn your means than to languish in wealth and inherit it. Or indeed, to marry it by taking a wife you despise, merely for her dowry."

"A man is able to do that," I retorted, "but what of women? We are nothing more than chattel to be treated as our owners see fit—forced to marry men *we* despise to further others' causes. 'Tis little wonder we think only of ourselves. Do you think I care what happens in the world outside? I have no control over my own destiny, let alone that of others. What I think or feel is irrelevant to anybody but myself. I am merely a possession, a tool to be used for others' personal gain—

as you have done yourself."

"Do not condemn me for seeking an honest wage. I have worked and fought hard for it all my life."

"I know nothing of your history, Monsieur, but for the past few sennights, your 'honest wage' was earned by brokering my sale to Lord Mortlock, whoring me out, and acting as a stud to produce an heir for your master."

He did not reply, and I picked up a bandage, giving him a look of hatred. "I believe my definition of honesty differs from yours."

He set his jaw into a hard line, and the scar on his chin whitened. I applied the herbs to the wound then bound it, securing the bandage with a knot.

"I will need to see this wound again in case the infection spreads. You may go now."

He nodded curtly before rolling his sleeve down. Without another word, he turned his back and left the room.

I was not summoned to the solar that night. Initially, I was relieved to be left unmolested but as the night wore on and sleep eluded me, I lay, watching the dim light of my candle and felt nothing but an acute sense of loneliness. Eventually, I fell asleep, my dreams disturbed by images of reddened, wounded flesh and a piercing pair of brilliant blue eyes.

****

I woke the next morning to the sound of Harwyn moving about in my chamber. I felt so tired and struggled to sit up. She rushed over to help me dress, and I let her administer to me in silence, standing up after she had secured my veil over my hair.

"Come, Harwyn, to the garden."

We spent the morning collecting calendula flowers. I had spotted their bright orange color in the garden and remembered how Maman had pointed them out to me at Shoreton, telling me of their healing properties. I had helped her make salves and, though I was unsure of the exact proportions, I was confident I could produce something far more effective in treating infected wounds than the herbs in my store.

When our baskets were full, we returned to my treatment room, and I sent Harwyn to the kitchens for oil, beeswax, and a large boiling pot, while I started to pick off the delicate petals. She returned with everything we needed to make the salve, including jars for storage. By the time the daylight began to fade, we had picked off all the petals and left them to soak in the oil in a bowl. It was too late to start the process which would draw out the healing compound, so we left the petals steeping in the oil and tidied up the room.

It was only when we went to leave, I noticed a piece of folded parchment under the doorframe. With a sigh of frustration, I picked it up and unfolded it, immediately recognizing the hand which had penned the words written on the parchment.

"Oh, lady, 'tis him again is it not?" Harwyn sighed. "You have gone as pale as a lily. What does he say?"

It was another poem extolling the beauty of my hair, likening it to the midnight black of a clear night sky. Again, he had finished with a brief note of comfort, but what made me gasp was the final line.

I would have you write to me, dearest Lisetta. Let me know you have not lost hope. I will await your answer by the seat in the rose garden when the sun sets tonight. Your loving friend and protector,

Tarvin de Fowensal.

Not only had he asked me to respond, but he'd signed his name.

"Tarvin…" I breathed.

"There is no man of that name here," Harwyn warned. "It must be a trap."

"If he's aware of the danger here, he would hardly use his own name," I replied. "He risks much by writing to me."

"Surely you're not going to respond?"

"I must. This is my chance to identify him. I will write a response, and you shall keep watch to see who collects it."

She shook her head, worry lines creasing her forehead. I took her hand. "I need not write anything incriminating, Harwyn. I still trust none but you."

She sighed, knowing I would not be dissuaded. My beloved Harwyn would always do what I asked of her, no matter how foolish the request.

****

Immediately after supper, I heard Harwyn's knock at my door and let her in.

"Someone took the note?"

I didn't need to ask. The look on her face said it all.

"One of the stable boys. Cedric, I believe his name is."

"You know where he is now?"

"Aye."

"Then hurry. We have no time to waste."

We saw Cedric almost as soon as we reached the stables. Carrying an armful of straw, he was a mere child. On seeing his mistress he dropped the bundle. His features were delicate and as he shook with fear my heart went out to him.

The source of his fear emerged from behind the stables. A thick-set man, with blonde hair thinning at the temples and a shaggy unkempt beard, trampled across the yard. The head groom. I disliked him, thinking him a brutish animal. On seeing the pile of straw in the mud, he lumbered toward the boy, his hands clenching into thick mud-streaked fists.

"Foolish, lazy boy! Do you want another beating?"

"No!" Harwyn cried. On seeing us he hesitated then resumed his path toward the child.

"Stop that!" I said.

"The whelp is lazy and needs to learn obedience."

"How dare you address me so! I gave you an order and expect it to be obeyed. Now leave us."

"But my master—"

"I am your mistress," I interrupted. "Go. Now. Or I'll have you whipped."

Cursing, he turned his back and returned to the stables, leaving the boy alone. A thin, solitary figure, the boy stood in the mud, his eyes large in his malnourished face. Ashamed of my own cowardice, I looked at him coldly, too fearful of my own safety to show him any gesture of comfort.

I nodded to Harwyn who approached him.

"You there! Cedric, is it not?"

The boy nodded, his eyes widening as he looked from Harwyn to me and back again.

"What has become of the note you took?"

The poor child looked like he was about to faint. He opened and shut his mouth but no sound came out. His whole body trembled, and he took a step back.

"I want no trouble, lady."

"Remain where you are in the presence of your mistress," Harwyn ordered.

I spoke softly to Harwyn so only she could hear. "Harwyn, there is no one here to see us, or to punish us for a little kindness."

Cedric shook his head. "He said he would beat me if I told."

"Lord Mortlock will do far worse if you disobey your mistress' orders," Harwyn said. "I only have to tell—"

"Harwyn, that's enough," I interrupted. A tear rolled down the boy's cheek. The urge to make him feel protected was too strong, and I held my hand out to him, ignoring Harwyn's protests.

"Tell us, child, and I will not betray you. You have my word."

He seemed more surprised at the softness in my voice than the fact I had spoken. Harwyn placed a warning hand on my arm as the boy nodded.

"I will show you."

He led us round the back of the stables and pointed to the wall.

"See the loose stone there, lady, the one covered in moss? I was told to put it there, behind the stone."

"Told by whom?"

"I knew not. He came up from behind and said he would kill me if I looked at him, so I kept my eyes shut. He said I must pick up a letter by the rose bush and hide it behind the stone."

"When did you put it there?" Harwyn asked.

"Just now," he replied, "before I went to fetch the straw."

"Show us."

Cedric ran to the wall and pulled out the stone. His cry of surprise was genuine.

"'Tis gone!"

There was nothing there.

"But that means…" my voice trailed off. For the note to be gone already, whoever had taken it must have been there while we were speaking to Cedric. My eyes met Harwyn's as the same thought crossed her mind. He might be watching us now.

"Leave us, child." I spoke sharply, eager for Cedric to be gone. He ran away gratefully.

We looked around us, but there was no sign of anyone.

"Come away, lady," Harwyn said, taking my hand. "There's nothing we can do. We must pray that this man, whoever he is, did not set out to trap you, for that trap has now been sprung."

Chapter 7

Harwyn and I spent the next morning making the salve. The oil which the flowers were soaking in had turned a rich, warm yellow overnight. Its delicate, healing aroma soothed my senses, and I picked up the bowl, swirling the oil round. Harwyn set a large pot of water over the fire, and I placed the bowl into it, stirring the contents as the water bubbled into a low simmer until the yellow gradually turned into a vibrant orange. Taking the bowl off the heat, my hand slipped, and I cried in frustration as some of the precious oil splashed out.

"Lady, your hand!"

Some of the hot oil had spilled onto the back of my hand. Harwyn ran over with a dish of cold water and plunged my hand in. She sat me at the table, insisting I do no more that morning. I obeyed her reluctantly, but was soon grateful for her care, for my hand started to feel very sore. Under my direction, she finished the process, straining the oil through a cloth into a clean bowl and stirring in the beeswax before pouring it into jars to cool. The color had now dulled to a soft ochre. I nodded approvingly. We now had enough salve to last several months.

Harwyn took my hand out of the water. The skin was an angry red and a blister was already forming. Once the salve cooled, I would be the first patient to use it.

I sent for Sawford during the afternoon but by sunset he'd still not come, so I sent for him again. While tearing strips of cloth for bandages, I heard his voice behind me.

"What is it you want, madam?"

I was used to the sneering tone, but his ability to move about so soundlessly still unnerved me. I had not even heard him enter.

I motioned to him to sit. "Your dressing needs changing, and I must check the wound."

"I have no time to waste on frivolities."

I bristled with anger but kept my voice cool. "You'll be lucky to avoid further infection, and are a fool if you choose to ignore the risk. Unless, of course, you consider having only one arm to be an advantage."

On seeing the jar of salve in my hand, his eyes narrowed.

"Hold out your arm, Monsieur."

He did so, watching me with what looked like amusement until he saw my bandaged hand. He grasped it but released me the instant I winced.

"It appears I am not the only fool."

"A simple accident," I replied, not disguising the scorn in my voice. "Not all ladies are engaged in frivolities, despite what those around us may think."

"Lord Mortlock would not share your sentiments. He does not wish to see flaws in his wife."

"Are you referring to the burn on my hand or to my character, Monsieur Sawford?"

He curled his lip in amusement but said nothing. I unwound the bandage on his arm, cleaned the wound and, as delicately as I could, spread the salve with my fingertips.

"Tell me if it pains you."

He remained silent while I applied a fresh bandage. I secured it with a knot near his wrist, and he took my hand, curling his fingers round mine. The shock of the contact made me look up. His eyes were fixed on my face, and I caught a glimpse of something in their hidden depths, an understanding between him and I which separated us from the rest of the world. He looked away as he removed his hand.

After dismissing him, I turned my back and resumed tidying the room. I did not hear him leave but when I looked round he was gone.

Before I visited my husband that night, I removed the bandage from my hand, remembering Sawford's words about a flawed wife. The burn pained me greatly but its appearance concerned me more. The skin was an angry red, and the burn had puckered into blisters. With luck, in the dim light of the solar my husband wouldn't notice it.

Standing before him once more, I removed my nightgown, suppressing a cry at the stab of pain of the fabric brushing over my hand. Sawford heard, for he immediately took my wrists, holding them behind my back. My husband did not tell him to release me. Instead, he nodded his approval, leering at the way the position pushed my breasts forward.

After my husband had finished, Sawford held my nightshift up to place over my head. I stepped closer to him and caught the tangy aroma of the salve mingled with his masculine scent. He nodded toward my arms and deftly slipped the garment on, taking care not to touch the burn as I lifted my arms. Taking my hand, he led me out of the solar.

On entering my chamber, I tried to ignore him while I replaced the bandage on my hand, but his presence dominated the room. I could almost taste the raw male power in the air.

He spoke softly but his voice conveyed strength and the inevitability of what was to come. He was not a man to be denied.

"Lift up your arms, so I may remove your gown."

I backed away and shook my head, my heart hammering in my chest.

"I'll not ask again, and you would not wish to explain a torn nightgown to Lord Mortlock."

I sighed in resignation and lifted my arms, letting him undress me. He took my shoulders and, as on countless nights before, pushed me toward the bed, until I fell back onto the straw mattress.

Slowly, painfully slowly, he removed his shirt, revealing the planed muscles on his chest. His physique was not that of a servant. The calluses on his hands and scars on his body were the marks of a warrior, relating far more of his history than any words could. He removed his chausses and hose and stood before me, utterly naked for the first time. His manhood stood thick and erect, almost brushing his stomach. Fear coursed through my veins. Until now he had taken me swiftly, but the expression in his eyes told me tonight would be different.

He approached the bed and lay beside me, the bed ropes creaking under his weight. His skin was hot to the touch, and it seared my body as he moved over me, trapping my legs with one of his own. I closed my eyes and started counting, breathing in and out, but his hand caressed my face, and my eyes flew open.

"Ah no, lover. Do not hide yourself from me tonight."

Was there nothing this man did not know? I tried to turn my head, but he held it firm, silencing my protest with his mouth. He moved his lips possessively over mine, knowing I would surrender. He brushed his hand down my neck, circling his fingers round my throat. Those long, skilled fingers traced a path to my breasts, sweeping in smooth circles until his palm rested lightly, cupping one breast in a soft caress. He rubbed the tip with his thumb and my chest tightened in response.

He drew his hand back, and I made a small involuntary sound at the sense of loss. He smiled, knowing my defenses were almost gone, and bent his head to brush his lips against my throat. I tipped my head back to expose my throat to him. The heat from his lips sent trails of warmth across my whole body, pooling in my stomach before spreading downward. I closed my eyes. When his lips found my breast, I let out a cry at the sensation. He covered me with his hot mouth and suckled gently, teasing my now-sensitive nipple with his tongue. He increased the pressure, nipping me with his teeth. I arched my back at the sweet agony of it, burying my hands in his hair to keep him close.

He pulled away, and I whimpered in protest. I curled my fingers in his thick mane, trying to draw him to me. He chuckled at my wantonness.

"Tonight, I will only take you if you beg me."

I shook my head. "I will never—"

"Ah but you will," he said softly, leaning over to take my mouth again.

Tears formed in my eyes as I yielded to my body's need for his touch. They spilled onto my cheeks as he continued to administer his sweet, torturous caresses. He must have done this to countless others just as dispassionately. Was I merely the latest in a long line of conquests? I did not care to know. He dipped his hand between my thighs and caressed me intimately where he knew my body wept for him. I bit my lip to suppress a moan.

Once again, that unfathomable ache formed inside my core. I knew not what it was, only that it always hung suspended, not quite within my reach, taunting me, driving me almost mad. He thrust his tongue into my mouth again, drawing my own tongue into his own. Instinctively I lifted my hips against his hand, surrendering to the craving that surged within me.

He slipped a finger inside me and my body shattered. It was as if I had come truly alive for the first time. Air rushed into my lungs, and I cried out at the wonder of it. He muffled my cries with his mouth, and I heard a low rumble in his throat as I clung to him, shaking, while the deep pulsing sensation in my body subsided, leaving me breathless and weak.

He nudged my thighs apart with his knee, and I clung to him, waiting. Yet this time I was not afraid. I wanted to give myself to him. He moved on top of me and the tip of him nudged hard and unyielding against my sensitive flesh. I waited for him to take me, but he moved only slightly, teasing me until I thought I could bear it no longer.

An instinctive urge impelled me to touch him. Reaching down, I curled my hand round him, my fingers caressing his skin. The soft silken exterior masked the unyielding steel within. I squeezed him gently, and he jerked in my hand. A deep growl bubbled up from within his body, and he closed his eyes, issuing a hoarse groan, so quiet I thought I imagined it.

"*Lisetta...*"

A sense of triumph nestled within the cloud of desire for him. I was a weak woman but here, in my own chamber that was my prison, I had the power.

He shifted position, and I cried out as he found the very spot where my body ached for him. His mouth twitched into a knowing smile. He had been toying with me, teasing me. In a heartbeat his slick, rhythmic motions shifted the balance of power and once more, I became his to command.

"Please..." I whispered.

"Please what, *cherie*?" his voice was quiet but demanding.

He stopped moving, and I whimpered at the loss, arching my back to offer myself to him.

He lifted his body away, and I let out a wail of despair.

"Ah, you wish for me to leave?"

"No! Please, I beg you..." my voice broke as we both recognized my surrender for what it was.

"Do you want me, woman? Are you begging me to take you?"

Blinking away the tears of shame—shame which was surpassed by my need for him, I nodded.

"Yes."

"Show me, woman. Show me how much you want me."

I shook my head, and he moved back.

67

"No!" I clung to him, pulling him toward me. He said nothing but remained, his body still covering mine, yet he did not move. He was waiting for me to obey.

Closing my eyes with shame, I shifted my thighs further apart, pulling him close until I felt him once again, hot and hard against my body.

"Now tell me what you want," he demanded.

"I want you."

I gave a strangled sob, and he kissed me again before he drove into me, claiming his complete ownership. But this time, instead of lying passively I met him stroke for stoke, opening my thighs hungrily to receive him. I wrapped my legs around his body and locked my ankles together to draw him in further. I dug my hands into his shoulders, feeling the iron hard lines of muscle ripple back and forth with his exertion. That burning hot flame ignited in me again, this time deeper, stronger, building with each thrust until I thought I might die from it. I clung to him, crying out with need.

He began to sound as if he were in pain—groaning, louder and louder until he lifted his head and let out a primeval roar. My whole world disintegrated around me, as if my body had been smashed into a thousand shards. I screamed and gripped onto him while my body rippled and melted. I was lost as my senses were torn apart.

Sawford always left quickly after taking me, but this time he stayed on top of me, holding me as fiercely as I held him, his head buried in my shoulder, his breathing ragged. I uncrossed my ankles and let my legs fall though I kept my arms round him, wanting to take comfort from his strength. He lifted his head, and looked at me, and I met his gaze, my vision blurred by tears.

For several heartbeats, we simply looked at each other while we strained for breath. His eyes widened. They showed arousal and something else. Recognition, perhaps? Discomfort and doubt, as if he questioned himself? Finally, they showed anger. He blinked and they glazed over into that emotionless expression I knew and hated.

At length he moved away to sit on the bed with his back to me, casually dressing as if nothing had happened between us.

"I knew you would beg me to take you." His voice was flat, toneless.

"Get out," I said, equally coldly, ignoring the pain of the burn on my hand as I curled it into a fist.

"As my lady wishes." He gave me a mock bow before leaving. Tears were already falling before he closed the door behind him.

****

From then on, I struggled to maintain my resolve. During the day I avoided Sawford, barely able to maintain the mask of indifference in his presence. But when he took me to my room at night I surrendered to him, unable to fight my body's craving for his touch. Tender caresses and gentle nips at my skin brought me to the brink of satisfaction. There, he would wait until I offered him my body, pleading and pulling him to me before withdrawing in shame. The intensity of the pleasure rendered my body limp, save for the gentle aftershocks which rippled through me. My body called him to return inside me; my need for him surpassed my fear of discovery.

We spoke not at all during the day and very little at

night. I hated what he made my body do, yet I yearned for the feeling that, when he lost himself at that final pinnacle of abandonment, a part of him cherished me, if only for the briefest moment.

The only fragment of hope came from my correspondence with Tarvin. His letters and notes became more frequent, and increasingly they convinced me that the gentle, heartfelt words I read were genuine. My emotions were so torn to shreds at Sawford's hands. I could not contain them. I finally succumbed and wrote to Tarvin, telling him how desperately I needed a friend and how frightened I was. He responded, begging me, for my own safety and his, not to try to discover him. I promised I would not. I alternated between hiding my letters to him in the rose bush and the stone in the stable wall. Though I burned with curiosity, I kept my distance afterward and bid Harwyn, who had taken it upon herself to spy on Mortlock, to do the same.

I wrote of my loneliness and a little of my childhood. In turn, he wrote about his own life. His letters were full of stories of adventure. He had not been a favored son and left home seeking adventure only to be almost killed on the road by robbers. A knight had rescued him and employed him as a squire, teaching him the arts of warfare and of stealth, until he was able to give his services to his lord. I smiled at his stories, which reminded me of the tales my mother had read of King Arthur's knights and their daring but chivalrous exploits. Tarvin's outlandish tales took me to another world: a world of romance and honor, where men fought bravely and where they loved, cherished, and protected their women. I was grateful to him, not only for his friendship, but for giving me those few precious moments when I could read his words and forget about the harsh realities of the world I lived in—the world of pain, treachery, and loneliness.

It became clear that Tarvin was loyal to the king. Could I trust him enough to reveal my own loyalties, worthless as they were? At first, I dared not, but as our correspondence continued he wrote more openly of his sentiments, warning me of traitors in our midst. He had shown trust in me, trust I would not betray him to my husband.

Would he ever reveal himself and take me away from here? I ached to know his identity, to see him with my own eyes. I had an ally, someone who held me in high enough regard to place his faith in me. He cared enough to risk his own neck for the sole purpose of giving me comfort. Lord help me, was I falling in love? The very notion terrified me. Maman died not only because she loved a man other than her husband, but because she lay with him. She had given her body and her heart to another. Now, two years after watching my mother's weakness, I was here: a woman married to a traitor to the king, with a cruel streak and a host of men at his beck and call, who willingly gave her body to one of those men, and her heart to another.

****

While replacing the stone in the stable wall to conceal a letter to Tarvin, I heard voices. The high pitched, coarse female tones grew closer. I shrank back against the wall, trying to think of an excuse for my being here. I almost laughed at the irony. Two gossiping maidservants shirking their duties should be more afraid of their mistress, yet I was the one crouched in fear of discovery.

One of them sounded upset, her voice broken with angry sobs. Her companion spoke harshly.

"Calm yourself Edith. He's just a man and there are plenty of others willing to take your favors."

"Just a man!" The second voice was punctuated by sobs. "I want not the others, Celia, and you know it!"

More sobbing. Edith was a pretty girl who worked in the kitchens and was popular with the men; she was harmless, but not very bright. Celia, however, was the woman who had taken me to the solar and tried to seduce Sawford in front of me. Edith was pleasant enough, but I could not bear Celia's insolence. Where most of the servants dropped a deep curtsey or bow on seeing me, Celia stood that little bit higher, challenging me with her sharp eyes. The hatred in her expression, when I caught her watching me, was unmistakable.

"…Sawford…"

Lost in thought, my mind jerked back to their conversation on hearing Sawford's name.

"You want him for yourself, Celia! You always have."

"Aye, 'tis true, Edith. 'Tis also true that his tastes have widened to include that scrawny sack of bones. But he will always prefer a real woman."

"Such as yourself?"

Celia's voice was proud. "I know how to pleasure him; unlike you and certainly unlike *her*."

Edith resumed sobbing and Celia spoke more kindly, her voice laced with false charm. She had used the same charm on Sawford the night she took me to the solar. For that night at least, her attempt at seduction had failed.

"Edith, Sawford will never kiss any of his women

on the mouth, and he refuses to let them kiss him. You should not have tried."

"Aye, he's said that, but…"

"But you thought you could be the one to change him? Little fool! 'Tis too personal an act with him. Enjoy the pleasure he gives you between your thighs, and expect nothing else."

Edith continued to sob and though Celia shushed her comfortingly, I detected exasperation in her voice along with a sense of triumph. Eventually sniffs replaced the sobs.

"For the love of God, Edith, stop that. Here."

Edith blew her nose, and her voice lowered to a murmur.

"He is an—energetic—man," Celia said. "A comely wench such as yourself will not be banished from his bed for long."

"But he said never…"

"Shush, fool! With your pretty face he'll soon relent and spread your legs again. Then, between us, we will banish all thoughts he has for that witch."

I almost smiled to myself. The jealousy in Celia's voice belied the manner in which she reassured Edith about Sawford's interest in her. However, my smile faded at her next words and a cold fist punched through my chest, squeezing my heart with icy fingers.

"Sawford's interest in her will wane. Mortlock will use her adultery to dispose of her soon enough, but we need not let him know 'tis Sawford who is rutting his wife."

I sank to the ground, my legs crumpling under me.

Edith's sobs turned into a wail. A sharp crack resounded followed by a shriek of pain.

"Be quiet, you fool, or I'll strike you again," Celia hissed. "Sawford is too clever to arouse suspicion. Another man will take the fall for her adultery and find his head on a pike."

The voices faded, but I waited to ensure they had gone. My hands shook as I brushed the dust off my overgown. I could not help but run a finger across my lips. Sawford had kissed my lips both savagely and tenderly. Under a torrent of passion, I had kissed him back.

'Tis too personal an act with him.

A hand tapped my shoulder.

"Lady?"

I jumped in fright, letting out a small cry.

"Percy!"

"Forgive me, my lady. Are you well?"

I nodded, regaining some of my composure.

"Aye, Percy, but what are you doing here, at the back of the stables?"

"I…I heard something." His nervousness and lack of assurance reminded me how young he was.

"Did you follow me, Percy?"

He shook his head, but the fear in his soft eyes told a different story. My own gaze flicked instinctively to the stone in the wall where my note was hidden, and I smoothed my expression into a smile, holding out my hand.

"Come, Percy, I am a little unwell and would have you escort me to my chamber."

He colored and helped me to my feet. Crossing the stable yard, I saw Edith and Celia standing beside the door to the kitchen. They were deep in conversation, their backs to us. At that moment, Sawford emerged from the building, walking toward the stables. He stiffened and stopped, narrowing his eyes. He looked at me so intensely that I gripped Percy's arm, in need of support.

Celia called his name, lowering her voice to a drawl. I raised my eyebrows at Sawford. He mirrored my gesture, a faint smile on his lips, before he turned in her direction.

I continued across the yard with Percy, acutely aware of murmuring voices, one deep and strong, the other sultry and seductive. Though I looked straight ahead as we passed them, I knew Sawford watched us.

Chapter 8

The next afternoon, while I worked in the treatment room, Harwyn rushed through the door, a look of wild terror on her face.

"Dear Lord, Harwyn, what has happened?"

"Oh, my lady," she panted. "Lord Mortlock grows suspicious of you."

"Of what? He's the one who ordered a stallion to service the mare."

Harwyn shook her head, trying to catch her breath.

"Then what has frightened you, Harwyn?" I lowered my voice to a whisper. "Is it Tarvin?"

"No, but I overheard a conversation between Lord Mortlock and Monsieur Sawford. I managed to get close enough to hear much of what they said."

"Harwyn, I have told you before not to place yourself in danger."

"I pledged to your Maman that I would face all the dangers in the world to keep you safe," she said. "I was well concealed; you need not fear for me."

"What did they speak of?" Sawford would hardly wish to incriminate himself if what Celia told Edith was true. Was he already trying to incriminate another?

"Your husband said he grows suspicious of the way you carry yourself."

"But I have been so careful not to reveal my feelings."

"That is what concerns him, my lady. He feels you should be more—afraid. He is a jealous man and has demanded to know if…if the mare holds affection for any of her studs."

"*Any* of them?"

"Aye, it seems the plan was for no individual to be given exclusivity over you."

I sank onto the bed, sickened by what I was hearing.

"So, I'm to be handed around his men? And what would happen if he suspected I held a…a stud in my affections?"

"He said any man with a loose tongue would pay with his head. And with yours."

"Mon Dieu," I whispered. "He cannot know Sawford takes me for himself. Who does he think I'm being given to?"

"I know not, lady. I was only able to hear part of their conversation before I deemed it too dangerous to stay. I saw Percy listening, too."

"Good God! Percy?"

"Aye. He was not as well concealed as I. He risked us both being discovered so I left. It seems there are spies everywhere."

"Spies for whom?" I wondered aloud. "Mayhap Percy is not all he appears to be."

Harwyn's eyes widened. "Surely you don't think—Tarvin…"

I found it difficult to believe it to be someone so young, but Percy had come upon me at the back of the stables, just after I'd concealed my letter. What possible reason could he have for going there?

****

The following morning, after I had broken my fast, I was summoned to the stables. I expected to find my husband brandishing my note to Tarvin, declaring my adultery before taking me to the courtyard for punishment. However, instead, a hunting party awaited me, most of them already saddled.

"I have been neglecting my lovely wife," my husband croaked from atop his gelding.

"Nay, you have been an attentive husband."

"Do not seek to contradict me, woman," he said. "I would have you ride with me on the hunt today."

I understood the necessity of hunting to provide food, but disliked the relish the participants took in the savagery of the hunt. But, I was fond of my horse and would take pleasure in riding her today. I had not ridden her since the first time when Wyatt forced his attentions on me, and I'd been reluctant to ask permission to ride again for fear he would accompany me. Though I kept my knife about me, I did not wish to be placed in a situation where I'd have need of it.

I stroked the mare's nose, knowing I had no choice but to join my husband.

"Here, madam." The skin at the back of my neck tightened at the familiar voice. Sawford touched my elbow and guided me to the mare and helped me to mount. His hand was that of a hunter who already had his prey in his grasp and was merely toying with her before the kill.

The hunting party was small—about a dozen of us. Mortlock took the lead with Sawford beside him on a large black stallion, together with another man leading the deerhounds. I was glad to see Percy among the party. He drew alongside me as we crossed the drawbridge which spanned the moat surrounding Mortlock Fort.

"I trust my lady is feeling better?" His face colored as he spoke, and I nodded, giving him a smile.

The hounds picked up the scent of their quarry almost as soon as we entered the forest. Most of the party set off at a gallop, but I followed at a more leisurely pace. Though I would have preferred the solitude, I was grateful to Percy for hanging back while the rest of the party disappeared through the trees. Perhaps now was the time to find out where his loyalties truly lay.

My curiosity rose when he began to speak of the king, but before I could steer the conversation, my horse pulled up, and I lost my balance on the saddle and fell to the ground. For a moment, I lay face up on the forest floor, watching the sunlight dance across the leaves of the trees in the breeze, until a shadow stepped over me and Percy's concerned face came into view.

He helped me to my feet, blushing furiously as his fingers touched mine, and my heart sank. The poor young man had a crush on me. I doubted he was my secret correspondent. The deep, heartfelt words I had read were not those of a tender-hearted boy. Tarvin would be too aware of the danger to risk such an outward display of affection. However, Percy might still be useful. If he were loyal to the king, he might know Tarvin's identity.

"You have my thanks, Percy," I said. "Twice in two days you have shown gallantry."

He smiled and bowed over my hand, kissing it at the wrist where the flesh was exposed.

"What are you doing with Lady Mortlock?"

The voice behind us was instantly recognizable.

Sawford stood by a tree, his face darkening with anger as he raked his gaze over me, taking in my disheveled appearance and the mud on my gown. Curling his hands into fists, his body betrayed more emotion than I had ever seen before.

A slight tickling sensation on my skin made me look down. A long scratch ran across the back of my hand, droplets of blood already beginning to form. I lifted my hand to inspect the wound and heard a low hiss from Sawford. He stepped toward me, jaw set firm, teeth gritted, shoulders shaking. But with what? Anger, fear? What could he possibly have to be afraid of?

"What have you done, boy!" he roared.

Percy stepped back, his face ashen with fear at the force of Sawford's anger.

I glared at Sawford. "He has done nothing; my horse pulled up. Why are you not at your place by my husband's side?"

Sawford ignored me and spoke to Percy.

"Return her ladyship's horse to the stables."

"But she is lame. It will take hours if I must walk her back."

"Do not make me ask again."

"But how will my lady…"

"I will ensure she's returned to her place by her husband's side." Sawford spoke quietly but his voice held a dangerous edge. Tall and muscular, he towered over both of us in the dappled light of the forest. Percy glanced at me, and I nodded at him to do as he was bid. He mounted his horse and Sawford led the mare to him. He lifted up her front left foot.

"She has lost a shoe. Take her directly to the

blacksmith. A gentle trot should suffice. Nothing faster or you'll lame her."

The young squire nodded at Sawford before giving me a stiff bow and taking his leave. Sawford furrowed his brow and reached out to touch my sleeve which was covered in mud from my fall.

"How do you propose I return to my place by my husband's side?" I said with a sneer in my voice.

"You will ride with me."

The stallion was tethered beside a tree, waiting patiently for his rider to return. Sawford took my arm and led me toward the tree. His grip betrayed his discomfort, the tension in his body reverberating through his arm. His loss of control was unsettling.

"Let me go." I tried to pull free, but he was too strong. He grasped my other arm and pushed me back against the tree, the hard lumps of the bark digging into my shoulder blades. As I opened my mouth to protest, his mouth crushed mine, and he forced me harder against the tree with his body. His kiss was brutal, and I cried out as he grazed my bottom lip with his teeth, then soothed it with his tongue. He grew hard as he moved his body against mine, rocking his hips, a low growl in his throat. A savage instinct made me respond to his kiss, and I bit his lip, drawing blood. He gasped and let go of my arms. Immediately, I reached out to him, clutching his hair. Digging my nails into his scalp, I pulled him to me until our mouths met.

He lifted my skirts and rammed himself into me so hard that my back jarred against the tree trunk. The air was forced from my lungs in mewing gasps as he pounded in and out, slamming me into the tree. With each powerful thrust, the pain of the rough bark digging into my body morphed into intense pleasure, and I urged him on, wrapping my legs around him. He drove into me harder and faster, until I was engulfed by the inferno inside of me. A demonic hunger screamed to be quenched. The urgency of his movements increased sharply and my body tightened in recognition of what was to happen. He then bellowed out his release. His horse stood placidly, unaffected by our frenzied coupling.

I held him tightly, my heart beating furiously, until my vision cleared, and I looked into his face. His breathing was hoarse and labored, his eyes tightly closed. When he opened them, they showed the same doubt and uncertainty as before. Something tormented him, and I had to ease it. I brushed my lips against his mouth and lifted my hand to stroke his face, wanting the pain in his eyes to disappear. He placed a hand over mine. His touch was so tender I gave a low moan of anguish before kissing him once more. I laid my head on his shoulder and sighed as he caressed the back of my neck.

At the sound of the hunting horn, he curled his hand into a fist in my hair and yanked my head away from him. The cold demeanor returned and once again the predator replaced the man. Shaking, I pulled my skirts down, though they would never hide my disgust at what we had done, what I had let—nay—begged him to do. He pushed me toward the horse, helping me onto the saddle, before he swung himself up behind me.

We followed the sound of the horn and rejoined the hunt. Sawford explained the incident with the mare to my husband in a casual tone, as if nothing had happened between us. Yet, for the remainder of the hunt, I could smell his desire and feel his hardness against my lower back as the movement of the horse rocked our bodies together. By the time we returned to the stables, my nerves were torn to shreds, and I was only too glad to leave Sawford to check on my horse.

I found Percy helping a groom rub the mare down. On seeing me, he waved the groom away.

"How fares the mare, Percy?"

"She is well. You'll be able to ride her again tomorrow."

I stroked the animal's forehead, rubbing her nose and smiling as she nickered in delight.

"'Tis good to see you smile, Lisetta."

I started at Percy's familiar use of my name. He lowered his voice.

"I know you are unhappy, lady, and I wish I could change that."

"Do not be kind to me, Percy," I warned him. "My life is as it is. Kindness, however well intended, will only make it more difficult for me to maintain my resolve."

"I can help you," he whispered.

I smiled and held out my hand. He curled his fingers limply round mine. I felt warmth and friendship, but nothing compared to the burning heat of Sawford's touch.

"You must think of yourself, Percy, not of me."

He squeezed my hand again. "I'm not only loyal to you, lady, but the king—"

His voice broke off abruptly, and he looked up. Sawford stood at the stable door. I lowered my voice.

"My loyalty is aligned with yours, Percy, but while that black cockroach of a manservant creeps about the place, I can do nothing."

"But I can. You have a friend in me. Have you not always seen that?"

I pulled him closer, dropping my voice. "Tarvin?" I whispered, "is it you?"

Before he could respond, Sawford joined us and dismissed Percy, telling him to return to his duties. I watched the young man leave. Sawford reached for my arm, but I had anticipated the move and snatched it away before he could gain purchase.

"Do not touch me," I snarled.

"That's not what you said when you were mewling like a she-cat in heat as I rutted you."

Swallowing my self-loathing, I swept past him without reacting. He called after me.

"Be careful whom you attempt to befriend, madam. For your sake and theirs."

****

The following morning, I woke earlier than usual, exhausted and a little nauseous. Rather than wait for Harwyn, I dressed myself, unable to shake off a lingering sense of dread.

The previous night, my husband had shown a particular relish while pleasuring himself in the solar, licking his lips while watching me with his fetid eyes. Sawford returned me to my room as usual to take me for himself, but he had been unexpectedly gentle. To my shame I had cried in his arms at his touch and before leaving me he held me close for a brief moment, his heart pulsing against my chest. After dressing, he reached out to wipe the tears which moistened my cheeks, but I jerked my head away, turning my back until I heard the door close behind him.

Harwyn entered my chamber just as I finished dressing. My cries of ecstasy from the previous night rang in my ears. I dismissed her and spent the day in my treatment room. Their echoes continued to mock me there. As hard as I tried to shake my head to disperse them, they grew louder—shrill cries, ending in a single high-pitched scream.

An atmosphere of anticipation lingered over the household. When I passed them on my way to the garden, the men stopped their training to stare, only resuming when I told them to show their mistress respect. I spoke in a hollow voice, knowing what little power I wielded here. Lord save me, had they heard my cries? Did they listen at the door when Sawford took me?

As the day drew to a close and the sun began its descent, my husband summoned me to the stables with a message that we were going hunting. However, when I arrived, only he and Sawford were there.

"Where is the hunting party?"

"I have instead decided to take you on a tour of the estate. I have a particular view I think you will appreciate."

Sawford watched me carefully as if to gauge my reaction to my husband's words. He looked uncomfortable. Had my husband discovered the identity of the stud who was servicing his mare? I raised my eyebrows in question, but he blanked his expression and looked away. Something was amiss and he knew it.

The ride itself was uneventful. Mortlock led us round the grounds and through the village. On seeing us approach the peasants scattered, the oppressive atmosphere affecting their spirits as much as it did mine. My husband pointed out various landmarks and buildings of interest, as if we were a young couple in love enjoying an evening ride. Once again he referred to the view awaiting me at the end of our excursion. My fear rose when, on the road back to the drawbridge, Sawford drew closer until our horses almost touched, while my husband followed immediately behind.

On passing the drawbridge and entering the bailey, the silhouette of the main building came into view. A small group of crows circled an object which stood out in the rays of the setting sun.

A head on a pike.

I pressed my lips together and rode closer until I could make out the features. The mouth was locked open, as if he had been screaming the moment his head was severed from his body. His lips were drawn back, showing his teeth. There were gaps where they must have pulled some of them out before they killed him. The jagged edge of his neck told me it had not been a clean cut; the axe-man must have made several attempts before succeeding. He would not have died at the first stroke. Big droplets of blood had formed around the rough lines of flesh, some sending thin streams which had trickled down the wall, following the spaces between the bricks before coming to a halt where they dried.

The most horrific feature was his eyes. They stared out blankly like dark, hollow sockets. My own eyes began to throb and ache. A crow flew at his face, driving its beak into one of the sockets, causing a spatter of blood to drip onto his cheek. The features were distorted and by dawn tomorrow they would be unrecognizable. Yet I recognized him.

It was Percy.

Chapter 9

I closed my eyes but could not erase the image of the black, gaping holes in Percy's face where his eyes had been. The lurching movement of my horse became more pronounced and a rush of nausea almost overwhelmed me. I took a deep breath, and my body shuddered. I tasted blood on my lips and realized I had bitten them.

A low chuckle burbled from behind.

"I think my wife approves of our treatment of traitors. What say you, Sawford?"

"Who can tell what she thinks, my Lord?

My husband laughed. "Aye, Sawford. She clearly thinks little of her lover, no?"

"Mayhap she knows nothing of love."

Sawford—how could he? To mock me with my own words while that poor gentle soul lay mutilated for all to see. Full of hatred I lifted my gaze to him. He narrowed his own eyes, showing small creases around the edges. I dropped my gaze, unwilling to let him see my tears. I focused on my hands which curled and uncurled around the reins. My horse, sensing I was no longer in control, lunged her head forward, jerking my arms. I struggled to steady her as we rode into the stable yard.

Another surge of nausea welled up inside me. I fought to control my breathing. I counted: one, two, three. Keeping my eyes closed, I drew on images of happier times—life with Maman, moments alone in the wild garden, occupation in the treatment room with Harwyn—anything to drive out the black and red images of Percy's severed neck, the drops of blood and the crow's vicious beak, pulling in and out...

"Lady."

I jerked my head up as a hand touched my wrist.

Sawford watched me.

I swung my leg over the saddle and dismounted. The ground came toward me at speed, drawing closer and closer until I could make out a small stone across which a black beetle crawled, dragging its hind legs. Its back, shiny and poisonous-looking, reminded me of my husband. I closed my eyes again, wanting to obliterate everything and a slow, pulsating, swirling sensation shifted my body as the ground beneath my feet began to spin.

My head began to pound, and I heard something—almost like a howling from within my mind, urging me to shut out the world. Desperate to succumb, I squeezed my eyes together more tightly, but a strong grip on my arms pulled me back. I reached out and my hands met cloth, which I grasped to steady myself.

The spinning sensation faded, and I opened my eyes.

I was in Sawford's arms.

I pushed him away, biting my lip to stop my voice from trembling, and eyed him with loathing. This was the man who in all likelihood was the one who murdered Percy or, at least, gave the order.

"The ground is uneven is it not?" He spoke calmly.

"Take your hands off me."

He said nothing. Instead, he lifted his hand to my face and wiped his thumb across my bottom lip. I saw a smear of red on his thumb which he wiped on his sleeve.

"Take care, madam. Lord Mortlock does not like to see a flaw on his wife's face."

I turned my back on him and addressed my husband.

"I would beg to be excused so I might dress for dinner."

"Of course," Mortlock croaked. "Come here."

To my horror he drew me to him until our mouths met. I thought I heard a sharp intake of breath from Sawford. Revulsion drove out all other sensations as my husband ran his lips over mine, roughly pushing his tongue in and out of my mouth. He tasted of decay and evil, his breath a fog of putrefaction. The kiss only lasted a brief moment, but I felt tainted and unclean, as if the sickness of his mind would permeate my soul and condemn me to hell.

He broke off the kiss and laughed.

"You see, Sawford, she is repulsed by a bastard and pushes you away. Yet her noble husband is not thus rejected. My wife has discerning tastes."

"Aye, she has."

I bowed my head at my husband and ignoring Sawford, turned and walked across the stable yard. Only after I entered the building, assured of my solitude, did I break into a run. On reaching my room I burst through the door and collapsing on the floor, retched. The ground began to spin again, and I gasped for air, my vision dimming. Once again, darkness rushed toward me, but this time I welcomed it, knowing it to be the precursor to oblivion.

I opened my eyes as a cool hand touched the side of my face, and I jerked my head up in fright.

"Shhh, lady. 'Tis me."

Harwyn sat beside me on the floor, cradling my head in her lap. Grief overcame me as she stroked my forehead, making soothing noises. She sang to me softly, and I clung to her, my body shaking with sobs.

When I quietened, she helped me sit up. The sorrow and compassion in her eyes only made my tears return.

"Poor young man. He did nothing wrong. My insane husband and his vile servant mutilated his body."

"Shhh, lady, I beg you not speak of it so loudly. Why do you think they killed him? Perhaps he was the author of the letters?"

I shook my head. "Nay, Harwyn. Percy was simply a kind, young man, loyal to the king, who liked me and was murdered for it. I know not who Tarvin is but I must ask him to stop writing to me. He puts himself in danger."

"He puts you in danger also."

She held out her hand, and I took it, letting her pull me to a standing position.

"Lady, do you love Tarvin?"

"I cannot afford to, Harwyn. I cannot risk loving anyone here." A sob rose in my throat. "Oh, Harwyn, 'tis too much for me! How can I continue this charade of feigning indifference? I know what happens here: evil, treachery, and the murder of innocents."

"Lady, you must. Your Maman would be proud of you." She lowered her voice. "Lord Mortlock is an old man. He won't live forever. Not all lords are like your husband—or your father."

"Aye, Harwyn, but my husband has family. His cousin de Tourrard is a powerful man and considerably younger. He would inherit."

"Then you must ensure he has no influence over you."

I shook my head. "The only way to achieve that, Harwyn, is to leave here after my husband dies…"

A sharp knock at the door made us both jump. We looked at each other in fear. Had they heard us?

Harwyn opened it to reveal Sawford, his powerful frame towering over her.

"I have come to escort Lady Mortlock to the solar."

"But she is dressed for dinner." Harwyn protested.

"She will dine alone with her husband tonight."

I shivered at the prospect of spending an entire evening in the solar with my husband, but I held my head high and regarded Sawford haughtily.

"I can find my own way there. I'm sure one such as yourself has duties elsewhere."

He raised an eyebrow sardonically. "One such as I?"

"Aye—a bastard."

His lips curled into a smile but his expression remained cold. He narrowed his eyes and held out his hand. When I took it, he stroked my skin with his thumb. I caught a breath in my throat but stared straight ahead, refusing to look at him while he led me to my husband.

At the threshold of the solar, he pulled me to him, his voice laced with warning.

"I advise you to do everything your husband

wishes tonight. Show nothing of the foolish behavior you displayed this afternoon."

"You have no right to issue orders to your mistress," I hissed, pulling my hand from his. But he merely gripped it more tightly.

"For the love of God, woman, do not be a fool. Heed my words. Remember what I told you about your husband."

I did not understand his meaning but as he pushed me into the solar, my senses were assaulted by a strange odor. The odor was faintly reminiscent of Sawford's wound, when I'd first treated it—the smell of rotting flesh. A table was set for three in the center of the room. Each placing had an eating knife and a trencher. On two of the trenchers someone had ladled out the venison stew eaten regularly at Mortlock. My husband sat in front of one of the trenchers, wearing a nightshirt. On the third—where the odor emitted from—someone had placed Percy's head.

"Ah, my dear. Come and join us." My husband beckoned to me. "Your lover and I are taking supper together and think it only fair you be permitted to partake. Sawford, bring her here."

Sawford pushed me forward and sat me next to my husband.

"Eat, wife. 'Tis good stew."

Bile rose in my throat. With a trembling hand, I jabbed at a piece of meat with my knife. Holding it up, I tried to avoid looking at the thing on the table opposite me. On seeing the small lump of flesh impaled on the blade, my mouth went dry, and I dropped it on the trencher.

"I believe the stew is too poor a fare for her

tonight."

Mortlock's words were directed at Sawford who merely nodded, though his eyes were on me.

"Perhaps my wife wishes to retire tonight?"

My husband eyed me as a spider, about to drain the lifeblood from its prey. Not recognizing the danger I nodded. "I would be grateful, husband."

He gestured to Sawford again. "Make sure she is ready for me; and in my bed this time."

"Aye my Lord."

Heaven help me! Not only had my husband expected me to dine alone with him tonight but, also, lie with him. He continued eating, making casual comments about the taste of the sauce and the cut of the meat, while Sawford undressed me before laying me out on the bed, as if I were being placed on a sacrificial altar.

"Good, Sawford. Now leave us."

Much as I hated Sawford, the prospect of being left alone with my husband terrified me. I looked up at him, unable to conceal the plea in my eyes.

"My Lord, might I suggest—"

"No, Sawford, you may not. Remain outside the door until I have finished with her."

As the door clicked shut behind Sawford, my husband rose and slipped his nightshirt over his head. His form was bent and wizened. A lifetime of evil had ravaged his body from the outside as well as withered his soul from the inside. Yet, I could see he was aroused.

"I must thank your lover, wife. In delivering his punishment, I find I'm at long last able to enjoy you properly."

At last Sawford's warning became clear. My husband's appetite for me was fueled by cruelty, death, and his relish over Percy's demise. But I understood it all too late. Only when in a particular frame of mind, Sawford had said, would my husband wish to force his disease-ridden body onto a woman. I could do nothing but await my fate as he approached the bed.

****

When my husband finished with me, I wanted nothing more than to drive my knife into his heart. At first I had wondered if all men were the same. Would my body betray me and succumb to his whims, as it did when Sawford took me? But I felt only revulsion at my husband's touch, as if maggots were crawling along my skin.

He called for Sawford to return me to my room. Though Sawford must have known of my humiliation, he said nothing. He pushed me through my doorway but came no further in himself. He merely ran his fingertips across my forehead before cupping my chin and lifting my face up. My eyes were wet with the tears I refused to shed in front of him. He showed no sign of seeing them. Instead, he leaned forward and brushed his lips against mine, then released my chin and closed the door, leaving me alone.

I ached for a bath to rid myself of my husband's foul stench. But, if I ordered one, he would find out. Feeling dirty and degraded, I crawled into bed, wanting nothing more than to not wake up in the morning—or any day after.

****

The sound of crackling flames surrounded me. The smell of fire reached my nostrils and I heard the snapping sound of burning wood igniting, along with the chants of the crowd…

…witch, adulteress, traitor…

My mother's voice broke through the chanting. At first she sang a lullaby, then she began to cry. Her cries sharpened, turning into screams. The crackling of the flames increased and the smell grew stronger. I wanted her to stop screaming—surely she must be dead by now. Her beautiful face came into view, smiling at me, but her eyes were no longer there. They had been replaced by black voids. Huge birds flapped around her, tearing strips of flesh from her face. The strips morphed into another face; Percy's. The crows flapped around me, their beaks grew large as they reached my eyes, the beat of their wings whooshed in the air. I lifted my arms to fend them off and opened my mouth. The screaming became louder, the birds tearing at my own eyes while I was powerless to stop them…

I sat up, my throat aching while I gasped and sobbed, struggling for air. I was in my bed but it was dark. I opened my mouth to cry out but a gentle hand touched my arm while another covered my mouth.

"Shhh, you're safe." The voice in my ear was a whisper, unrecognizable above the pounding heartbeat in my ears, but it sounded like Maman.

A hand stroked my forehead.

"Here, drink this."

The rim of a cup touched my lips. I choked as it was tipped into my mouth. I could not fight my body's instinct to swallow and cool liquid ran down the back of my throat.

"Drink it all."

I complied, not caring whether the cup contained

poison, for if that hastened my death it would free me from this life. When I drained the cup, gentle hands pushed me back.

"Sleep now, sweetling."

I heard the sound of flint being struck and saw a brief flare of light and a pair of eyes, full of kindness.

"Maman!" My voice weakened as the drug began to take effect. She had come to me when I needed her most and would guide me in death. Her eyes were bluer than I remembered but their expression was soft and loving.

"Maman, am I going to die?"

She did not answer, and I closed my eyes, embracing the heavy blackness which draped over me. I was able to whisper a few words before it fully engulfed me.

"I am coming, Maman. I love you."

****

The next time I opened my eyes, my vision was blurry and my head felt heavy. The glare of the light hurt my head. A hand brushed my forehead.

"Maman?"

"No, dear lady. 'Tis I, Harwyn."

"Harwyn. Are you dead also?"

I lifted my head. It was morning and judging by the pain in my head, I was very much alive.

"You must rest. You are ill."

"I've been poisoned." My voice was hoarse.

Harwyn tut-tutted as one would to a child with an active imagination.

"Nonsense, lady. You're tired and overwrought after your ordeal. Perhaps you took some wine to help you sleep?"

Images flashed before my eyes—a blurred shape, Maman's face and gentle fingers clasping my own as they lifted a cup to my lips. Yet, there was nothing in my room. The table beside my cot, where I usually kept a flagon of wine and a goblet, was empty. I must have imagined it, unless the ghost of my mother had visited me. Was I going mad?

"Lady?" Harwyn's face and voice were full of concern. Though I longed to tell her of Maman's visit, I was terrified she would think I was losing my sanity. I shook my head.

"'Twas only a dream." I said. I swung my legs over the edge of the cot and stood, but I lost my balance and fell against Harwyn. She held me steady.

"Come, you must stay abed today. You are unwell."

"Nay, Harwyn, I need fresh air." And solitude. I longed for the wild garden. I wanted to be free from the fog of evil embedded within the walls of Mortlock Fort. I shook my head again, trying to expel the drowsiness, while Harwyn helped me dress.

The day was dull, the sun unable to penetrate through the leaden clouds. Thick, cold moisture hung in the air, penetrating my cloak despite its dense, woolen material. The building seemed to loom higher the further I walked from it. I could make out the silhouette of poor Percy's head. One of my husband's men had replaced it on the pike for all to see.

I drew my cloak around me, shivering not from the cold alone. I sat on the bench underneath my tree. Driving out all thoughts other than the soothing lull of the wind in the trees and the babbling of the stream, I was able to relax a little. I cherished the stolen moment of peace. A part of me hoped my unseen lover might come to me here and reveal himself. Perhaps he might even carry me away and protect me. But I knew that, unlike the legend of King Arthur's knights, I did not live in a world of honor and chivalry. So I clung to the dream and imagined a different life, where I would be free—free to live and to love as I chose.

A wave of nausea overcame me, and I bent forward, retching. The memory of the cup at my lips grew stronger. Someone had drugged me, though I did not understand why. Had they meant to kill me? Perhaps the poison worked slowly, and I would sicken gradually. I took in a deep breath, and the nausea subsided as the fresh air filled and cleaned my lungs.

The nausea returned the next day but did not worsen. The poison had not done its job properly, unless the intent was to disable rather than kill me. Nonetheless, I was careful of what I ate, and I avoided wine. My husband did not seem to notice, but Sawford's eyes stayed focused on me in the dining hall as I shared a trencher with my husband and pretended to sip at my wine.

After that terrible night in the solar, my husband did not touch me again. He resumed the previous routine of commanding me to strip and stand naked before him while he took his own pleasure. Then, Sawford would return me to my room and take me for himself. Though I tried desperately to keep my passions at bay, my body betrayed me. To my shame, I willingly opened myself to Sawford.

One night, after Sawford had taken me, I turned my back, expecting him to dress and leave as usual, but his hand touched the back of my neck. My skin tightened at his touch, sending a jolt of longing to my core, which still pulsed faintly from the pleasures he'd given me.

"Who is Tarvin?"

My stomach lurched in fright, but I kept my back to him.

"I know not what you say. I've never heard that name before."

The bed ropes creaked as he stood up.

"You called out his name."

"You must have imagined it," I said coldly.

"Perhaps you have another lover? Are you such a whore that you do not wish for exclusivity with me? I should be affronted, madam, for I have not yet left any of my women unsatisfied."

Sawford was goading me, but I refused to take the bait.

"You know well enough, Monsieur, you are the only man forcing his attentions on me. Given my husband's desire for a stallion—any stallion—to service his prize mare, I hardly think a servant such as yourself should have any cause for complaint. We are both livestock in Mortlock's eyes, though I am the one with the bloodline." I turned and looked him in the eye "Perhaps Lord Mortlock may prefer a destrier to service the mare than a mere carthorse."

A flare of rage lit up his eyes and the muscles of his jaw tensed. My arrow had found its target.

"Ever the cold-hearted bitch," he said, "though you are less discerning when I am between your thighs."

To hide the hurt in my eyes, I turned away. I cared not for his opinion, and it was safer for me if they all thought me devoid of feeling. But I still ached for a kind word or a gentle touch. Eventually, I heard him sigh before the door closed after him.

Chapter 10

I strolled in the garden with my husband as the oppressive summer heat pricked against my skin. He gripped my wrist and turned me to him. I fought down my usual, instinctive shiver of revulsion at his touch. Despite the heat of the summer, his cadaverous fingers were cold.

"We have guests arriving tonight, wife. I wish for you to dine in your room. We have much to discuss that is not for the ears of a woman. My guests would not welcome the...distraction."

"Aye, husband." I was aware something was afoot. The chatelaine had been busying herself with preparations, overseeing the guest rooms. The kitchen maids ran to and fro preparing enough food for a feast. Though I was curious as to the guests' identity, I was glad my presence was not required. The less time I spent in the company of my husband or his allies, the better.

I noticed that Sawford was busy—too busy to be lurking in the shadows, and I was grateful for that, too. Instead of having him watch me, I turned the tables and observed him. Underneath that stony demeanor, he began to look wary—almost strained. I doubted if anyone other than I could tell the difference. The day before the guests' arrival, I spotted him walking toward the solar. The way he carried himself, the occasional glance over his shoulder, told me he was not carrying out Mortlock's orders. He was on some errand of his own and did not wish to be discovered. I followed him but, almost immediately, it became clear he knew, for he stopped and called out.

"I suggest you contain your lust for me until tonight."

In shame, I fled and avoided him for the rest of the day, choosing instead to hide myself in my garden at every opportunity. He seemed to be perpetually aware of me—always knowing where I was and what I was thinking and feeling.

On returning to my room, my knees grew weak as I spotted a familiar piece of paper on the floor. With trembling hands, I unfolded it to read the written words:

Courage, Lisetta. Stay safe.

Tarvin

My heart leapt for joy. He was alive! A nugget of hope grew inside me. There was someone who watched over me and wanted to protect me. I was sure he would do nothing to put himself—or me—in any danger. His warning must refer to my husband and his guests. In all likelihood, they were plotting against the king, hence why my husband did not wish for my company while they remained here.

That evening, I dined in my room with Harwyn. The almost continual sound of hoof beats and shouting signaled the arrival of guest after guest, but my husband did not send for me. I told her about the note from Tarvin. She was still concerned Tarvin's motive was entrapment, and she urged me to use caution. Her own resolve, however, had started to falter. She was beginning to believe, as I did, that I had a friend here.

He might be Baldwin—the knight poor Percy had served. He was about two score in years, with graying hair. He seemed more honorable than the rest of the men in my husband's employ. I knew little of him, having only seen him occasionally. It made some sense, and would explain Percy's behavior. Poor young man! Had he known the risks he took and that they would lead to his death? His head was still on the pike. But now it was indistinguishable. The crows had done their work.

The next day, the household was quiet. The guests were possibly with my husband in his study. What were they plotting? Though I was curious, the memory of Papa's beating was still vivid. My husband was likely to do something far worse if he caught me spying. I might even share Percy's fate.

As the day drew to a close, I became so lost in my thoughts I did not notice the man approaching me in the passageway outside my chamber.

"Cousin."

He was tall, lithe, and softly spoken. His handsome features were surrounded by soft, dark blond hair which fell just short of his shoulders. He smiled, but the smile did not reach his eyes. He was dressed in a brilliant, rich-red tunic, embroidered with gold thread. He extended a hand to me; rings glittered on his fingers as he stretched them out.

My husband's cousin, Wulfric, Baron de Tourrard.

I took his proffered hand, and he gripped mine so tightly I winced.

"You have no idea what a great pleasure it is to see you again, my dear."

He leered at me, looking me up and down, as a

snake might size up its prey before striking. There was little resemblance between the angular planes on his handsome face and my husband's wizened features, except perhaps around the mouth. Much as my husband disgusted me, I was glad de Tourrard was already married when Papa had begun looking for a husband for me. The prospect of being owned by a man with a reputation for cruelty, surpassing even Lord Mortlock's, was unimaginable.

He lifted my hand to his lips and kissed my fingers, drawing them into his mouth. He ran his tongue over them and grazed his teeth over my forefinger before biting it. I pulled my hand away.

"'Tis a great pity, Lisetta, that you belong to my cousin."

"What of your own wife, Monsieur?"

He chuckled, "I would gladly have taken you, had my late wife not been alive, at the time your father was brokering you around. You are wasted on my fool of a cousin."

"Your wife is dead?"

"Aye," he took my hand again. "Your eagerness for me is showing."

"You are too familiar." I tried to pull my hand away but his hold was firm. I could not disguise the hatred in my voice, but he merely laughed and lifted his hand to brush my face, rubbing his thumb over my lips.

"I want you, Lisetta, and will have you. I hear my cousin is impotent, and you need a real man under your skirts."

I closed my eyes, his touch making me sick. He stroked my face as gently as Sawford did but, instead of the heat that came at Sawford's touch, a coldness swept over me, turning my blood to ice.

"All in good time, cousin," he whispered. I opened my eyes to see his face close to mine, his eyes dark with lust. He moved his hand to my neck before curling his fingers around it and gripping firmly. As he pressed his thumb against my throat, the pressure on my windpipe grew painful.

"I could show you many intricate delights in my bed, Lisetta. Lord Mortlock will not live forever. I am an extremely patient man. Malford Hall is in need of a mistress. Mayhap I will take you with me when I leave here."

He released me and bowed. I fled, clasping my throat which throbbed with pain. Rounding a corner, I came face to face with another of my husband's guests, and I cried out in recognition.

My father.

Arms outstretched I ran toward him. He was a harsh man, but he was my father. I craved a familiar face and still clung to the memories of my childhood. Those days with Maman, before I more fully understood the ways of the world, were happy. For a few short years, as a young child, I had been happy at Shoreton and I missed it dreadfully.

"Papa!" I cried, "I had not known you were visiting. Why did you not send me word?"

I threw my arms around him and buried my head in his chest, breathing in the smell of him, a familiar smell which brought back memories of my home.

He took me by the shoulders, shaking me roughly.

"Foolish child! What are you doing running about the building like a common villager? I thought I had brought you up to behave like a lady."

"Papa I'm sorry, I was just—"

"I care not for your excuses, Lisetta. I must speak to Mortlock. He needs to rein you in, if you wander around so freely." He lowered his voice, gripping my arms so tightly I groaned with pain. "I expect you to be a dutiful wife as I expected you to be a dutiful daughter. Has your lover's head on that pike taught you nothing? If you behave as your mother did, you will share her fate. 'Twould be no more than you deserved. Clearly the whelp has inherited the bad blood from the bitch. You disappoint me. You're nothing better than a whore."

"Papa…"

"Get thee from my sight. I will speak to your husband to tighten your leash and beat the wantonness out of you. How many other lovers' heads will soon be lined up to display evidence of your lustfulness to all?"

I pulled away from his grip and, sobbing, ran away blindly. I could bear it no longer. I had to go: to the village; to the woods; to anywhere but here. I would take my chances. If I could get to the stables, I could take my mare and seek sanctuary at the convent. Even if the abbess turned me away, a lifetime of penury and starvation would be better than this. At that moment, I cared not for Tarvin—or even Harwyn—my instinct for flight was too strong.

I reached the door leading outside and fumbled at the handle, panic rising when it would not turn. Eventually, it swung open and I ran through, barely aware of my surroundings until I collided with what felt like a solid wall. I found myself in the arms of a man.

Sawford.

He drew his arms around me, holding me tighter as

I struggled.

"Let me go!" I cried. "Oh God, please let me go. I cannot bear it!"

I clawed at him, trying to free myself, aware of nothing but the urge to run. I heard a tearing sound, then a sharp pain on the side of my face pulled me back from the brink of panic. Sawford had struck me.

I stepped back, rubbing my cheek.

"Please let me go," I whispered, "please—Vane."

At the use of his name, his eyes widened. My mask had crumbled to dust. I took his hand and begged him with my eyes, not caring what he—or anyone—thought of me.

"Please," I begged. "No one need know how I escaped. Tell them anything. Say I died, or ran off with a lover, I care not. But you have to let me go. Please!" My voice cracked as I began to cry again. Now my barricade had come down, months of unspent emotions flooded through, threatening to engulf me.

"So, madam, outside of my bed there beats a heart beneath your cold shell." His voice sounded triumphant, and he touched my face, wiping the tears away.

"You would not get far, madam. My lord prizes his mare too highly."

I pulled away. "You are too familiar."

"Nay, lover, I am not and well you know it."

"Lover," I said bitterly, "Papa wants my lover's head on a pike."

He raised his eyebrows. "Baron Shoreton is here?"

I forced a laugh. "So, your master does not tell you everything. Mayhap the brood mare has greater worth to my lord than a…a cockroach."

"You are well aware of my worth, madam." He pulled me to him and kissed me roughly. I drew back my arm and scratched him across the face, taking care to score a mark with my fingernails. He pushed me away, and I glared back defiantly, challenging him to strike again but he merely laughed.

"I see my lover has a set of claws."

He stepped toward me and I backed away.

"Return to your room. Even if you survived an escape attempt, a pampered creature such as yourself would not live long in the real world."

As if to prove his point, he nodded toward my gown where it had torn in the struggle. Beyond him, in the light of the setting sun, a group of my husband's men stood by the bailey wall watching us.

I had no choice but to obey. Never had I felt so trapped. The shame at losing my self-control in front of the very man I strived to protect myself from was too much to bear. I felt ill again and only just reached my room before I bent over, retching.

The poison must be working again. Perhaps someone was slipping something into my food. I had two options—die slowly here at Mortlock or die more quickly in an attempt to escape. The latter seemed preferable but I could not leave without Harwyn.

Harwyn. I heard her exclamation of horror on seeing her mistress collapsed on the floor yet again and felt her hand on my head.

"Lady, you are unwell again."

She helped me up and undressed me, easing me into my cot. I reached out my hand and she took it.

"Harwyn, we have to leave," I whispered. "I'll ask Tarvin to help."

She shook her head. "Nay, lady, 'tis too dangerous. We know not who he is yet."

"I care not, Harwyn. I am tired, so tired. I cannot stay here any longer and would rather leave—or die trying."

She squeezed my hand in comfort. "Then I will help you."

****

My husband's guests remained at Mortlock for almost a month, but I managed to stay away from them, confining myself to my room. I used Harwyn as a lookout when I slipped out to the wild garden for air. If they were plotting against the king, I wanted to leave as soon as possible but Harwyn warned me of the danger of corresponding with Tarvin while the guests were here, especially Papa and de Tourrard.

The evening after the guests left, my husband summoned me to the main hall for dinner. Harwyn was brushing my hair when another wave of nausea caught me, and I lurched forward, feeling faint. She sat me on my cot, facing the window, my back to the door while I leaned forward, taking deep breaths until the nausea passed.

"Lady, I have to ask. Are you breeding?"

"Harwyn?" I lifted my head weakly. "No. Dear Lord. No."

"I've not had to supply you with extra cloths for some time. This sickness of yours—forgive me—'tis obvious. Your Maman suffered much the same with you."

Lord save me, I was with child.

"My husband must not be told, Harwyn. He'll never let me out of his sight if he knows."

She placed a gentle hand on my shoulder and I took it, trying to make sense of what was happening to me. Escape was now an imperative. I could not live with myself if I allowed a child to be brought up here. Lord Mortlock was a vile enough husband but what of Baron de Tourrard? He had made his intentions clear when he accosted me. A life with him would be even worse. I would not let any child of mine be used by either of them.

Eventually Harwyn patted my hand and picked up the brush again, running it delicately through my hair before braiding it.

"Harwyn, is there anything you can give me for my sickness?"

"Aye, I will brew you an infusion tonight."

"Thank you, Harwyn. But be careful. My husband must not find out. Nobody must know I am carrying Vane Sawford's child."

A noise made us both turn round. Neither of us had heard the door open, nor the approaching footsteps of the man who now leaned against the doorframe, his eyes fixed on me. Harwyn took my hand and I stared in horror as Vane Sawford inclined his head toward me in a slight bow before turning his back on us, leaving as silently as he came.

Chapter 11

Neither my husband nor Sawford said anything in particular to me during the evening meal, but I was nervous, nonetheless. Though confident I gave nothing away, I dared not look in Sawford's direction.

After the stew had been cleared away my husband waved a servant over who placed a dish in front of me, laden with honeyed figs—my favorite food. Fighting a wave of nausea I picked one up.

"Do you like them?"

My husband watched as I bit into the fig and licked my sticky fingers.

"Aye, husband. Thank you."

"I find them repulsive myself, but Sawford was very particular about serving them tonight."

My eyes met Sawford's and he dipped his thumb into the dish of figs in front of him and lifted it to his mouth, curling his tongue to lick the honey off, an echo of my wedding night when I had taken his thumb into my mouth. I dropped my gaze and took a second fig, the sweet taste lessening the churning in my stomach. My husband gave a low laugh.

"It seems my wife has regained her appetite. You must be careful, my dear, not to overeat and lose your looks. I do enjoy your visits to the solar."

I instinctively placed a hand over my stomach. After Sawford had left my room earlier, Harwyn had lifted my gown to inspect my thickening waist. She deduced I must be at least five months' gone. I had cursed myself for having assumed the changes to my body had resulted from poisoning. My monthly flow had not come since I'd arrived at Mortlock. Sawford's seed must have taken root almost as soon as he had taken me.

When I visited my husband in the solar that night he said nothing about my changing shape, but when Sawford returned me to my room I shook with fear. He must have heard my conversation with Harwyn but he showed no sign of it. Later, that night, after he'd gone, I curled into a ball and wept with fear for the child growing within me and with shame at my reaction to Sawford's skillful touch. I had cried out and writhed underneath him as he touched every part of me with his hands and mouth, and I had pulled him to me as greedily as I'd plundered the bowl of figs, relishing the honey on his lips. His touch had been gentle when he finally claimed me, easing into my body while he covered my mouth with his own. His tenderness elicited a more passionate response than his brutality, and I groaned with the shame of revealing myself to him. Had he been colder, rougher, I could have withstood it better.

Celia had spoken the truth. Kissing was too personal. Not for Sawford, but for me. I had to get away before it was too late. Not only did I fear we would be discovered, but I knew if I stayed here much longer I would lose the strength of will to leave.

The next day I woke aching for the taste of the figs. After sending Harwyn to the kitchens she returned with a small dish of honey and a piece of bread which I ate greedily, the rush of sweetness filling my mouth. We spent the morning in the herb garden, replenishing our supplies before tying them up to dry in the treatment room. Another note was slipped under the door and though Harwyn rushed to the door and flung it open she neither saw nor heard anyone. It was as if a ghost delivered them.

Another wave of nausea struck me, and I bent over, groaning. Harwyn admonished me for working too hard and insisted I go outside for some fresh air. I needed little persuasion and within moments I was on the path to the wild garden. I felt a flutter in my stomach and placed my hand over it.

My child. The need to escape was more acute now I had another to think of; an innocent life I was responsible for. Sitting by my tree I opened Tarvin's note. He told me to be brave, but what would he think when he discovered I carried another man's child—the child of a servant? Would he call me whore as Papa did—as Sawford did?

Unobserved I could let out my feelings and a sob escaped my lips.

"My poor child. How I wish your father was another. Oh Tarvin! Where are you?"

I heard a noise and looked up. My stomach clenched in fear, as I saw a dark mass moving among the trees. I was being watched.

"Who's there?" My voice sounded feeble. The shape moved and I forced myself to step toward it, fumbling in my skirts for my knife.

"Show yourself!" I cried, more boldly than I felt. I drew the knife and moved toward the trees and the shape became more defined. A man.

"Tarvin? Tarvin!"

He broke into a run. By the time I reached the edge of the trees he was gone.

Dejected, I returned to my room, caring neither for subterfuge nor discretion. I scribbled a note pleading with Tarvin to take Harwyn and me as far away from Mortlock as possible. Harwyn begged me to be cautious but I was desperate. I wrote that I had fallen in love with him and if he refused to help I would leave of my own accord and seek sanctuary in a convent. With hindsight it was reckless but the need for freedom was too strong. By revealing my loyalties I placed my life in his hands, hoping he would be spurred into action by my declaration of love.

Eager to keep me from danger and discovery, Harwyn bade me wait in my chamber while she hid my letter in the stables.

I felt another stirring in my belly and placed my hands over it, wanting nothing more than to protect the precious life within. I lay on my bed, drawing my knees up, whispering softly to the babe I carried. In my naïveté I imagined a time when I was far from here, settled in safe obscurity, away from intrigue and treachery, my child in my arms and Tarvin by my side. Closing my eyes I could picture it—a small dwelling in the middle of a lush green countryside. I could almost smell the fresh air; see the ears of wheat in the fields surrounding our home, moving gently in the breeze while we walked among them, hand in hand.

The pounding on my chamber door brought me to my senses. Before I could call out, the door burst open, and Wyatt rushed in.

"What are you thinking of; disturbing me like this?

Where is my maid?"

He took me roughly by the arm. "You are to come with me immediately."

"For what purpose?"

"Your husband demands it."

"But—"

"Be quiet, woman."

"You have no right to address me so," I said, the anger in my voice tainted by the undertone of panic.

Ignoring my words, he pulled me to my feet. Tightening his grip on my arm, he strode out of the chamber and I struggled to keep up without tripping.

"At least tell me where you're taking me."

"Lord Mortlock instructed me to tell you nothing."

He took me to the courtyard. Had his hold on my arm not been so firm I would have collapsed with fear at the sight awaiting me. Two men-at-arms held a crying, whimpering figure, its shoulders hunched and head bent. Standing beside them my husband beckoned to me.

"Ah, here she comes. Wife, we have a traitress in our midst."

The figure between the men groaned and lifted its head up. The face was bruised and battered, barely recognizable.

"Harwyn."

My voice came out in an anguished whisper and my husband smiled.

"Aye, my dear. We caught her delivering a missive to your lover."

"Forgive me!" Harwyn's voice was thick with pain, and she cried out as one of the men delivered a kick to her side.

"No! Leave her alone!"

"Silence, wife, unless you want the same."

"I don't have a lover. Let her go," I pleaded, but my husband shook his head.

"She has betrayed you, my dear." He held up my letter to Tarvin, and Harwyn's body shook with sobs.

"It took little persuasion for her to tell us of your plans to leave. She was gracious enough to show us where she had concealed your letter."

He moved toward me until his face almost touched mine ,and he lifted his hand, running a finger along my lips.

"I am disappointed to find you as much of a whore as my other wives. But we can remedy that when you share their fate."

"My lord," a familiar quiet voice resonated behind me.

"Ah, Sawford. Just in time to administer justice upon two more traitors."

"Two?"

"It seems the mare sought freedom. Here." Mortlock handed the note to Sawford whose eyes narrowed as he read the words I had written.

"You know what to do, Sawford. I want them both executed immediately."

Harwyn wailed piteously at Mortlock's words and I struggled against Wyatt's hold.

"Let her go, my lord," I pleaded, "'twas not her doing."

"Nay," he said, "'tis time I found a new wife."

Sawford folded the note, keeping his eyes on me. "My lord, put the servant to death if you will; but as to your wife, I would counsel you to wait at least until after the birth of your child."

Wyatt increased the pressure on my arm. A slow smile crept across my husband's face.

"My wife is with child?"

I drew in a sharp breath. Amid Harwyn's sobbing my husband laughed. He took my chin in his hand and forced my head up.

"Is it true? Woman?"

"Aye," I whispered.

"Then she has performed her duty, Sawford. Has she been examined?"

"Aye, my lord."

I did not know why Sawford lied but hoped I could turn it to my advantage. I pleaded with my eyes, hoping news of a child might instill some compassion in my husband's heart.

"I will need a maidservant, husband, to care for me. Harwyn tended to my mother throughout her confinement."

Mortlock nodded his assent and my body sighed with relief.

"I will find a replacement among the wenches in the castle."

"No!" I cried.

"Sawford, deal with my wife," Mortlock said. "Wyatt, the axe."

Wyatt handed me to Sawford who circled his arm around my waist, pulling me against him.

"Do not struggle or 'twill be the worse for you," he hissed in my ear. "You may still share your maid's fate."

I wanted to close my eyes but could not. Instead I watched, a morbid little corner of my soul transfixed, as they dragged Harwyn toward a thick, wooden block. Wyatt approached her brandishing an axe, its iron head catching in the sunlight where the blade had been honed. Its sharp, cutting edge curled into a sadistic smile to match the leer on my husband's lips.

They pushed Harwyn to her knees and held her head against the block while she wailed and struggled.

"Harwyn, be brave!" I cried, "Heaven awaits—" I was cut short as Sawford's hand clamped over my mouth.

"Be quiet, madam. Heed my warning."

My poor maid's body began to shake as terror overcame her. When the first blow fell, I shuddered, almost feeling the iron on my own neck. A strangled cry told me the blade had not struck cleanly, and I prayed the next blow would be fatal and deliver her a swift death. The second caught her across the shoulders, and her arms twitched against the force of it. Sawford's hand muffled my screams and tears blurred my vision. Wyatt raised the axe once more and this time he struck cleanly. Harwyn's head fell to the ground and rolled toward my husband's feet.

"Wyatt, see to it that the servant joins the other traitor. Sawford, my wife is in need of her rest. Make sure she does not place herself or my child in danger."

My gown felt too tight, constricting my chest. Sawford loosened his hold, and I stumbled, my legs unable to support my weight. My heartbeat rushed inside my head before the ground gave way under me. The last thing I saw before the door closed between the world and my consciousness was a pair of dark blue eyes looking into my own. I fought my body's instincts to shut down and looked at him with loathing.

"You will burn in hell for this," I choked.

"Aye, I will," he said quietly, and swept me into his arms before blackness engulfed me.

Chapter 12

I woke to find myself lying on my cot which rocked gently as if I were in a boat. On sitting up the rocking intensified and I collapsed back. I had been drugged again.

"So, you're awake." A woman spoke, coarse and unfriendly. I knew that voice.

"Celia. What are you doing here?"

"I have replaced the traitor."

My poor Harwyn. What would I do without her?

"I need no maid, Celia. Leave me."

"No," she retorted, "I am to look after you until your brat is born. Lord Mortlock knows the difference between a loyal servant and a treacherous bitch. You do as *I* say."

I rolled onto my side. My prison walls had closed around me. Celia would not help me; instead, she would relish the chance to wield any power she might have over me.

As for Tarvin—with the note discovered, how long before he shared Harwyn's fate?

Forgive me, Tarvin.

"What did you say?" Celia demanded, but I closed my eyes, letting the drug coursing through my veins give me peace again, if only for a while.

I was confined to my room permanently, mostly lying in my cot, my senses dulled. During brief moments of clarity I fumbled about the chamber, but the door was always locked. The window was large enough for me to climb through, but when I looked out, the ground far below swirled before my eyes, increasing the nausea which constantly threatened to expel the contents of my stomach. I bent over, retching, desperate not to be sick, knowing it would burn my throat and subject me to Celia's punishments. Had I been on my own, I would have risked falling to my death to climb out. But the urge to protect the life inside me was too strong. I could not risk my child. There had to be another means of escape.

Celia fetched my meals, feeding me herself to ensure I ate and drank everything. For my own sake I would have resisted, though I felt so weak, but I submitted for the sake of the babe.

After each meal, the food lay heavy in my stomach and I curled up to sleep as soon as I had eaten, wanting to shut out the world. Each day Celia grew more confident in her cruelty, gleefully telling me how she would be rewarded after the babe was born and I had been disposed of. I ignored her taunts, became numb to her rough handling when she dragged me to the privy to see to my private needs. Sometimes, on the brink of oblivion, I saw dark shapes moving. Muffled voices surrounded me, punctuated by howling noises; wild animals and demons marking my descent into madness.

****

As time passed, the air within the thick walls of my chamber grew colder, signaling the end of summer. Celia grew lazy, letting me feed myself, watching me with scornful eyes. She laughed at my attempts to rise, mocking me as I stumbled across to the food. On one occasion my hands shook so much I spilled the stew. She strode over and slapped me on the side of my head.

"Disgusting wench!" she cried, "I'm not paid enough to put up with one such as you." She flounced out of the room, slamming the door behind her.

The pain where she struck me honed my senses and the sound of the door closing was sharp and clear. I took a deep breath, and my head almost cleared: the air in my lungs brought forth a moment of lucidity. I was neither ill nor insane; they were still drugging me. I picked up the flagon of wine, staggered to the window and threw the contents out before finishing my meal.

Over the next few days I began to feel better and my vision cleared as the drug wore off. I played my part carefully, stumbling against Celia when she helped me up and lying still on my cot when she was in the room, trying to sleep to conserve my strength.

On the third day after I threw the wine away the source of the demonic noises was revealed. I woke one afternoon to the sound of a beast being speared. Opening my eyes, I saw Celia pressed against the door, her head twisted to one side, mouth wide open revealing blackened teeth. The noise had come from her—guttural sounds of animal pleasure as the man behind her drove into her relentlessly. I squeezed my eyes shut but the sound only magnified. The pounding against the door increased in unison with Celia's howls though the man was oddly silent apart from his breathing which came out in harsh puffs.

Celia's scream pierced the air, and the pounding stopped. I heard a rustle of clothes before she spoke, the desperate need for reassurance in her voice.

"Did I please you?"

"Well enough."

It was Wyatt. His terse answer was followed by the sound of coins clinking.

"Surely I pleased you better than that?"

"'Tis more than you are worth."

I heard the door open and slam shut. After a pause, Celia spoke again, lowering her voice to a sultry tone.

"And what of the pleasures I can give *you*? You know my worth, do you not?"

Another man was in the room.

He said nothing but must have responded because she continued, her voice sulky.

"Then why did you agree to meet me if only to give me to Wyatt? It's you I want. I told you I am willing, and I would let you give me your seed."

"I will father no bastards."

The voice was Sawford's.

"What about the brat that bitch over there carries?" I almost flinched at the hatred in Celia's voice but Sawford merely laughed.

"The child is Mortlock's, Celia. Anyone claiming otherwise risks their neck."

"But she has a lover. Is it you?"

"I have no time for haughty ladies, Celia. I despise them and all they stand for. I prefer my women lush and earthy.

"But you want her?"

"Jealous, love?" His tone was mocking yet Celia persisted.

"She's not the woman for you, Vane. Not like your Celia…"

"No woman shall lay claim to me; not even you. I take who I want whenever I want."

"Do not take *her*, Vane," she murmured, her voice thick with seduction.

I heard the crack of a hand striking flesh.

"You bastard! You dare hit me?"

"I do what I please, woman." His voice rose in anger and I heard a scuffle before he struck her again.

"Get off me you bastard! I only kissed you!"

"I told you before I don't kiss my women. Do not try it again! You think I would father my bastards with you when you use that term to belittle me?"

"Then take me for a wife," Celia pleaded, "I can give you endless nights of pleasure in your bed."

"You're a whore, Celia, only fit to be rutted in the dirt on your knees."

"You liked me well enough in the past." The coaxing tone returned to Celia's voice.

"Fawning does not become you—you who freely give your pleasures to every man in the castle, nay, the country." Sawford's voice turned into a snarl. "Get out and find another willing to settle for soiled goods."

"And leave you in here with *her*?"

"I said get out!" Sawford roared. I heard a curse and scrambling feet before the door slammed shut.

The cot shifted under his weight, and he sat beside me, the warmth from his body seeping into mine. Every nerve in my body screamed at me to open my eyes.

His hand touched my arm. The gentleness with which he brushed his fingers over me contrasted sharply with the cruelty of his words to Celia. His touch was so delicate I almost couldn't feel it, yet my skin tightened with want. He flattened his hand and moved it slowly, tentatively, toward my rounded belly. The child within me moved, and he drew in a sharp breath. My instincts took over, and I moved my hand to protect my baby. Sawford's body stiffened.

The cot shifted again as he stood. The door opened, and he issued a sharp order before he moved back to the cot.

"I will tell Lord Mortlock to expect you at his side tonight. I have sent for someone to help you dress."

Not waiting for an answer he left the room. I cursed his arrogant confidence; he knew I was awake. Expecting me to comply, he did not even deign to argue the point.

That evening he came to deliver me to my husband. I wore my pale gray silk gown through which my swollen belly was more visible. Though I hated Sawford I was thankful he had sent Edith to dress me. Her hands would never be as gentle as my beloved Harwyn's but she lacked Celia's streak of cruelty; Celia who took pleasure in tugging my hair viciously as she drove the comb into my scalp.

Still unsteady on my feet, I clung to Sawford's arm as he led me to the dining hall. We walked past the trestle tables while the men stood, watching me in silence until we reached my husband who sat on his ornately carved chair, two empty places either side of him.

"Ah, wife. I'm glad to see you recovered from your—illness."

I sat beside him, repressing a shudder as his clammy fingers circled my wrist, the nails biting into my skin. A servant approached with a flagon of wine but Sawford waved him away before sitting at Mortlock's other side.

"Quite so, Sawford," my husband said. "My wife

has had enough of our wine, has she not?"

The company watched us with anticipation, and the men shifted their feet as they stood waiting. My husband cleared his throat.

"I am pleased to tell you my wife has recovered from her illness and can grace us with her presence again."

A polite ripple threaded through the room.

"I also wish for you to share our joy. Tonight I announce we are soon to be furnished with an heir."

A cheer rose. Some of the men stamped their feet while others banged their wine cups and tankards on the surface of the tables. I searched their faces, to see if any of them showed recognition, but I saw none. No evidence signaled that Tarvin was in the hall. My gaze rested on Sir Baldwin, the knight Percy had served; but he was engrossed in conversation with Wyatt. At a signal from Mortlock the company sat down. Platters, trenchers and wine cups were filled, and everyone began to eat.

My husband held a piece of meat to my lips.

"I trust you understand, wife, that as you have no more need of my good wine and are now more precious to me than ever, I must assign some of my men to— hmm—*protect* you."

His smile did not reach his eyes. He knew what I'd done with the drugged wine. I looked past him at Sawford, loathing him with every fiber of my being. His betrayal had cost me my only advantage. Rather than trust the drug to keep me docile I would now be guarded. Mortlock ate the stew with gusto while I picked at it with my knife.

He drained his wine, and the red liquid ran down

his chin, as Harwyn's life essence had flooded over her shoulders. As if he saw the image in my mind, he smiled and licked his lips. The slurping smacking sound turned my stomach. I looked away in disgust but not before he caught the expression in my eyes. I flinched as he touched my shoulder, tracing a line with his fingertip across the front of my gown, dipping his finger in the valley between my breasts.

"I am glad you are recovered, wife, for I have missed you. I shall enjoy your company later tonight."

He stood up, instructing Sawford to return me to my room and send for Celia to prepare me.

Chapter 13

A sulky Celia escorted me to the solar. On seeing her bruised face I felt a small spark of compassion for her, even though she hated me and brought her misery upon herself. We were victims who could never unite against our common enemy. The balance of power between us having shifted in my favor, I dismissed her with a sharp word at the door.

After pleasuring himself, my husband rubbed my belly, licking his lips with relish as if he wanted to devour the little life growing inside. I couldn't bear the thought of my child being subjected to a life with him. Worse, still, was the idea of him growing up to be like the man who would acknowledge him as his heir.

Him. Now I felt the babe move almost daily I imagined him growing into a fine man. Yet at Mortlock he would be corrupted. His soul would rot and decay from the evil surrounding him until he mirrored my husband's twisted form. I could not let that happen. Not only would I die to protect my child, I would also be prepared to kill. Despite my captivity I still had my knife.

Returning to my chamber with Sawford, he pushed me inside and tugged at my nightshift.

"Take it off."

I backed away until I met the hard resistance of the door. Visions of Celia slammed against the wood while

Wyatt rutted her from behind flashed across my mind.

"No." I held out my hands to fend him off. "You have done the deed and my husband knows it. You have no need to touch me again."

"You forget, madam, I only receive my reward on the birth of a healthy son. Until then I see no reason why I should not seek my pleasure where and with whom I see fit."

"Then find one who is willing," I snarled. "I'm sure Celia would oblige."

"Jealous, love?"

I turned my head away at the same derisory tone he'd used on Celia, but he took my chin in his hand and pulled me to him until our mouths met. His hard body radiated heat into my own flesh, and he let out a low groan before teasing my lips with his tongue. He played my body with his hands, caressing me where he knew he would elicit sighs of pleasure. He brushed his hand against my breasts before teasing them with his fingertips, sending shocks of pleasure coursing through me. My body melted, and I opened my lips to invite him in while he ravaged my senses with his tongue, probing, searching my mouth until I gave a sob of surrender and drew my arms around him.

"I have found one who is willing," he whispered, tearing my nightshift down the front and dropping it on the floor.

"Leave me alone," I whimpered, covering myself with my hands, shivering at the rush of cold on my bare skin. "You will harm the babe."

He laughed softly. "You underestimate my talents. I know how to pleasure all manner of mares, in all sizes and shapes."

He drew me toward the bed and pulled his clothes off, his eyes never leaving my face.

"Please," I begged one last time as he lay beside me.

"For what do you beg, lady? For me to take you?"

"No," I said quietly, "for compassion."

"Look not for compassion here, for you will find none."

He kissed me before turning me on my side, my back to him. His powerful frame imprisoned me. He began to caress me again, running his hand across my body in soft, sweeping movements, teasing my breasts until they ached with longing, touching my belly possessively before dipping lower. My very core jolted with longing as he slipped his hand between my legs, before easing a finger inside me. My body pulsed with desire, and he growled with pleasure as I clutched the sheets, burning need surpassing my shame at responding so wantonly to his touch.

"Mine."

The soft rumble of his voice against my neck sent a rush of longing through my body, igniting my flesh which rippled under his expert touch. I clenched my teeth but couldn't suppress the low growl of pleasure that erupted from my throat, my body calling to him.

"Lean back," he whispered. My body involuntarily obeyed the soft command, and I tipped my head back. He claimed my mouth with his own and continued to administer his exquisite torture, eyes darkening, mouth capturing every whimper that escaped my lips as each slick circle he traced drew me closer to completion.

I felt him hot and hard against my back before he teased my legs apart and took me swiftly and smoothly.

His movements inside me were so unlike the base, hard thrusting I had expected. But he was merely using his gentleness against me. My body was weak against his brutality, but it was his tenderness that conquered my mind and soul.

He seemed to know how to draw me to the brink of pleasure, to that moment of madness which precedes the dissolution into ecstasy. Urging him to move faster, I arched my back, offering myself to him, caring only for my body's need to have him deep within me.

He smiled against my mouth and stopped moving.

"No!"

The pleasure began to fade. I shifted my legs wider, reaching for his hand, urging him to continue. He pulled his mouth away from mine and whispered in my ear.

"Tell me you're mine."

Unable to respond I parted my thighs wider, but he began to withdraw.

"Please…"

"Tell me, Lisetta."

"Yes!" I cried, "I'm yours."

Nipping my earlobe, he dipped his hand between my folds again while my sensitive flesh quivered at his touch before he slammed into me and my world exploded. My body's reaction caught me unawares, sending wave after wave of exquisite, pleasurable torture. My legs writhed and danced as I cried out with the force of it. The deep pulsing within my core grew more powerful, crossing between agony and pleasure. Sawford's cries matched my own, as if he felt the same agonies as I, until he let out a shout, his hands tightening their hold on me while he drove into me one last time with a deep sigh.

We lay there, utterly exhausted, my heart thudding in my chest. Sawford's breath, fiery and erratic, brushed against my neck. His own heartbeat pulsed against my back, and he molded his body against mine, wrapping his arms around me. Gradually our breathing eased until our chests rose and fell together in unison, joined together as if we were a single creature. He moved his arm until his hand rested lightly on my swollen belly where the life within slept on, undisturbed by what had happened on the bed. Before sleep overtook me he murmured into my ear.

"Mine."

I woke the next morning with a clear head, to the sound of knocking. I had slept well, experiencing no nightmares.

Someone was outside the door. I tried to move but could not. Sawford lay beside me, cradling my body with his own, his embrace protecting rather than possessive. He had remained by my side throughout the night.

Stirring in his sleep, he caressed my belly, a loving, gentle gesture. Soft feathered kisses brushed against my neck, and he murmured my name, his voice thick with emotion.

The knocking grew louder and his body stiffened.

"Lady!"

At the sound of Celia's voice he leapt from the cot and gathered his clothes. There was no time to question why he'd stayed; the danger of discovery was too great.

"A moment, Celia," I called out before gesturing to him.

"Get under the cot," I whispered, pulling the sheet

over my body to hide my nakedness.

He only just made it in time. His foot disappeared under the bed as she walked in.

"I have come to dress you," she said, not bothering to hide her dislike.

"I find myself indisposed this morning, Celia. Pray tell my husband this."

She gave me a sly smile, "I will find Sawford and tell him."

"No!" Her eyes widened at my reaction before her mouth curled into a smile.

"Aye, I will, lady. He would welcome me into his room—and his bed."

"Don't be a fool, Celia," I snapped, and she stiffened at my tone of authority.

"Go to Mortlock directly. Say I will be well enough tomorrow."

She looked at me mutinously, and I sat up straight, glaring at her. Some of my old resolve returned, and I became, once again, the ice cold mistress rather than a weak rival.

"Do as you are bid," I said with a cruel edge to my voice. "As the mother of Mortlock's heir I have more value than a lazy disobedient servant. A word or two in the wrong ear and you could find yourself on a pike. After all, one whore is easily replaced by another."

She paled at my words but fear for her own skin overcame her urge to retaliate, and she fled.

I leaned over the bed.

"Begone before you share their fate also. Quickly!"

He rolled out from underneath and slipped his clothes on before handing over my torn nightshift. He cupped my face with his hand.

"Is your heart softening, lady?"

"I want no more deaths on my conscience."

His eyes narrowed. A glimmer of emotion swam in their depths before his usual, dispassionate expression took over.

"You forget. Your maid brought about her own end. She betrayed you. She was weak-minded and treacherous, as all women are."

"Not all of us, Monsieur," I said bitterly. "Your hatred for us blinds you."

"Hatred? Of women? Far from it. I enjoy them frequently. But I understand better than others what your purpose is—to serve a man's needs and nothing more. Women with ideas outside their station are either whores or lovesick fools."

"And which am I?"

"I will leave that for you to decide."

He smiled, tracing an invisible line with his fingertip down my throat to the swell of my breasts before he reached a nipple and flicked it with his thumb, curling his lip into a smile as it peaked under his touch. Leaning forward, he kissed my cheek before taking my earlobe between his lips where he had bitten it the night before, marking me as his.

"Remember who you belong to."

He bowed and left the room. We played a dangerous game. My worth as the bearer of Mortlock's heir was not limitless, nor would it last forever.

After he had gone, I noticed a piece of paper on the floor near my cot. It must have fallen out of his clothes.

My letter to Tarvin; the letter which had condemned Harwyn to death.

With trembling hands I picked it up and held it

against my breast before concealing it in my trunk where I'd hidden all the notes and poems Tarvin had written to me over the months.

Was he alive?

****

Over the next month I did not see Sawford. It was as if he had disappeared. Had my husband finally discovered the identity of the stallion? Had Sawford shared Harwyn's fate? While Celia saw to my needs, I watched her carefully for a sign that she knew anything. But she remained sullen and quiet, and I dared not enquire.

Though I was not permitted to go outside, my husband granted me freedom within the confines of the building. He did not summon me to the solar again but insisted I dine with him each night. He seemed to grow daily in strength and stature, eating his meals with an increasingly voracious appetite. The very air was thick with anticipation. There was a lot of activity among the men, their excited whispers echoing in the stone passages. I saw Baldwin and Wyatt thick in conversation. It sickened me to see the knight chatting amiably with the very man who had tortured and mutilated the young man who'd served him.

Sawford was noticeable by his absence. To my surprise my heart ached with regret at the possibility that he might be dead.

So I had an unexpected fright when I woke in the middle of the night, a large hand covering my mouth. Sawford's eyes pierced through me as he held a knife to my throat.

"Come with me now, lady, or you die tonight."

Chapter 14

Sawford hissed savagely in my ear.

"I'm going to remove my hand, but one sound from you and I'll tie a gag so tight you will struggle to breathe. Do you understand?"

I looked at him, frozen still with fear. He shook me roughly.

"Answer me!"

I nodded.

"Get up. Now."

I rubbed my eyes to clear them from sleep and felt a soft thud against my chest as he threw something at me.

"Put that on."

Before I could answer, he went to the door and looked outside, body tense, ready to spring into action. The garments in my hands, a brown kirtle and overgown, were made from a rough, homespun material. I was glad of my nightshift, for they prickled my skin, even through the soft silk.

Noises outside grew louder—yelling, shouting, the occasional clash of metal on metal.

"What's happening?"

"Be quiet," he snapped, still looking outside. "A traitor dies tonight."

My instincts told me I would never set foot in my chamber again. I hurried over to my trunk and took out the precious contents, tucking them down the front of my gown, placing Tarvin's letters against my heart. Would I ever hear from him again? My knife I slipped into the belt of the kirtle, concealed beneath the overgown. I was just in time. As I smoothed down the skirt, Sawford took my wrist and pulled me to him.

"Do everything I say."

He led me through the door and ran along the passage, dragging me with him. Closing my eyes only heightened my other senses as I stumbled behind Sawford who drove on relentlessly. I screamed as we came upon a body—one of Mortlock's men, his chest a mass of mangled flesh.

Sawford gripped my wrist tighter, snarling through gritted teeth for me to be silent. He stepped over the body, urging me to do the same, and I kept my head level, fighting a morbid voice in my mind which goaded me to look into the dead man's sightless eyes.

The all too familiar smell of smoke and oil burned in my nostrils. Closing my eyes I saw her once again; my mother, holding her head high, as she tried to greet her fate with dignity, before succumbing to the pain, as the flames licked up against her gown.

A traitor dies tonight.

Fire.

Sawford was leading me to my death.

"No!" I cried, struggling against his grip, "Dear God have mercy, no!" I would face death when the time came but not now, not when I was with child. I lashed out like a wild animal caught in a snare, screaming for mercy, for help, in the hope that someone would prevent this.

The screaming intensified. The crackling of the

flames and cries of pain from men who knew they were meeting their death swirled inside my head, beating out a rhythm before culminating in a huge explosion, and I fell into blackness.

When I opened my eyes I was outside. The whole building was ablaze. My ears rang and my jaw throbbed in pain. I groaned and almost immediately a hand pulled me upright, and I came face to face with Sawford. He touched my chin where he had struck me, and sighed as I flinched. Our eyes met, mine smarting from the smoke, his showing something—regret, perhaps?—before they hardened and he lowered his hand.

"'Twas necessary."

He led me away from the building. We were outside the bailey, at the edge of the moat where it was narrowest at the back of the Fort. He gestured toward the dark water.

"Can you swim?"

"Aye."

"Then jump."

I pulled away. "No."

"Does a lady not care to get her feet wet?" he mocked. "We cross the water now, or I leave you here at the mercy of Mortlock's men."

I turned my back and jumped. The shock of the cold pierced me like a knife. The woolen gown hampered my limbs, and I struggled to stay afloat. Was death by water a worse fate than death by fire? A splash beside me signaled Sawford's entry. Strong hands took hold of me, and he swam across the water, supporting me until we reached the other side. He scrambled out and pulled me up after him before we set off at a run again.

I was almost grateful for the hard pace; my limbs began to warm with the exercise. Eventually he slowed at the edge of the forest where a large black horse was tethered by a tree. The animal pricked its ears up on seeing us. Behind the saddle, bulging panniers had been strapped to the horse. Sawford had prepared for this.

"Please—tell me what is happening."

"Your husband is a traitor," he said savagely, "and tonight the traitor was betrayed."

"By you?" I whispered. "*Mon Dieu.*"

He laughed, "I think you will find God on *my* side tonight."

"But innocent lives will die! Servants, children…" I cried, thinking of Cedric, still a boy.

He shrugged his shoulders. "The casualties of war."

"I hate you," I said with all the passion I could muster, "God would never be on the side of a man who caused such destruction. The Devil himself would gladly walk beside you after what you have done."

"Enough!" he roared, pushing me toward his mount, "get up on the saddle. I have no time for tattle."

A shout rang out from behind.

"Treacherous bastard!"

Wyatt ran toward us brandishing a sword. Sawford pushed me out of the way and reached into one of the panniers, pulling out a sheathed sword. The air hissed as he drew the sword from its scabbard and raised it the very moment Wyatt reached him. The clash of steel rang through the night, punctuated by heavy breathing and grunts as the two men fought savagely. Wyatt was a skilled fighter but what surprised me more was

Sawford's prowess. For a mere servant he fought with the skill of a knight. In the months since my arrival at Mortlock I had never seen him wield a weapon, but it was clear he was a practiced fighter; a warrior. Who was Sawford, and what did he want with me?

Sawford lunged at Wyatt and drove his blade through his heart, pulling it back and cleaning it even before the other man's body had fallen to the ground.

Frozen to the spot, I had not thought of escape while they fought. Though shapes were discernible in the moonlight, I wouldn't need to run far into the forest before I'd be completely concealed in the shadows. As if he read my thoughts Sawford turned toward me, his face grim, and he motioned to the saddle.

"Get up—hurry, woman."

Behind him, another man appeared. I recognized Sir Baldwin, who raised a finger to his lips to warn me to be quiet. Holding his sword aloft, he advanced toward Sawford. His eyes were on me, almost glowing in the darkness. I saw my life split like a fork on the road. One path led away from Mortlock, to Sawford, the man in whose power I had been almost since I had arrived here. The other led me back, to the man my father had given me to, the man who would take my child and dispose of me.

Baldwin paused about five paces away. In that moment I made my choice.

"Vane!" I screamed.

Sawford spun around as Baldwin's sword came down. It narrowly missed his head but he took a glancing blow to the shoulder and lost his balance.

"Bitch! You'll be next," Baldwin snarled before lunging for Sawford again. Grunting in pain, Sawford kicked out at Baldwin, who crashed to the ground. The two men rolled over, arms and legs flailing, fighting to the death. I pulled out my knife and held it up but they were moving so fast I was terrified I might hit the wrong man if I threw it, still uncertain who the wrong man was. Who was the enemy?

The next moment it was all over. Baldwin screamed before making a gurgling sound. Thick red liquid poured from a long gash in his throat, running down his tunic with slow, steady bursts as his heart pumped the last of the life out of him. Sawford threw the body to the ground and cleaned his blade before looking up. For a heartbeat he stared at me, the intensity of his expression making me uncomfortable until his gaze dropped to the knife in my hand. He shook his head almost imperceptibly before his lips curled into a sneer.

"What did you intend to do with that against a man with a sword? Little fool!"

I tucked the knife back into my kirtle.

"You're no ordinary servant. Who are you?"

"'Tis nothing to you. Get up on the horse."

"No," I said. "I'll do nothing until I have answers. You owe me that, at least."

"I owe you nothing."

"Are you a knight? A nobleman?"

"Would you prefer me if I was such a man?" he mocked. "All women are the same! Whores the lot of you—you would willingly open your legs for nobility, casting aside a respectable man to be ridden by one with a title."

I had given him the warning that saved his life yet still he despised me.

"What do you know of respectability?" I cried. "No respectable man would do to any noblewoman what you have done to me."

"Noblewoman no more, my dear. You're now a peasant—worse, even, for without your husband you are nothing."

"How dare—"

"Enough!" he roared. "Do as I say, woman, or I'll leave you here to rot."

He pulled me to the horse and helped me up. I dared not ask where we were going but he knew my thoughts.

"We ride to the next village. Ask me no more tonight."

We had not ridden for very long before patches of light shone through the trees. Sawford guided the horse past a number of huts until we reached a small dwelling next to a smithy. He motioned for me to stay on the horse while he dismounted and tapped on the door. A sliver of light appeared, and I heard low voices before he led the horse to the building and held out his hand. Again, the notion of escape crossed my mind—I had only to snatch the reins and be gone. I fingered the rings on my hands—jewels which would pay for my passage and entry to the convent. But something prevented me; a small spark of concern in Sawford's eyes as they met mine. My desire to be rid of him faltered until it drained from me as assuredly as the blood from Baldwin's throat.

I took his hand and dismounted, leaning against his warm body to steady myself, my legs trembling. Wanting to draw strength from him yet afraid to show dependency I resisted when he tried to draw me closer.

Shrugging his shoulders, he pushed me toward the door.

"Say nothing, do you hear?" he warned, "or 'twill be the worse for you."

The smith's home was split into two rooms, separated by a cloth hanging. The smell of stale sweat and human waste lingered in the front room. I wrinkled my nose but said nothing. The smith sat at a table in the center of the room and eyed me curiously. A woman lay asleep on a pallet. Three children huddled together under a blanket on another pallet beside her.

Sawford pushed me into the back room and threw the panniers at my feet.

"You'll find dry clothes in there."

He returned to the front room to speak to the smith. I hastily stripped off my clothes, pulling on a fresh kirtle and setting my wet clothes out to dry. I drew the hanging back to see Sawford holding the smith's hand.

"My thanks," he said.

"Be gone in the morning," the smith grunted, giving me a pointed look before joining his wife on the pallet. She stirred and drew him to her, offering her lips in her sleep. As Sawford let the hanging fall, I heard her sighs of pleasure.

"Are we to stay here?" I asked.

"Just for the night," Sawford replied. "Do not cause trouble. I had to pay him extra to let you stay."

"Does he know who I am?"

"I told him you are my whore. You look the part."

I turned my back, touching my chin which throbbed where he had struck me. I heard him rummaging in the bag.

"Come here," he said. I turned to see him lying on the pallet, holding his hand out.

"You wish me to play the part of your whore?"

"I am in no mood for you tonight," he sneered, "but I wish to keep you close. You belong to me now. Do I need to bind your hands?"

"No," I said wearily. "I have nowhere to go."

I sank onto the pallet beside him, exhausted in body and mind, barely noticing him curl his body around mine. The last thing I remember before sleep took me was the sound of lovemaking in the room next door.

Chapter 15

When I woke I was cold and stiff. Sawford had gone. Patches of light peeped through the oilskin covering the window. Unused to the hard pallet my bones ached. I touched my belly and the child rewarded me with a small kick. Despite my situation I smiled. Though I was alone, lying on the dirty floor of a peasant's house, my child and I were free from Mortlock.

I struggled to my feet, rubbing my lower back, and drew aside the hanging. The outer door was open, letting in a shaft of sunlight. The smith's wife sat at the table along with three children. She scowled at me.

I offered my hand to her. "I must thank you for giving me shelter."

"Don't thank me. I would not have the likes of you in my house, no matter how much he paid us."

I withdrew my hand. "You're not accustomed to entertaining a lady."

"Lady!" she laughed. "Nothing but a whore! I suffer your presence in my home—and near my children—for the coin. I carry the shame to ensure my children eat this night. One such as you carries no shame."

She thought me Sawford's whore.

"You have no right to judge me," I snapped. "You suffer my presence against your moral judgement for

146

the sake of a coin. How are you better than a woman forced to sell her body to survive? You think she does it out of choice?"

She stood up and spat in my face. "You're nothing but dirt, you hear me? A diseased whore who serviced the men in that traitor's castle while the villagers starved around him. You should have died in the fire along with the rest of them."

She prodded me with her finger. "I doubt you even know whose seed spawned that little bastard in your belly."

I jumped back. "My child is innocent."

Tears stung the backs of my eyelids at her cruel words. Had I escaped the confines of Mortlock Fort only to be subjected to the cruelties and injustices of a judgmental world?

"It is not innocent," she said. "It has been tainted; conceived in sin and God will make it suffer."

"How dare you!" I cried.

"What is the meaning of this?" Sawford stood at the door next to the smith. I had never seen him look so angry, and I shrank back in fear as he strode toward me and took my arm.

"Stop causing trouble," he said through gritted teeth and he dragged me through the hanging. The smith called his wife out of the house, and she left, deriding him for letting a whore into her home.

"Keep your mouth shut," Sawford said.

"But she insulted—" I began, but he shook me roughly.

"I care not what she said, madam! We're still in grave danger this close to the Fort. If you speak, you'll reveal your identity. Your accent betrays you."

"You want me to speak like a whore?" I glared at him. "That woman judges me as one!"

"She would judge you a great deal more harshly as the wife of Mortlock now his treachery has been revealed and punished. Do you wish to die a traitor's death? You would be condemned by association."

I opened my mouth to protest, but he held his hand up to silence me.

"Enough. We leave when the sun sets."

Before I could answer, he left. With nothing else to do I folded the clothes which were now dry and packed them into the panniers. Inspecting the rest of the contents I found food, a bag of coins, along with two jars of my salve.

When I had finished I felt sick again. I needed fresh air. The house was now empty and I was glad of it. I had no wish to be subjected to any more scorn from the smith's wife. Stepping outside I breathed in deeply, stretching my arms to fill my lungs.

"Mistress."

The smith watched me. Shading my eyes against the sunlight I saw kindness in his face.

"Are you well?"

"Yes," I replied. "Forgive me, I had to come outside. The smell in the house..." My voice trailed off and I blushed with embarrassment.

"Nay, 'tis I who should apologize, not only for the state of my house..." he lifted a hand and smiled at my protests, "...but also my wife's words. You're our guest, and she had no right to say what she did. She's a pious woman and takes her faith seriously."

"As do I sir. Might I know to whom I am indebted?"

He shook his head. "Your companion, Sawford, does not wish it—neither does he wish me to know your name, so do not speak it."

He held out his hand. "I would welcome you to my home."

A large red mark ran along his forearm. I took his hand.

"You're hurt."

"The hazards of being a smith."

"Have you anything for it?"

"Time, mistress; just time."

I released his hand. "I have something that will help. Come inside."

He followed me into the house, and I darted into the back room to fetch the jar of salve, tearing a strip from my silk nightshift as a makeshift bandage.

He sat patiently while I opened the jar and spread the salve over the burn before binding it.

"Change this once every two days," I said, tying the ends of the bandage in a knot. "The pain should lessen by tomorrow and will heal within a sennight."

He smiled at my crisp instructions and took my hand.

"You are no ordinary whore, are you?" he said gently. "Perhaps you're no whore at all."

I lowered my head, and he patted my hand in the manner of an indulgent parent.

"It matters not, child. You're under Sawford's protection, which is good enough for me."

I lifted my head and smiled. He was the first man since poor Percy who showed me genuine kindness.

"Get away from her, John!"

His wife stood in the doorway, Sawford beside her.

She jabbed a finger at me.

"Leave my husband alone. Have you no shame?"

Sawford's voice was smooth but his eyes betrayed his anger. "She will look for trade wherever she can, but I keep her in line."

The smith began to argue, but I shook my head and rose from the table. His wife pushed the jar of salve toward me.

"Take it back, whatever it is."

"But…"

"Do as she says," Sawford barked. With trembling hands I picked up the jar, retreating to the back room. The woman's shrill voice continued, berating me for tainting her home. Sawford joined in, apologizing for burdening them. Distraught at the injustice of it all, I curled up on the pallet, drawing the blanket over my head to shut out their voices.

After a while Sawford's footsteps approached and a hand tugged at my blanket.

"Leave me be," I pleaded.

"The smith and his wife have gone and won't return until we leave. I will be gone a few hours. Do not leave this room."

I covered myself in the blanket again.

"Did you hear me?"

"Yes!" I cried. "Go! I pray that I never see you again."

When he returned I had fallen asleep again. My sleep had been punctuated by dreams of flames surrounding my mother's face. Twice I had woken up screaming for her. When he shook me awake, I cried out again, and he covered my mouth with his hand. He smelled of smoke and I pulled away, the flames still vivid in my mind.

"Mortlock," I croaked.

"Aye, I have been there," he said grimly. "The building is destroyed and all are dead. You are a widow."

"All dead?"

"Some of the women and children survived, but the men either perished in the flames or were killed trying to escape. Those captured by the king's men were executed. Your husband has been declared a traitor and everything he owned is now property of the king, to dispose of as he sees fit. That includes you."

His next words sent a chill down my spine.

"That is why you will marry me tonight."

"No," I gasped, "I'm finally free. Why would I consent to marry a traitor who served my husband then betrayed him in turn?"

"I am no traitor. I'm loyal to Henry and will be richly rewarded." I heard the pride in his voice and boiled with anger.

"You betrayed and caused the death of many. What could a murdering bastard know of loyalty?"

He gripped my throat. "Do not use that word in my presence! I serve my overlord with honor. He was prepared to employ me despite my birth. Most of the nobility has little time for those of us born on the wrong side of the blanket. You give us nothing but your scorn. But I have the upper hand now. As Mortlock's widow you are a traitor by association."

"I've done nothing!" I protested.

"Nevertheless you would be given to the king for his pleasure. With luck you might warm his bed until he tires of you, but he has discerning tastes. In your present state I suspect he would hand you to his men before giving you a traitor's death."

"I am with child. The heir to—"

"The heir to nothing. The child of a traitor."

"Then I shall tell them my husband is not the sire. You know that to be true."

"You will simply be acknowledging your own adultery and branding yourself a whore. I think you know the penalty for adultery. Did not your mother reap the fruits of her sins?"

"How dare you!" I cried, striking him across the face with all the force I could summon. "Do not speak of her so!"

He rubbed his cheek. "Strike me all you like, but you know your sin would not go unpunished. The world is well aware of the weakness of women. Your own maid betrayed you."

"She was brave and honorable," I said.

"Brave!" he scoffed. "At the first sign of danger to herself she squealed, spilling all the sordid little details about your love letters and your wish to leave your husband. She begged for her sorry skin without a thought for you."

"Harwyn did not deserve to die."

"She was a coward. Like all women. Eager to betray at the slightest test of her resolve."

"I would never betray one I loved," I said vehemently. "I'd do anything I could to protect them."

He reached out to me, and I shied away, cradling my belly. His voice grew softer.

"If you wish to protect your child then prove what you say. Do as you are bid and marry me. After all, I am the child's father."

At that moment I hated him. He staked his claim on me and my child, yet in the same breath he told me of my own sins, even though he had taken me at my husband's bidding.

"My child cannot help having you as his sire. I intend for him never to find out."

"I am a loyal subject; my name will protect you both."

My freedom had been an illusion. I was a fugitive, the widow of a traitor—lost, alone, to be hunted down. I hated Sawford for what he had done to me, for how he made me feel. Yet, with my child to think of I had no choice but to yield. I clung to the hope that Tarvin was out there somewhere; that he would come for me.

"Tell me, sir, the honest truth if you can. Was every man killed at Mortlock?"

"Aye. Every single man. They're all accounted for; even the two we encountered in the forest."

I was alone. Tarvin was dead.

"Tarvin..." Tears rolled down my face. There was nothing left now, apart from the need to protect my child.

"Tarvin." Sawford's voice was harsh. "Your lover?"

"No," I said, "but he was a better man than you could ever hope to be. He was brave and noble, whereas you are nothing. I feel sick at the very thought of your name and his being spoken in the same breath."

I looked up at him defiantly, expecting to see anger in his eyes, but their expression was softer, almost sad before he turned his head away.

"But you will wed me?"

I hung my head.

"Aye."

"Then make haste. We leave now."

Chapter 16

"See to my meal, wife."

Sawford threw a rabbit at my feet.

We had been travelling for almost a month. Unaccustomed to hard riding and sleeping rough my whole body ached. During the day we rode whether it rained or not. Sitting astride the horse behind my husband I could not relax, having to grip his waist for fear I would fall and harm the babe.

My husband.

Once again I was a bride. Six months ago I had entered Mortlock Fort a hopeful child, dreaming of a long, fulfilling marriage and the comfort of occupation as the lady of the castle. That naïve child no longer existed. Neither did the lady. I was the wife of a servant, a man I craved to be near but longed to escape from at the same time. We had married the night we left the smith's hut having ridden straight to the abbey near Mortlock. The abbot who'd joined us, his face wrinkled with drowsiness, had refused at first to conduct the ceremony. But the point of Sawford's sword and a handful of coins had persuaded him otherwise.

Our first night as man and wife we'd slept under cover of trees. He sealed our union with a quick, rough consummation, his breathing quickening against the back of my neck as he came to pleasure. I had woken later that night, his lean, hard body against my back while he slept—the sleep of one undisturbed by the screams and flames that haunted me since we left Mortlock Fort.

As the days passed, the smell of smoke clinging to his clothes had been replaced by the damp, almost sweet smell of the leaves lingering on the ground, their bright reds and yellows fading to brown.

Our food had grown scarce. Each time we had rested, the piece of bread he gave me was smaller than the last, until one evening after lighting a fire he'd said there was nothing to give me, before disappearing without another word. He had returned with a rabbit, which he swiftly and expertly gutted before roasting it over the fire. Since speaking my vows I had said very little, answering his questions with a nod or shake of my head. I was tired, so tired. Each time we stopped, I dropped to the ground, curling up and closing my eyes, though sleep eluded me.

"Did you not hear me?"

I looked up, lost in my thoughts. He stood over me, body tense with expectation. Picking the rabbit up by its ears I drew out my knife. The body was still warm, a gaping hole in the flesh where Sawford's arrow had impaled it. A huge, black sightless eye stared at me reproachfully, and I dropped the knife, unable to slice into the animal's flesh.

"I have made a poor bargain if my wife cannot fulfil her duties."

Irritated by his tone I sheathed my knife. "I am neither peasant nor servant. See to it yourself if you are hungry."

"You think the circumstances of your birth make you better than me?"

"The circumstances of anyone not base born makes them better than you," I retorted.

A sharp intake of breath told me my arrow had hit its target.

"Shall I tell you what makes me better than *you*, woman?" he sneered. "I don't need others to perform every small task for me. I feed myself, clothe myself, even bathe myself. As fine a lady as you think you are, you are a commoner now. In my world you are nothing, incapable of lighting a fire or even laying the blankets. You wouldn't survive one day without me, whereas I would last far longer without being burdened by you."

"Then I propose you unburden yourself, Monsieur. I am not, and will never be, your whore."

"No"—his voice had a dangerous edge—"you are my wife. My whores may do as they please, but my wife is bound to me by law and by the church."

Struggling to my feet, I ignored his proffered hand and walked toward the stallion. The animal pricked its ears up, and I patted him on the nose before pulling out the blankets from the panniers. I hid my face from Sawford to conceal my tears. His words had confirmed my worth to him; an item of property to do with as he pleased. By marrying him I had surrendered my freedom. I could better bear the stigma of being his whore than the prison of being his wife.

However, he was right. Though hateful to admit it, I was a peasant now. I had a duty to care for my child and in order to fulfill it, I first had to learn to care for myself.

After laying out the sleeping blankets, I returned to where Sawford was gutting the rabbit. He looked up and raised his eyebrows. I gestured toward it with my knife.

"I will see to it."

He nodded and turned away to tend to the horse, the flicker of a smile dancing in his eyes. Ignoring him, I busied myself with the rabbit, driving the spit through its mouth to impale the body as I had seen him do, before placing it over the fire, turning it occasionally.

After a while, the smell of roasted meat made my stomach growl. It was ready to eat. Sawford did not answer my call and on looking up I saw why. He sat on the blankets, propped against a tree, his eyes closed. I had not seen his face at rest before, and it was as if a different man sat before me. While awake, he wore a similar mask as I; both of us concealing our true feelings. Were we really so different?

Since we had left the smith's hut, he'd worked continually, setting up camp, providing food, while I dropped to the ground to sleep as soon as we stopped. While awake, he seemed impassive, emotionless as the statues that graced the altars of the abbeys. Asleep he looked tired, almost vulnerable.

I touched his face. He had not shaved since we left Mortlock and the scar on his chin was completely concealed beneath his beard. Now his eyes were closed I noticed the thick, dark lashes which framed them. Though his skin was pale, the hue under his eyelids was darker—the only sign of fatigue. His mouth was full and sensual as it had ever been. The cheekbones were well defined and his nose, which I had at first thought to be perfectly straight, had a slight kink, evidence it had been broken in the past. Would my child resemble him?

I dropped my gaze to his hands; to the scars I had

seen when I first met him. How had he come by them? What hardships had he suffered to become the man he was? Would I ever understand him or, as I feared, had he taken me for the child, to then abandon me without a backward glance? What did he want with me?

The back of his hand was badly grazed. Out in the open, with little clean water, it would be prone to infection. Reaching over to the panniers I drew out the jar of salve along with the remnants of my torn nightshift. I applied the ointment before binding his hand as gently as I could so as not to wake him. On impulse I turned his hand, palm upward, and stroked the calluses with the tips of my fingers.

Looking up I gave a start. His penetrating blue gaze was on me.

I tried to let go, but he gripped my fingers. For a moment we looked at each other, and I held my breath, waiting for a sneering comment, but none came. The heat rose in my face, and I needed to break the silence.

"Your meal is ready, Monsieur."

"Monsieur!" His voice was soft but he mocked me. "So formal, still? Why not address me as you ought?"

"Husband," I whispered.

He lifted my hand and brushed his lips against my fingers.

"Come, wife, we shall dine together."

Though we ate in silence the air had been cleared a little. The wall of hostility between us had lost some of its height. There was a little meat left on the rabbit after we finished, and I wrapped it in a cloth before handing Sawford the waterskin. He drank slowly, his eyes on me, before handing it back. Aware it was nearly empty, I took a small sip, but he shook his head.

"You need water. Finish it. I'll find us more tomorrow."

Squeezing the last drops out of the skin, I handed it back before sinking, exhausted, onto the blankets. Listening to the sounds of him moving about the camp and the crackling of the fire, I closed my eyes and waited for him to join me. For the first time since we'd left Mortlock, I fell into a dreamless sleep.

I woke as he lifted the blanket and crawled in behind me. The night was freezing, and I moved closer to his warmth, turning sleepily to face him. My eyes flew open as his lips covered mine. My body responded before my mind could object, and I opened eagerly for him, drawing his tongue into my mouth. He moved his lips over mine and pulled me toward him, his body hard and ready.

"Lisetta," he whispered, kissing me on the jaw, following a heated trail down my neck while he caressed my arms. He cupped a breast, and I sighed, arching my back to offer myself to him.

"Lie back."

I was his to command, not only in the eyes of the world, but my body yearned to obey him. I relaxed against the blankets and closed my eyes as he unlaced my gown. I possessed neither the strength nor the desire to resist. His hands set every nerve on my skin ablaze before his hot, wet mouth came down on my breast. I cried out as he laved me with his tongue and grazed my nipple with his teeth, and I buried my hands in his thick, dark locks, holding him close.

His touch was so gentle and previously unshed tears spilled onto my cheeks. He pulled my skirts up, and I shifted my knees apart. I shivered at the exquisite sensation of a light fingertip which ran along the inside of my leg, stopping to stroke me tenderly where my thighs met. A rush of warmth flooded my body, and I parted my thighs with a sob of resignation. He hushed me gently as a mother would a crying babe and slipped a finger inside me, releasing a shockwave of pleasure. I cried out as my whole body shook with it.

He knelt up and drew me to him, holding my hips firmly in his hands, until the head of his thick member brushed against my throbbing core. With a low growl, he claimed my body, and I wrapped my legs around him to pull him deeper inside. I reached out, and he took my hands, our fingers interlocking. My body dissolved as waves of pure pleasure shook me. He moved faster and faster until I sobbed aloud, begging him not to stop, and I heard him shout his own pleasure. Our twin cries echoed into the night, before fading until nothing remained except the sound of our breathing. I lay back fully sated, struggling for air, and opened my eyes. His own eyes, almost black in the dim light, were wide open, staring at me in surprise and wonder.

He uncurled his fingers from mine. Eyes fixed on me, he eased my skirt back down before pulling his chausses up. Without a word, he rolled me onto my side and pulled the blanket over us both. His heart beat a gentle rhythm against my body, and his soft voice whispered my name. He stroked my hair before taking my hand, moving it to cradle my belly where our child slept peacefully within. I closed my eyes, my body at peace.

Before I fell asleep, I realized I had cried out a name as I came to pleasure—not Tarvin's, but another name.

Vane.

The crackling of the fire penetrated my sleep, and a voice called my name.

"Lady Lisetta." A young man's voice. He sat before me, his youthful face bathed in red light; sightless eyes trained on me. He turned his head, and the red light glowed more brightly; thick, scarlet liquid which poured down his face.

Percy.

The crackling turned into a deep roar and two voices joined Percy's.

"Lady!"

"Daughter!"

Maman and Harwyn sat beside him. The flames were closer now, the heat scorching my skin. Maman held up her hand, blistered and blackened, and she opened her mouth to scream, the shrill sound cutting through my dreams.

"Maman—no! Don't leave me!" I cried, reaching out to her, but I was bound tightly and unable to move. She gripped my hand and the flames engulfed me. My flesh began to melt until the bone gleamed through it. Maman opened her mouth wide and flames shot out with a piercing screech...

"Wake up!" another voice broke through as I struggled against my bonds. I thrashed my limbs, fighting to free myself until a resounding crack brought me to my senses.

Sawford held me in his arms, crushing me against his chest.

"I saw them!" I cried, looking around in panic. "My God—the fire!"

"We're alone here. The fire is almost out."

He spoke the truth. The night was still, the only sound the occasional sputter from the fire, which had nearly died down. I sat up as he released me to place another piece of wood on the fire. He blew on it gently until a small flame burst into life. Had I not been so distressed I might have laughed at the sight of a man conjuring up a flame in a world where the women—not the men—were persecuted for witchcraft.

"Who did you see?"

"Maman. Harwyn," I choked. "Percy."

He sighed and sat beside me, taking my hand, but I pulled it away.

"Did you kill him?" I asked.

"Does it matter?"

"Aye, it does!"

He shook his head. "It was not my hand on the axe."

"But you gave the order?"

"Aye."

"Dear God." I hung my head.

"You weep for him?" Sawford did not attempt to hide the anger from his voice.

"He was my friend."

Sawford's jaw ticked as he gritted his teeth at my words.

"His death was necessary."

"Necessary?" I cried. "To take an innocent life?"

"We're none of us innocent," he growled. "That young whelp died because of your foolish indiscretion. You're as much to blame for his death. You were content to play the lady, ignoring the harsh realities of the world with little thought for the lives of others."

"I did not murder him!"

"If you remember; I warned you," he said, coldly. "His blood is on *your* hands."

He held out his hand. "Come, wife. Let us return to our bed. We have a long day travelling tomorrow, and I need my sleep. I have no wish to be disturbed again by your foolish fancies."

"Then sleep elsewhere," I said, drawing my knife, but he shook his head.

"I think not."

I thrust my knife at him, but he caught my wrist.

"You think that pathetic little blade can stop me?"

He squeezed my wrist until I dropped the knife. Immediately he picked it up and handed it back.

"Next time you draw that blade be prepared to use it. I will not show leniency again."

He bent down swiftly, and I jerked back in fright, but he merely laughed.

"Have no fear, madam; I will not touch you again tonight." He picked up a blanket and, turning his back on me, moved toward the horse.

"What are you doing?" I asked.

He kept his back to me as he sat down, drawing the blanket around him.

"Sleeping. I suggest you do the same. We rise with the sun."

Sickened at the feelings I had begun to experience for Sawford, I huddled under my blanket; but the image of Percy's face still haunted me and sleep eluded me for a long time.

When I woke, the fire had gone out, and a thin film of mist hung in the air. The sun struggled to pierce the clouds. I prayed it would not rain.

I sat up, stiff, sore, and tired from lack of sleep. As

soon as I moved, a piece of meat was dropped on the ground before me.

"The last of the food. Eat it quickly."

I nibbled at the meat, grateful for something to ease my grumbling stomach. The sickness from being with child had passed but would return if I went too long without eating. I swallowed the meat, and a wave of nausea struck me. Leaning forward, I took a deep breath until it subsided.

A gentle hand touched my shoulder, and the waterskin was pushed into my hand.

"Drink," he said quietly, "it will make you feel better."

I snatched it from him ,and he sighed before sitting beside me, tearing at the joint of meat in his hand with his teeth like a man starved. His face looked thin and his features had changed from the softness I had seen in repose the day before. The hard, shuttered expression had returned. The fragile bond between us had been broken, and the wall had regained its height.

"Might I ask where we are going—husband?"

He appeared not to hear me and sat chewing thoughtfully before he sighed and tossed the bone into the ashes of the fire.

"We go to stay with my brother and his wife. With luck we should arrive before the onset of winter."

"You have a brother?"

"I had two."

"Had?"

"My youngest brother is dead."

"I am sorry. How did he die?"

"Over a woman," Sawford replied. "You make fools of us all. Ask me no more. We leave now."

He'd not spoken of his family before, but his clipped speech and angry gaze prevented me from voicing my curiosity, and we spent the day in silence. As the sun broke through the clouds, we rested beside a stream where I washed my face and filled the waterskins. Our food had run out and Sawford was unable to catch anything to eat. I dared not ask how soon our journey would end.

Chapter 17

The air grew colder the further we travelled. On some mornings when Sawford shook me awake, the leaves on the ground were dusted with frost; tiny icy fingers spreading into the veins until the leaf crumbled and rotted. The frost penetrated the blankets at night, and we huddled together, sharing the warmth of our bodies.

In the dark of the night I set aside my conscience and forgot what Sawford had done to Percy, succumbing to my body's craving for him, relishing the tender touches on my skin as his expert hands carried me to another world. Each time he took me, my body's reaction intensified, my need overpowering any desire for freedom. But in the frigid, gray light of the dawn, the lover turned, once more, into the tormentor; the man who owned me.

One evening, the rough path began to look more like a road and Sawford told me we were nearing our destination—Balsdean. A small town came into view, buildings straddling a well-trodden road, beyond which a river ran. Though the sun was setting, the town was alive with activity—merchants shouting their wares, a farmer walking his cattle along the road. Gaudily dressed women propositioned men near a tavern from where raucous laughter could be heard through the open door above which a sign swung in the breeze.

Some of the townsfolk stared at us. We must have looked an odd sight—a shabbily dressed man and woman astride a large black horse. Sawford steered the animal along the main thoroughfare, past a smithy from which I heard sounds of activity until we reached a two-story house outside which a pile of barrels was neatly stacked.

Sawford dismounted and helped me down. I bent over, rubbing my aching legs, too glad that our journey was over to be concerned about our destination. He thrust the reins into my hand.

"Wait here."

I nodded, leaning against the horse for support. He knocked on the door, and a voice called out before the door creaked open.

"What are you wanting at this hour?" a male voice rasped.

"'Tis me."

A pause was followed by an exclamation.

"Devil's holy cock! We thought you were dead."

"Forgive me, Jack. It's been a long time…"

"Three years, brother. Three cursed years and hardly a word!" The man was furious.

"'Twas necessary." Sawford's voice was quiet. "Are you well? And Lily?"

"Aye, we are well," the man replied. "My God! Lily! Lily!" he roared before speaking to Sawford again.

"Are you staying? You are most welcome."

"If you have room."

"Aye we do. There's just the two of us. We have not been blessed with children."

"I am sorry. I know how much you and Lily

wanted—"

"No matter," the man interrupted. "You have returned to us. You are much loved here; I trust you know that."

He gave a hearty laugh. "In fact, you're so loved I'll wager the bed of every whore in town will be warmer and their smiles broader within a sennight."

"Brother." Sawford's voice was a low growl before he called to me.

"Come here, Lisetta."

I opened my eyes and shifted to stand beside my husband. The man in the doorway was shorter and stockier than Sawford, and I saw little resemblance at first glance. He glanced at me then shook his head.

"Brought your own whore? Lily won't have her in the house, much as she loves you."

"This woman is my wife, Jack."

Jack's eyes widened. Despite my shabby appearance, I had my dignity and I held out my hand.

"I assure you, Monsieur Sawford, I am no whore."

He took my hand and kissed it before Vane pulled me back.

"My brother's name is not Sawford. It's Cooper. Jack Cooper."

Light footsteps approached and a woman joined the man in the doorway. She gave a shriek of surprise.

"Valentine!"

She began to cry and Sawford embraced her, muffling her sobs, speaking soft, soothing words. A hot flame of anger choked in my throat. He'd only ever shown me coldness and contempt, yet he had a genuine affection for this woman. She was taller than I with a soft, round body and the kind of warm, earthy beauty only peasants possess; beauty which could bring a man to his knees.

"Lily, you are as comely as ever. The years have only enhanced your beauty."

She held him at arm's length before kissing him affectionately. Only then did she notice me, her gaze lingering on my swollen belly.

"Who is that?" Her voice was hard.

I tipped my chin and spoke haughtily, my voice equally hard. "I am his wife, Lady Lisetta of Shoreton."

Ignoring me she turned to Sawford. "Your *wife*? But I thought, after William you vowed never…"

"Who is William?" I demanded.

"No concern of yours," Sawford snapped. "Lily, I thank you for taking us in. See to it that she makes herself useful."

Lily raised her eyebrows, looking at me as if she could not believe I would have any use. Sawford took my elbow and propelled me forward.

"You are not the pampered lady now. You're the same as the rest of us and will work for your living rather than expect others to serve you."

I bit my lip, hanging my head in shame.

A light hand touched my shoulder, and I looked up to see Jack's face, his expression kind. His eyes were as blue as his brother's but their gaze was warm and curious rather than dispassionate and searching.

"Lily, my love, show her where she can rest. She must be tired after her journey."

I smiled, grateful for his kindness, even though it was the cause of the tears pooling in my eyes.

"Such beautiful eyes, my lady, should not be marred by tears."

"Sister," I said.

"Lady?"

"Call me sister; 'tis what I am. My husband is right. I am not a lady, but the same as you."

"Then you are welcome to our family."

He drew me in and embraced me swiftly before handing me to his wife who led me inside.

****

When I woke it was morning and a small ray of sunlight stretched across the blanket covering my body. The previous night Lily had taken me directly to a bedchamber where I'd collapsed on the bed and fallen asleep. I had awoken some time later, Sawford's warm body against mine, before sleep claimed me once more. Now, however, I was alone.

A murmur of voices came from somewhere, and I crept out to investigate. The daylight revealed the true size of the house. It was larger than most, clean and tidy. The upper floor had three rooms. A narrow wooden staircase led to the ground floor, which consisted of one large room and another room behind a door.

Reaching for the door handle, I heard voices from the other side and froze.

"I tell you Jack, she must be his whore."

"Hush, Lily. My brother may have bedded every whore in the country but he would not disgrace us by bringing one into our home. He says she was Lady Mortlock so we must believe him. You can tell from her voice she's no peasant."

"But *married*, Jack? To a *noblewoman*, the widow of a traitor barely cold in his grave! He must have abandoned reason if he expects us to conceal her while

171

he's off with de Beauvane."

"He left her in our care, Lily, and we must trust him."

The voices were silent for a minute until Lily spoke again.

"She is with child."

A chair scraped on the floor, and I heard a low cry.

"I'm sorry, Lily," Jack said, his voice low and soothing.

"Why, Jack? Why am I not given a child when women like her—undeserving whores—are more fortunate?"

"Shhh my love; come here."

Her cries were muffled, and I imagined Jack taking her into his arms. I couldn't hate her, even though her anger was directed at me. The harsh top notes of bitter hatred in her voice were tempered by a deeper tone of sadness born out of years of longing for a child. She had a husband to love and cherish her, but no child of her own. I had been blessed with a child, but my husband did not love me.

In my mind's eye, I pictured them together at the hearth; Jack holding his wife, stroking her head; a man and a woman living together, loving each other openly and honestly, as equals. I closed my eyes and imagined a different husband and wife—Vane, smiling down on me as I placed his child in his arms. Would he love me, when I gave him a child?

Unwilling to intrude on their pain I waited until Lily's cries subsided. Eventually she sniffed and spoke again.

"Who do you suppose sired the child? Valentine said 'tis not the traitor's brat."

"Valentine himself, I would assume."

"No, Jack." Lily's voice was firm. "That woman was widowed barely a month ago, and she's nearing her confinement. He would not be so disrespectful as to flaunt the fruits of an adulterous relationship in my home. He's a good man."

"Then why marry her?"

"I know not. 'Tis plain he loves her not. That whore Elizabeth was his undoing, and he will never love another as he loved her. After what happened, do you think he would cuckold another man under his very nose; a man he served, even if he was playing the spy for de Beauvane?"

"You don't know my brother as well as I."

"I do, Jack!" Lily's voice rose in anger. "Oh, I know about his whoring, and he'll very likely continue that here. I know all he did to erase the memory of that bitch. But I also saw how it changed him. His fate was worse than William's. William is at peace, but Valentine lives his torment day after day. I see it in his eyes. The kind, loving man who was your brother was all but destroyed."

"Lily, please…"

"No, Jack! I'll defend him if you won't. You think that heartless mare upstairs cares for him? She saw him as a means to secure her future to avoid condemnation as the wife of a traitor. Another person who uses him for their own ends. Just like Elizabeth. Just like de Beauvane."

"De Beauvane is an honorable man."

"That man took advantage of Valentine at his weakest. Your brother was condemned by his entire family, even you, Jack! Only I saw how he cried over

173

William's body, how his loving heart was destroyed. The stigma of his birth has clung to him all his life. Your father died cursing him. Valentine does not deserve that, Jack. Under that exterior beats the heart of a good man. I believe in him even if nobody else will. Do not doubt my faith in him."

"You love him, Lily?"

There was a pause and I held my breath, terrified of her response.

"Aye I do, as a sister loves a brother. Even though God has seen fit not to give me a child, I love him as a mother would love her son—to atone for the mother who disowned him and declared him dead to her, in an attempt to assuage her own guilt at her weakness. She was a sinful woman who blamed her child for her sins—much as that bitch upstairs will."

I pushed the door open. The room was a kitchen; a small fire burned in a hearth at the far wall. Jack sat at a large table in the center, Lily standing beside him. Jack stood and smiled at me but my eyes were on Lily whose expression showed suspicion and hostility.

"Forgive me," I said, "I was looking for—my husband."

Lily looked pointedly at Jack.

I stepped into the room. "I assure you I *am* his wife."

Lily had the grace to look uncomfortable. "Forgive me for being blunt," she said, "but you are in my home and I must ask." Jack placed a steadying hand on her arm but she continued.

"Who is the father of your child? Was it Lord Mortlock?"

I shook my head, placing a protective hand over

my belly as if the very notion he was Mortlock's would harm the babe.

"Is it my brother-in-law?"

Two pairs of eyes watched me. Despite their opinion of me they were good people. They both loved Sawford. I could not bring myself to tell them what he had done to me, to destroy their good opinion of him. Life as a bastard could not have been easy and whatever tragedy had befallen his brother, he had clearly suffered from it.

My husband concealed his feelings but the scars still ran deep within, eating away at his soul. Yet I saw moments of feeling in him; in his abandonment when he cried out his passion as he took me; in the tender, affectionate way he treated these people.

Even Sawford deserved to be loved. For some reason of his own he'd saved my life and delivered me from Mortlock. If nothing else I owed him for that.

"Nay," I whispered, "'tis not him." I fixed my gaze on the table in front of me, unwilling to meet their eyes for fear my expression would betray the lie.

"Do you love him? The sire?"

I opened my mouth to deny it but shut it again, unable to speak. I nodded my head slowly, stifling a sob. When had my physical desire for him, the starving need in my body, crossed the bridge into love? Was it possible to hate someone and love them at the same time? Aye, it was. I hated what he did to me, hated myself for wanting him; but I could not face life without him.

"Who is the father of your child?" Lily demanded.

"Ask the lass no more," Jack reprimanded his wife. "'Tis a matter between Valentine and her. Whether she cares for him or no, she's part of our family now. If he wants her here we must make her welcome."

Lily sighed. "Of course. Let me get you something to eat. Valentine will be gone a day or so, he said, and I am sure he would wish to find you fit and well on his return."

Sawford returned the next day. I had spent the time helping Lily with her household chores, ashamed that although I knew how to run a household, I knew nothing of the simple tasks of day-to-day living. She warmed to me a little but it was obvious she neither liked nor trusted me. Her love for Sawford secured my good opinion of her, but I kept my feelings to myself. Though she spoke little of him, I learned a great deal from what she did not say. In Jack, I saw flashes of the man Sawford might have been had life treated him more kindly. What had happened to the brother he'd lost? Who was the woman he had given his heart to? I dared not ask.

He arrived in the evening while we ate in the kitchen. Jack and Lily were engaging in easy conversation—a husband and wife in partnership, Jack heeding Lily's words and smiling in thanks when she placed a bowl of stew in front of him. The door swung open, and my own husband stood at the threshold, tall and magnificent. The candlelight threw shadows across the strong planes of his face. He was clean shaven, the scar on his chin visible again. My heart leapt to see him, but his eyes were on Lily who ran to embrace him. The loving smile he gave his sister-in-law disappeared when he finally acknowledged me.

"Wife."

"Husband," I replied coolly, turning my head away

to hide the hurt in my eyes.

He sat and began speaking to his brother. I rose to serve his supper, but he ignored me, not even looking in my direction as I ladled stew into a bowl and pushed it toward him. Lily ushered me out of the room "to enable the men to enjoy their evening" and I turned my back on her ungraciously before retiring.

Vane entered our room some hours later, the movement waking me as he climbed into the bed.

"Husband, where have you been?"

"'Tis no business of yours" he said. "Mayhap I have found a better bed partner with a kinder heart and warmer thighs."

He sounded angry. When he'd arrived that evening his manner toward me had been indifferent but something had happened since then, for now he shook with rage.

"What's wrong?" I reached out to him.

He slapped my hand away.

"Go to sleep, woman, or I'll throw you out on your feet!" he roared, "I have no desire to have a cold-hearted shrew for a wife."

He turned his back, and I waited until his breathing steadied into the deep, slow rhythm of sleep. Hot tears of jealousy and sorrow flowed down my cheeks; jealousy of the easy, loving relationship he had with his brother and sister, jealousy of the other women he'd visited. My heart ached with sorrow for the feelings I bore for him which he did not return.

My body was safer in the life of a peasant compared to the perilous life of Lady Mortlock. But as for my heart—the key to my heart may have been unlocked by the loving words written by another, but the fragile treasure contained within belonged utterly and completely to the man lying beside me now; the man who would only spurn and reject it.

Lord save me. I loved Vane Sawford

Chapter 18

As the year drew to a close I settled into life as a peasant. The work was hard, harder even than it would have been at Mortlock had I undertaken the full duties as chatelaine. The skills I'd been born for were of no use here. The physical labor made my body ache and blistered my hands, but I was grateful for the occupation which diverted my mind and eased the pain in my heart.

Since his outburst, my husband resumed his uncaring manner. I treated him with indifference, though the easy affection he showed Jack and Lily tore through my heart. To see him capable of such feelings made me love him all the more. I ached for him to bestow even a portion of that affection onto me. Though Jack and Lily were kind, their manner toward me held little true affection. In turn I treated them coldly, only giving my feelings free rein during the snatched moments of solitude in the room I shared with my husband.

Most nights he was absent, and I dared not ask where he went. He discussed de Beauvane, whoever he might be, with his brother. Occasionally Lord Mortlock's name was mentioned, followed by pointed glances in my direction. He forbade me to leave the house. Someone was looking for me but whether they were connected to Mortlock seeking revenge or the king looking for the traitor's widow he didn't say.

The few nights he spent in my bed he took me with a soulless passion before turning his back and falling asleep. Each morning I descended the stairs, flushing with shame at the cries of pleasure he had elicited from me, cries which Jack and Lily must have heard.

We had come full circle, returning to the routine at Mortlock where he used my body to quench his lust then withdrew as if I did not exist. But this time it tested my limits of endurance, for now I loved him.

One afternoon on seeing Vane embrace his sister-in-law, a smile lighting up his beautiful blue eyes, I could stand it no longer and left the room, claiming fatigue. In Jack and Lily's house I saw the realization of my dream—a loving family, tending to each other—working, laughing together. How I longed to be part of it!

Alone in our chamber I retrieved Tarvin's letters, frayed at the edges where the water from my swim at Mortlock had almost destroyed them. Reading the words that were distinguishable and remembering those that were not, I cursed aloud at the unfairness of it all, that the man I loved displayed not one fraction of the tender feelings which those written words evoked.

I looked up to see Vane watching me, his gaze dropping to the letters in my hands. I interrupted his enquiry by slamming the door in his face, telling him I hated him, wanting to hurt him as much as he was hurting me. Having him near was unbearable, knowing he cared so little. Shutting him out should have numbed my feelings but it only served to increase the pain in my heart.

Lily and I managed the house during the day while

Jack toiled in his workshop making and repairing barrels. He employed two apprentices, and his business prospered. Lily worked as a seamstress and with my limited needlework skills I helped her a little. They were a relatively wealthy couple compared to the rest of the villagers, but I had no wish to be a burden to them and was determined to earn my keep. However, as I grew larger with the child I became increasingly tired and Lily would often shoo me upstairs mid-afternoon to rest before we prepared the evening meal.

One such afternoon I woke, screaming from another nightmare. Their frequency had lessened, but this one was different. The fire was ever present but Vane and Lily had emerged from the flames, locked in a passionate embrace before calling me a whore and pulling me into the fire. The door burst open and Lily ran in, but I screamed at her to leave me be, pushing her away as she approached the bed. I felt nothing but anger and jealousy toward her. She had taken me in with reluctance and treated me with kindness, but no real affection; my husband directed his smiles at her while he turned away from me.

I spent the evening in my room, listening to the voices downstairs, the deep timbre of Vane's voice punctuated by something I'd never heard from him before—laughter.

When he came into our room, I squeezed my eyes shut, pretending to be asleep as he crawled into bed smelling of ale. I bit back the urge to ask if he'd been wenching as well as drinking.

He was gone by morning. Hunger overcame my embarrassment, and I went to the kitchen, in search of something to eat. Lily sat alone, concentrating on her sewing, a pile of bandages and cloths on the table in front of her, along with my jar of salve. A pot of porridge simmered over the fire and my stomach grumbled in protest. Uncertain of my welcome I backed away, mumbling an apology, but she waved me over, holding out her hands. I reached out hesitantly, and she took my hands, turning them over to expose the blisters on my palms.

"How long have you had these?"

"Shortly after I arrived."

She sighed in exasperation as if I were a troublesome child, before reaching for the bandages.

"He was right; they need to be bound. Sit down."

She opened the jar and sniffed the contents.

"How much of this do I need?"

"Just a little."

"Forgive me," she said as I winced when her fingers brushed against a blister, "I should have realized you'd be unused to work."

The insult hit home.

"I cannot help my upbringing, Lily, nor can I help being in a situation where the skills I possess have little use. I have no wish to inconvenience you. Vane should not have brought me here."

"Perhaps he shouldn't have married you. Why did he?"

"That's his concern," I said, controlling my anger. "If he loves you as a sister I wonder he has not told you."

"Why did you accept him?"

"I had no choice."

"There's always a choice," she scoffed, securing a knot in the bandage.

I thanked her and rose to serve myself a bowl of porridge but she took my wrist.

"Valentine is a good man. I have no wish to see him hurt."

"I would never hurt him," I heard the bitterness in my own voice, "yet he—" I broke off, regretting my words as her eyes narrowed with hostility.

"My brother would never hurt an honest woman. He deserves a good wife after all he has suffered."

"What has he suffered?"

"If he loved you as a wife, he would have told you. I wonder why he did not?"

Stung by her words, I withdrew my hand and helped myself to porridge.

Before I finished eating, Jack entered the room. The atmosphere dissipated almost immediately. He nodded toward my hands while Lily served his breakfast.

"You should not have kept that to yourself, sister."

Lily turned her head sharply at his familiarity.

"'Tis nothing," I smiled back, grateful for a friend.

"You must rest from now on."

"No," I protested, "I have no wish to be idle. You were kind enough to take me in, and I wish to help. Nay, I insist."

"Well you cannot accompany me today," Lily snapped. She was due to pay calls on her customers in the village, delivering sewing and collecting further orders. Though eager to escape the confines of the house I had no wish to join her; her personal dislike of me was too thinly veiled to be ignored.

"Then you can help me." Jack lifted a hand to stop Lily's protests. "Valentine doesn't want her to be seen in the village, but he said nothing about the workroom. Nobody will see her there."

My heart sank at Jack's words. Was my husband so ashamed of me he did not want me to be seen? Would the whores he visited object to him having a wife at home—a wife expecting his child?

How could Vane and Jack be brothers? Their characters were completely different; one open, honest, and welcoming, the other cold, manipulating, and distant.

The day passed pleasantly in Jack's workroom. His gentle, easy conversation was so unlike anything I had experienced with anyone, let alone a man. He spoke honestly about his business, his love for Lily, and life in the village. He asked neutral questions about my tastes and preferences and avoided anything concerning Vane or my past. For that I was grateful, and I found myself relaxing and answering his questions honestly, for once able to conquer my fear that my words would be used against me.

By the time he closed his workroom and sent me to wait in the kitchen, it was late afternoon. Lily had not yet returned and there was no sign of Vane. I wanted to lay my head on the table and sleep but Jack had other plans for me. I had told him how I wished to be more useful in the home; to learn to undertake the domestic tasks I only understood how to direct others to perform.

My lower back ached and my skin felt stretched and sore, like a child's favorite gown she strives to fit into even though she has outgrown it. The babe moved and my belly tightened before it relaxed again. Placing my hand across where the child lay, I felt definite shapes and pictured his little limbs curled around his body inside me. I wanted him safe, warm, and protected from the world outside. If we stayed with Jack and Lily, he had a chance. I could trust Jack, grow to love him as a brother the way Lily loved Vane.

I could be happy here. They were kind people who worked hard for a living, unconstrained by the rules and traditions of the noble classes. Perhaps, in time, after I had given him a child and shown how I could work in the home to support him, Vane might come to care for me.

Jack breezed gaily into the kitchen, interrupting my thoughts. He held up two bags of flour, a broad grin on his face.

"Have you ever made bread?"

I shook my head.

"Then it's time you learned."

He spent the next hour showing me how to make dough and knead it, explaining that we would leave it to rise overnight before taking it to the bakery in the early morning.

At first the technique was difficult; my hands were clumsy, and I could not feel the dough's texture through the bandages. However, I soon found a rhythm, turning the dough over, pulling and rolling it, until it became smoother and more pliant. His gentle praise when I finished was balm to my wounded heart. Holding up the ball of dough I was so proud of, I swung round to place it on the hearth beside the fireplace. Losing my balance I knocked over one of the bags of flour, watching in horror as the precious contents spilled onto the floor.

Jack swore under his breath. The finely milled flour was expensive. It had been ordered by the sackload at Mortlock but here, in the village, even a small bag was costly. Jack would have toiled for many hours to afford it, and I had ruined it. Childhood memories chilled my blood—Papa beating me after I had spilled his wine, the blows to my stomach.

He stepped toward me, and I raised one arm to protect myself, curling the other around my stomach to protect the babe.

The blow never came. Jack stood over me, horror and anger in his expression. He moved, and I instinctively shielded my face again.

"Lisetta," he said, "lower your arm."

He held out his hand, but I shook my head.

"Devil's holy—I mean—heavens above, Lisetta, you think I would beat you? Over a bag of flour?"

"Forgive me, it was an accident."

"I'm aware of that. Take my hand." He reached out again, and this time I let him pull me upright.

"Are you hurt?"

Still trembling, I shook my head. He tried to draw me to him, but I pulled away.

"I am fine, Monsieur Cooper," I said evenly, smoothing down the front of my gown.

He sighed. "I think not. You hide much behind your ladylike airs."

Unwilling to trust him, I said nothing. Eventually he smiled.

"No matter; today is not the day to pursue it. Instead let me teach you the value of friendship."

Flinching, I stepped back as he raised his hand, but he merely plunged it into the remaining bag of flour on the table, pulled out a fistful and threw it at me. It hit me on the chest, sending a white cloud across my face, making me splutter.

"Now you do the same." He laughed.

Had he lost his wits? I shook my head, backing away, but he persisted.

"You must learn, dear sister, that family and friendship is worth more than a handful of flour." He nodded toward the bag. "I insist."

Family and friendship—something I longed for. I had begun to believe it might be possible. Not in a soulless castle where a woman's only comfort came from her status as a lady, but here, in a peasant's home, in an obscure little village.

I reached into the bag and scooped up a handful of flour.

"Go on."

Closing my eyes, I threw the flour in his direction, opening them again when I heard him cough. His face was covered, and he grinned, showing large teeth, his mouth a dark, gaping hole in his white face. His blue eyes twinkled with mirth, and I could not help smiling a little. He picked up the bag and tipped it over his head to leave a pile of flour on top. which dispersed into the air when he shook his head from side to side. He gave a courtly bow.

"Sir Wilbur Whiteface at your service, my lady."

The impulse to smile was too much, and he soon had me laughing at his antics. Jumping up and down, he clapped his hands in delight as a boy might at some childish prank. He took my hands in his, and my laughter died as his eyes met mine.

"'Tis good to hear you laugh."

I shook my head, smiling, "I cannot remember ever laughing like that."

"I'll wager you cannot remember the last time you

laughed at all. Do you realize how beautiful you are when you smile? Your eyes sparkle like liquid silver in the sunlight. I can see why my brother married you. He is indeed a fortunate man."

My smile died.

"He cares not for me," I whispered.

Jack squeezed my hands gently. "He does; or at least he will, in time. You are both welcome here, Lisetta—welcome to stay as long as you wish. It would gladden my heart to see you—both of you—settled and happy, here at Balsdean."

"You are kind." I dipped my head forward and brushed my lips against his knuckles.

"What are you doing with my brother?"

Vane stood in the doorway, his icy blue eyes on me. Dropping Jack's hands, I backed away.

"Nothing of any import, husband."

"We were making dough," Jack explained. Vane cast his eyes over the kitchen, the mess, the flour on the floor, and over our clothes.

"So I see."

"Come, brother, no harm done," Jack said, smiling.

Vane said nothing. The silence in the room thickened, the atmosphere full of tension which Jack tried to break.

"You're a fortunate man, Valentine; you have a lovely wife." Vane's eyes narrowed and Jack continued hastily, "almost as lovely as my Lily."

I rubbed my hands together, dispersing the flour, anticipating an angry outburst, but my husband merely turned his back and left the room.

Supper was a strained event, Lily the only one inclined to speak as she related gossip from the village.

She declined my offer of help when she cleared the table, and I followed Vane to our room. Though he'd hardly spoken, the tension in him at dinner was obvious. Spooning stew into his mouth, he appeared relaxed but his body was taut. As I sat beside him, I could barely swallow a mouthful. Following him up the stairs, I rubbed my aching back.

He threw off his clothes and sat on the bed, watching me while I finished undressing. Picking up my nightshift with shaking hands, I started in fright at the harshness in his voice.

"Leave that. Come here."

He pulled me onto his lap, his thick manhood bulging against my thigh. He took my head in his hands and turned my face toward him. I tipped my head up until our lips met but he pushed me away.

"No kissing, get up."

He pushed me onto my hands and knees on the bed. The tears that had threatened to form during supper spilled onto the blanket in front of me. An image invaded my mind; Vane plowing into Celia soullessly, using her body as a vessel for his lust.

"No," I pleaded.

"You forget you are my wife to do with as I please." He circled his hands around my waist.

"Not like this, please; not like *her*," I whispered so quietly I was unsure he would hear. The tears spilled down my cheeks, and I let out a sob.

"Vane!"

He stiffened at my cry before he huffed with exasperation and pulled away. I remained on all fours, too afraid to move. My nightshift landed against my thigh as he threw it at me.

"Put it on before I change my mind."

I obeyed him and slipped under the blankets but sat up when he pulled his chausses back on.

"Where are you going?"

"'Tis not for a wife to ask that of her husband," he said, "but since you ask; what you deny me I shall find elsewhere."

"No, you cannot!"

"I can, and I will." His eyes blazed with fury. "You dare question me when you seek to cuckold me with my own brother?"

I lunged at him, livid with anger that he could accuse me of such a deed. I loved him against all reason yet he cared nothing for me and accused me of the very sin he was about to commit. I swung my hand to strike him, but he caught my wrist.

"Do not provoke me, woman. A husband has every right to control an errant wife in any manner he sees fit." He increased the pressure on my wrist until I feared the bones would snap, before letting go as I cowered before him, cradling my hand.

"Go, then!" I cried, "for I care not. I hate you."

"Then I shall find love elsewhere tonight," he said. "There will always be plenty of willing women to console me for having shackled myself to a haughty shrew with a heart of ice. I should have left you at Mortlock, to the mercy of the king's men. Mayhap they would have warmed you up if the fire had not claimed you first."

His words tore into my heart as if he had plunged his sword into my chest. I bit my tongue to stop the scream building up in my throat, focusing on the sharp pain. Closing my eyes, I counted my breaths—one, two, three—until the door closed, and he was gone. There was nothing left to do other than pray sleep would come before he returned smelling of whores and ale.

Once again smoke and heat engulfed my dreams. Several figures stood before me, taunting, laughing, and holding torches aloft. The shrill cackles of whores mingled with deep laughter, the sound of my husband's mirth. His naked body entwined with Celia's as the whores moaned in ecstasy, squirming, wraithlike, in front of him, flickering in unison with the dancing flames.

"There are plenty of women willing," Vane laughed. "Why would I want you when I have *her*?" He lunged forward, thrusting his torch, and speared me in the middle. A burst of agony ripped through me, and I screamed.

I sat up, my throat hoarse. I was alone. Vane had not returned. Another nightmare, yet the pain had been so vivid. I massaged my stomach muscles which were rock hard with cramp. When the pain eased I lay back, whimpering softly to myself. But sleep eluded me for the rest of the night. Only when the first slivers of sunlight heralded the dawn did I close my eyes and drift once more into blessed oblivion.

Chapter 19

My body still ached as I descended the stairs the next morning. Vane sat at the kitchen table with Lily and Jack. My stomach clenched as he turned his blue gaze on me, but he rose and left the room, Lily following. I moved to the fireplace but Jack stopped me, insisting I sit while he ladled porridge into a bowl for me. I jumped as he took my hand.

"Are you well, sister? Lily and I heard you last night."

"I am fine," I whispered, blowing on the porridge to cool it.

"I would believe you had I not heard screaming," he said before withdrawing his hand. He did not press the matter but watched while I spooned porridge into my mouth. His careful scrutiny did more to loosen my tongue than demands or coercion.

"Sometimes I have bad dreams."

"Do they include my brother?" I started and looked up.

"You were crying for him, and I notice he did not come home until morning."

My appetite gone, I pushed the bowl away.

"Do not think badly of him, sister. He's a good man and has a kind heart."

"So Lily says," I replied, "yet he cares not..." I broke off and rose to leave but Jack took my hand.

"Perhaps if you know him better you'll think more kindly of him. The events in his life have scarred his heart, and he has yet to heal."

"Is this to do with William? The man Lily has spoken of?"

Jack's eyes narrowed in pain. "Aye, it is all to do with our brother."

Brother! "So, William was your brother? The one who died?"

"Aye," Jack said, "he was our younger brother. Valentine is the eldest but he was not my father's child; our mother had lain with another. William and I did not know he was only our half-brother and a bastard. Children don't question why one brother has a different surname. We loved him just the same. Father agreed to raise Valentine but never truly recognized him. Sawford was our mother's family name. When I became of age, father handed the business to me."

"Was Vane angry?"

Jack smiled, reliving the memory. "No. He was a generous-hearted brother and loved William and me very much. We agreed to run the business together. Lily and I had recently married, and he adored her, treating her as his own sister, comforting her when we were desperate for a child and our efforts were fruitless."

Pain flashed across his eyes.

"I'm sorry," I said, "my being here must be difficult for you."

"Nay, we are resigned to it, Lisetta, and will share your joy when your child arrives. I am glad Valentine has married."

"Yet you were surprised at the time? Because of William?"

"Aye."

"What happened, Jack? My husband will not speak of it."

He sighed. "Valentine had always given his heart too easily. He fell in love with the daughter of a knight serving the lord here. Elizabeth was a beautiful creature and Valentine was smitten. He offered for her and was accepted, or so we thought. However, when she discovered he was bastard born…"

"…she rejected him?"

"Nay, worse." Jack said. "She turned her attentions to William. Valentine caught her whoring herself with William in his bed. She told him she could never shackle herself to a bastard and that William had offered for her. The foolish young whelp also fancied himself in love, and she had managed to persuade him the child she carried was his, though I suspect it was Valentine's."

"Dear lord—does Vane have a child?"

Jack shook his head. "He lost his temper when he saw Elizabeth with William. She'd planned it, of course, but poor, foolish William had no idea. He told Valentine he loved Elizabeth and was going to marry her and raise the child. They fought and Valentine struck a blow. William fell and hit his head."

Jack closed his eyes as if uttering a brief, silent prayer before opening them again, moist with unshed tears.

"William never recovered."

I let out a low cry.

"Please, Lisetta, it was not his fault. He suffered greatly over William's death. Father threw him out, but what hurt him most was our mother's rejection. He left that night, and we did not see him for some years. After a while we thought he was dead. When he returned he was a changed man; scarred and hardened. The brother I knew no longer existed. Lily persuaded me to take him in. She has always seen the good in him. But he did not stay. He would disappear for months at a time. The last time was almost three years, before he returned with you."

"What happened to…" I struggled to speak her name "…to Elizabeth, and her child?"

Jack's voice hardened. "She married an acquaintance of her father's, someone prepared to take her though she carried another's child. She died in childbirth and took the child with her. The first time Valentine returned, I took him to her grave. He stood by the headstone and spat on it, declaring all women deceitful whores and that he would never fall prey to one again."

He laughed bitterly. "Little did that bitch know, Valentine eventually became everything she'd wanted. Her rejection of him was like the stone being thrown into a pond, sending out ripples of events, leading him to become the man he is."

I shook my head. "I don't understand."

"De Beauvane knighted him."

My eyes widened. "A knight? I thought him a mere servant."

"Yet you still married him."

"I had no choice."

His eyes narrowed. "Would you have been more willing had you known he was a knight?"

I shook my head. "No, Jack. It would have made no difference. I have spent most of my life subject to the authority, and whims, of lords and knights. Yet only during these past sennights in your house, have I understood how a man can be kind, even when he has nothing to gain by it."

He eyed me curiously. Anxious not to talk about myself I changed the subject.

"Does he still think of her?"

Jack sighed. "Nay, he does not, though it left him with a bitterness toward women."

"All women?"

"He loves Lily as a sister; she defended him against my father, more so than I did for I was grieving for William at the time. But as for other women—he was a changed man. 'Tis a pity."

I lowered my head, feeling the heat rise in my face. Jack took my hand.

"Forgive me, Lisetta. He has a loving heart, but conceals it."

He lowered his voice to a whisper while he caressed my hand. "He is much like you. I think you care—and love—a great deal more than you wish the world to know. Why is that?"

I shook my head, but he persisted.

"Do you think me blind? Your manner may be aloof but even if the tears you shed last night did not betray you, your eyes show a great deal. They contain fear but also deep sadness—and I see their expression when you look upon my brother. Do not try to convince me you are incapable of love…"

"Please, Jack, say no more." I pulled my hand away.

"Why do you not reveal your feelings?"

I stood, but he caught my wrist where Vane had

crushed it the night before. I groaned in pain and struggled against his grip. My body belonged to Vane as much as it had belonged to my father and Mortlock, who had abused and controlled it. But my mind and soul—I wanted to believe they were free, still mine to control. Yet Jack, who I had trusted, was probing my thoughts, wanting me to reveal myself to him.

"Please, let me go!"

He released me and held his hands up in a gesture of appeasement. "I will not touch you if you don't wish it. Sit down and finish your porridge."

I backed away, rubbing my wrist.

"Are you so frightened to trust us?" he asked.

I continued to move, not answering.

"Who did this to you, Lisetta? Who made you so afraid to speak of your feelings that you have built a fortress around yourself? What happened to you? I am no fool—I see your loving nature but it has been driven deep within you. You are terrified to show it."

I smoothed my face into indifference.

"You speak nonsense. I am merely tired and wish to rest."

He slumped his shoulders and sighed. "As you wish. But I am your friend, Lisetta. I hope one day you will see me as such. Go and rest. I will ensure you are not disturbed, but as a friend I would ask you to do one thing."

"What is that?"

"Give him a chance. Trust him. He married you for a reason."

Unable to reply, I left the room.

I was unusually tired that day, and I ached everywhere. The child moved and my body began to stretch around him, tightening into spasms. It seemed as if he shared my discomfort and distress, and I stroked my belly shushing him with soft words of love.

Perhaps in time I could trust Jack. When he asked me to give Vane a chance his eyes pleaded for a brother whose heart had been broken. If I told Vane I loved him, might Jack help him to grow to feel something for me—for our child? Lily clearly loved Vane; if I could convince her of my love for him she might help me, too.

What would it be like to have a loving family around me? Was it possible? Even at Mortlock I had seen occasional glimpses of something akin to tenderness in Vane's eyes. Jack's words wove through my mind as I lay, drifting in and out of sleep, on the bed. Perhaps I could tend to the wounds of Vane's heart as I had healed the wounds of his body. Perhaps those glimpses of empathy I had seen in his eyes were the small sparks of a flame I could nurture.

The pains in my body woke me later that night. Vane's muscular form lay against mine. A rush of fear overcame me as another spasm fluttered across my belly. My confinement was drawing closer, and I had been denying the fear of childbirth; the possibility I might not survive it. I wanted desperately to feel safe in his arms, to have him comfort me with his strength—the strength I did not possess.

The soft candlelight illuminated his face. Asleep, his features displayed none of the harshness he turned on me when awake. Jack was right; my husband wore a similar disguise to mine. Vane had just as much reason as I to conceal his feelings.

His chest rose and fell with each breath. Where had

he been during the day? Had he thought of me at all? Jealousy surged inside me at the thought of this woman Elizabeth who he'd loved so deeply. I ran my fingers along the stubble on his chin, tracing the line of his scar. He sighed, and the ghost of a smile played across his lips as he whispered one word.

"*Cherie.*"

I brushed my lips against the scar. He murmured in his sleep and reached toward me. I took his hand and held his knuckles to my lips. A single tear ran down my face and splashed onto his hand. I wiped it across his palm before kissing a trail where the tear had fallen. Holding his palm against my cheek I closed my eyes, whispering of my love for him.

His body stiffened before I heard his voice; harsh and cold.

"What do you want?"

I opened my eyes to see him staring at me, eyes the color of ice.

I had reached the point of no return and shattered the road leading back.

"You, husband." I kissed the tips of his fingers. "I want you."

I lowered myself over him and placed a soft kiss on his lips.

With a low growl, he rolled me onto my back and pinned me to the bed, thrusting his tongue inside my mouth savagely. He grasped my hair in one hand, forcing my head back against the bed. Ignoring my cry he fisted the top of my chemise with his other hand and tore it from me. The rush of cold air sent ripples of shock down my spine, tightening my chest. I gave a groan, part agony, part desire, as the need for him surpassed all else. His lips burned as he kissed my neck, drawing his lips together and sucking hard against my tender skin until I cried out again.

"Do you want me, woman?" his voice was rough and hoarse as he rubbed his hand across my breasts, pinching the nipples between his finger and thumb until I writhed against him, overcome by the twin sensation of pleasure and pain. He released my hair and sat back, his eyes hooded and dark.

"Oh, I wish to God it were so," he whispered, his voice loaded with pain. He ran his hands across my stomach where the skin stretched over the child. His hands faltered as my muscles contracted before resuming their path to my thighs. A flame burned through my veins where his fingers touched me, and my core pulsed softly with longing. His hot, wet mouth claimed my breast the same time he brushed his fingers against my flesh. It was exquisite—my sensitized body wept at his touch. He moved his fingers lightly, too lightly, against me. My body screamed for release, and I parted my legs, willing him to give me what I craved, what I knew his expert touch could do. He withdrew his hand and I whimpered at the loss.

"Tell me what you want," he growled.

"I want you," I cried, aching for him to touch me again, lifting my hips toward him. He started to caress me again, and my whole body tightened.

"Tell me again," he said, moving his fingers; teasing, probing, keeping me on the brink of shattering, withholding the satisfaction I craved.

"I want you inside me," I begged. Hot tears of shame welled in my eyes as I clutched the sheets on the bed and sobbed, "Oh, Vane!"

He withdrew his hand, unmoved by my sharp cry of frustration and loss which deepened as he moved off the bed.

"Vane, please!" I cried, but he turned his back and began to dress. A sharp pain in my belly racked my body and I caught my breath, squeezing my eyes shut and gritting my teeth until the pain subsided. When I opened them again he was fully dressed and heading for the door.

"Where are you going?" I struggled to sit.

"To find succor in the arms of another."

"No!" I wailed, "Don't leave me!"

"You think you can seduce me now my brother has rejected you?" He lifted his hand against my protests. "Do not deny it. I've seen you direct your smiles at him. Women! Whores, the lot of you! If I want a whore there are many in the village who are willing and would give me considerably more pleasure than you could ever hope to do."

"'Tis not true, Vane," I pleaded. "Not all women are like her. *I* am not like her!"

"Like who?" he said, his voice dangerously quiet.

"Elizabeth."

His expression darkened. He lifted his hands as if to wrap them around my neck but drew back, balling them into fists. He set his jaw into a hard line.

"Woman, if you wish to survive this night, speak no more."

"But…"

"I said enough!" he roared, his face contorted with rage. I stepped back in horror, tripping and falling back on the bed. He turned his back on me, slamming the door behind him, angry footsteps echoing down the stairs. With nothing else to do, I lay on the bed and wept with shame. My pathetic attempt at seduction had only served to drive him away, into another woman's arms.

****

When I struggled down the stairs the next morning there was no sign of him. Lily and Jack were talking quietly in the kitchen. As I entered they stopped, but not before I caught her sharp voice.

"…back in a sennight, though he has little to return to."

Jack laid a warning hand on her arm, and she turned to me, her expression full of contempt.

"He's gone," she said angrily.

"Do you wish for me to go also, Lily?"

"Aye," she sneered. "You drove him away last night. Mayhap your absence would bring him back to his family—to those who love him."

A spasm of pain gripped my body, and I fell against the doorframe. Jack reached toward me, but Lily pulled him back.

"Do not come near my husband!" she raged at me. "You think you can whore yourself out to every man who falls in your path? You probably don't even love the man who sired your child."

"I do!" I cried, the anger I felt against her injustice forced out by the pain in my heart and body. "I love him more than you could ever understand, and I will never love another! Surely you don't think Jack and I…"

"Be quiet, you whore!" Lily's usually kind face contorted with fury. "You have done nothing but disturb our peace since you—"

She broke off at my sharp cry of agony. A gush of warm liquid ran down my legs and splashed on the floor. Before I collapsed, Jack took me by the arms and pulled me toward the table. Clutching the edge with one hand I moaned as another wave of pain engulfed me. It felt as if my body were being ripped apart. Jack supported my weight, and I gripped his hand, not caring that I dug my nails into his palm. Through the haze of pain I heard his voice, calm and reassuring.

"Lily, take care of her while I find the midwife."

"No," I choked as a spasm of pain shook my body. "Don't leave me, Jack!"

I heard Jack's voice interspersed with Lily's sharper tones though the pain obliterated the words.

The spasm receded, and I breathed out. Jack tugged at my arm.

"Can you move, sister? You need to be upstairs."

I shook my head and my body tightened again causing a peculiar stretching between my legs. I tried to move but the feeling intensified, and I moaned in pain.

"Forgive me, sister. I won't try to move you." Jack's voice was kind. "Is there anything you want or need that I can get you?"

Aye, I need my husband. I shook my head, sobbing.

"Do you wish for my brother?"

I jerked my head up, hope springing in my heart which died on seeing the sad expression he wore. He kissed the top of my head, stroking it with his free hand.

"Lisetta—I am so sorry he's not here." He smiled weakly as if trying to convince himself of the truth in his next words, "I am sure when he returns he'll want to see you—and your child—safe and well."

I gripped the table as the pain overwhelmed me again, grateful for his strong arms supporting me as we waited for Lily to return with the midwife.

****

My confinement lasted several hours, and as night fell, I gave birth to a son. I had begun to deal with the pain of each contraction, and as my body stretched to accommodate his entry into the world, I grew calmer, determined to be strong for his sake. The midwife tried to send Jack out of the room, but he stood firm, holding my hand and ignoring Lily's admonishments. At one point, I looked up at the man supporting me and thought it was my husband. I cried out his name before turning my head in disappointment, realizing that the blue eyes looking back at me were not the eyes I had been praying with all my soul to look upon again.

When my body eventually tightened in the instinct to bear down, the pressure inside me was almost intolerable. Encouraged by Jack and the midwife, I gritted my teeth and strained as hard as I could. Surrendering to my weakness, as the child slid from my body, I screamed the name of the one person I wanted by my side.

"Vane!—Vane!!"

I collapsed forward, my body floating. I kept my eyes closed, sensing the oncoming blackness, and the welcoming relief from pain—both physical and emotional. The world swirled around me as I heard the midwife's voice.

"'Tis a boy."

A sharp cry returned me to the world—the pitiful wail of a child. The sound ripped through my soul and in that moment I understood my purpose. A mother's instinct told me my son needed to be safe in my arms. All that mattered was the urge to protect him. I struggled to my feet and held out my arms.

"Give me my son."

"Mistress, you must rest. Let your brother take you upstairs to your room first…"

"I. Need. My. Son," I said slowly and clearly through gritted teeth, shaking off Jack's steadying arm though my legs trembled.

"Give him to her, Edwina," Jack said softly, "I can carry them both."

The midwife wrapped my son in a blanket and handed him to me. As he opened his eyes to look at me for the first time I felt a warm rush of love. It was as if Vane himself looked back at me with the love I yearned for. I knew then that if I could not have the love of the father, the love of the son would be my solace. My tears splashed onto his perfect little face, but for first time in my life they were tears of joy.

I barely registered Jack as he carried me upstairs. Placing me on the bed, he held out his arms for the child, but I refused, clutching him to me as if my life depended on it.

"It seems I have a nephew." He smiled. "Have you thought of a name?"

"Aye," I replied, bending my head to kiss the top of my child's head, breathing in the beautiful scent of him.

"I will let you rest now, Lisetta. Edwina will attend you in the morning."

Before I could answer he had gone. The babe wriggled in the blanket, working an arm free. I held out a finger, and he curled his little hand around it, forming a tiny pink fist. My son—whom I loved as much as I loved his father.

"Welcome, my love," I whispered. "Geoffrey Valentine Sawford."

Chapter 20

The sound of crying interrupted my dreams. For a moment I thought Vane had returned, but I was alone in the bed and had been since the birth of my son. Geoffrey screamed in anger, his little body tangled in the blanket in the makeshift cot Jack had placed beside the bed. Lifting him out, I held him close, opening my nightshift. He instinctively turned his head to my breast and reached out with his little hand, stroking it as he took his nourishment. As the milk flowed from my body into his, I understood, at last, the true meaning of love, but I didn't fear it. I understood why Maman was willing to suffer pain, even death. Here, in my arms, lay someone I loved unconditionally and valued over my own life.

I wanted to get up, to smell fresh air and feel the sun on my skin, but the midwife had warned me of a virulent sickness in the village which had struck down a number of babies and children. Fear for Geoffrey's safety kept me inside.

Lily avoided me, making no effort to disguise her hostility. Jack visited me in my room but despite my daily pleas for Vane he could not tell me where his brother was, or even if he would return. I was grateful for Edwina's company. The midwife's caring nature and gentle hands were so like my beloved Harwyn's and under her care I recovered quickly. While tending to my sore body she sang to Geoffrey, the same lullabies Maman had sung to me.

When Edwina left the room, two days after Geoffrey's birth, Jack brought in a tray of bread and porridge.

"How is my nephew today?"

I smiled. "He is beautiful."

"'Tis good to see you smile thus. Your love is obvious. I cannot understand your reluctance to show it."

"Jack, please…"

"Are you so afraid to love, Lisetta? Afraid it will destroy you or, perhaps, you'll be rejected?"

"I have already been rejected."

He set the tray down and sat beside the bed, stroking Geoffrey's head.

"I'm sorry you and Lily never had children of your own," I said. "Lily would have been a wonderful mother."

"As will you be, dear sister."

I didn't reply, and he turned his blue gaze on me. "You have not been rejected, Lisetta."

"Then where is he?"

Jack leaned forward and kissed me on the forehead. "He will return to you. Have faith."

His voice was filled with uncertainty. He was trying to convince himself as much as me.

****

Almost a sennight later, Vane had still not returned, and I lost hope that he ever would, or at least that he would return for me. Jack's kindness was a comfort but Lily made it increasingly plain she did not want me in her home.

An idea, once pushed to the recesses of my mind, began to resurface. The convent near Shoreton, to where I'd thought to flee when I left Mortlock. It was somewhere safe where I could live with Geoffrey in peace, surrounded by a community whose purpose in life was contemplation, reflection, and healing. There I could lead a simple life, away from treachery, murder, and unrequited love. I still had my rings—trinkets to pay for my passage. The journey would be difficult in winter, but not impossible if I could find someone to help me.

Eventually I asked Edwina. The sickness in the village was spreading and many children had succumbed to it. My pleas for Geoffrey's safety, together with Lily's obvious wish to be rid of me, finally persuaded her. Though uncomfortable with the deception, at my bidding, she sold one of my rings in the village. An honest and trustworthy woman, she got a good price and used some of it to secure my passage to a market town several days' ride away. She tipped the remainder of the money into my hand. I gave her some, ignoring her protests, telling her there were few people in the world worthy of trust, and they had to be rewarded.

In the dark of the night, she led me out of the house to the tavern where a young man waited for me with a horse and cart. I had a basket over my arm with a loaf of bread and a change of clothes. Geoffrey, wrapped in a blanket in my other arm, was asleep.

"Tom here will take you to the tavern at Midford and will make enquiries there for someone to take you further."

"Can he be trusted?"

"I brought him into the world, my lady. I would trust him with my life."

"God be with you, Edwina. I'll never forget your kindness."

She embraced me. "And also with you. Take care of the little one."

"I will," I replied, choking back tears. "He is all I have."

Tom helped me onto the seat next to him and dropped my basket into the cart before covering my legs with a blanket.

"Take good care of her, Tom," Edwina warned, "or you answer to me."

Tom laughed good-naturedly. "You've already threatened to relieve me of my manly parts should any harm come to her in my care, Mistress Edwina. I value them too much."

He turned his gaze on me. "My lady, you have nothing to fear from me."

His voice was kind, and I nodded before addressing Edwina.

"Tell Jack and Lily I'm sorry for the trouble I caused them, and I wish them well."

Edwina nodded to Tom and we set off. I took one last look at the house where I had spent the last three months; where I had caught a glimpse of the life I dreamed of. I turned away, unable to look any longer upon the place where I'd finally realized my heart belonged, only to discover the man I had given it to thought less than nothing of me. I would always love him, no matter what. He had given me the greatest gift of all—Geoffrey. I held my son close, feeling a small ray of hope. I might never have the life of my dreams, but I would find contentment in the convent and fulfillment in the love of my son.

Tom whistled a merry tune, and I couldn't help smiling. His youthful joy for life was infectious.

Reaching the edge of the village I spotted a tall figure standing by the edge of the road.

"Tom—stop!" I cried. My hands shook. He had returned!

"Vane!"

The man took a step toward us, and I realized I was wrong. He was too short to be my husband and less muscular in build. I sank back against Tom, defeated.

"Forgive me. 'Twas my mistake."

We continued on our path, the stranger watching us. Before we rounded a corner, I took a last look back and shivered with fear as he raised his hand in salute. Though my knife was tucked into my gown, I would not feel safe until there were several miles between us and the man who had watched us leave so intently.

****

The journey to Midford took nine days. I had little money and wished to avoid being noticed so we slept rough each night and avoided the main roads. But it was no hardship; the cart provided shelter from the rain and Tom proved an adept hunter. We worked well together. Tom set up camp and hunted rabbit while I nursed Geoffrey. In turn I prepared the meals and packed our belongings each morning. What would Vane think of me if he could see me? I truly was a peasant now, but for the first time in my life I felt free. I had no need to pretend to be anything other than what I was.

Tom was good company. He had offered for a girl

in Balsdean village but her father had refused consent until he proved his ability to keep her. With the money he made from accompanying me, he could marry her on his return. He was touchingly devoted to her, and I resolved that once I'd paid for our food and lodging at Midford as well as my passage on to the convent, I would give him the rest of my money. He was so like Percy in his youthful innocence. I had not been able to do anything for poor Percy, but I could do something for Tom.

****

We arrived at Midford early evening. Tom drove the cart to the inn before helping me down, my legs stiff from the journey. Geoffrey slept on, and I held him close, taking Tom's hand as he led me inside the inn.

My eyes grew accustomed to the dark, the blurred forms morphing into the shapes of tables and chairs, casting shadows from the light of a fire at the back of the room. At one table a small group of men murmured to each other, turning their heads briefly to look at us before resuming their conversation.

"Hello there!"

At Tom's call, a door swung open at the back of the room, and a man shuffled out.

"What ye be wanting?" The thick, rough accent almost obscured his words.

"Are you the innkeeper?" Tom asked.

"Aye—who be asking?"

"My name is Tom." Tom nodded in my direction. "My sister and I have travelled a long way and seek board and lodging for one night, maybe more."

"Two rooms?"

"Just one. We have very little money."

The man hawked and spat on the floor. "Ye're in luck, boy, we have one room remaining. The village is busy for 'tis market today tomorrow."

Market day. With traders visiting the town we had a good chance of finding someone willing to take me on the rest of my journey. But the danger of discovery still lurked in the shadows. We'd have to be careful not to draw attention to ourselves—I had no idea whether someone was still looking for me.

Tom pulled out the bag of coins I'd given him. He tipped some into the innkeeper's outstretched hand, increasing the pile one by one until the man nodded.

"I'll send Gwenna to show you to your room."

"Have her bring our meal," I said. "We wish to dine in our room."

The innkeeper thrust his face toward me, sour anger in his eyes before addressing Tom. "Your woman speaks for you?" he leered. "You should control her better—she merits a beating for speaking thus, uninvited."

"How dare…" I began but Tom placed a warning hand on my arm. "Forgive us, good man. My sister is merely tired and wishes to retire."

"If she wishes to eat, she'll eat in the main room with the rest of us. We're too busy to tend to a woman who fancies herself a lady."

He spat at my feet then turned his back and roared for Gwenna.

A thin woman, barely out of childhood, scuttled out and led us to our room. I sank onto the bed, my body aching. It would be a relief to sleep in a bed rather than outside. The damp cold from ground hardened by winter frosts had penetrated the woolen blankets we lay on during our journey. Each morning I'd massaged my feet, numbed by the frost, flinching at the sharp needles of pain pricking at my skin as my toes returned painfully to life.

After fetching our belongings, Tom left me to nurse Geoffrey in peace. Placing my sleeping child on the bed, I dropped a kiss on his forehead before joining Tom in the main room. He had found a table tucked away in a corner and waved as I entered. I sat, surveying the room, my skin prickling with anticipation as if everyone's eyes were on me.

The room had filled since our arrival and was much noisier—an amorphous bustle of coarse words and laughter. My eyes smarted in the air, acrid with smoke from the fire which now burned more brightly, the shapes of the patrons silhouetted against the deep orange glow of the flames.

An occasional drunkard roared for ale, followed by cheers as a serving wench weaved her way between the tables. The woman shrieked with laughter as she dodged eager hands which reached out to fondle her, spilling ale as one man secured a hold on her skirts, pulling her toward him to plant a loud kiss on her lips.

"Well, well—what do we have here?"

A sour stench of sweat and stale liquor grew stronger and a leering, fleshy face was thrust in front of me. Having learned my lesson earlier I remained quiet, waiting for Tom to respond.

"Please leave us," Tom said, his voice trembling.

The man laughed and sat beside me. The stench of his body odor turned my stomach, which already churned in distaste at the greasy stew we had eaten.

"I'll wager you'd not miss your wife, young pup,"

he slurred. "I could warm her up for you."

Poor young Tom. His face paled and he shook his head, too frightened to respond. He had grown up in a friendly village where most of the inhabitants were related to each other—brothers, cousins, aunts, and uncles. Midford, a larger town, attracted traders and travelers from further afield—strangers with no ties of family or friendship. Tom was unused to such behavior.

I drew my knife and pressed it against the man's side. With a yelp of surprise he jerked away. but I lifted it, holding the tip of the blade against his throat. His eyes widened, but he stayed still as I twisted the knife, making a deep dent in his skin.

"I have much experience in defending myself against drunken animals," I said coldly. "Your wife has my sympathies."

"I meant no disrespect to you or your husband," he said.

I increased the pressure and a small patch of red appeared on his throat, growing to form a droplet. The man whimpered, and I leaned closer, ignoring the stench of his breath, and I gave him a cold smile.

"My husband is dead," I said. "I wonder if your own wife would care to join my widowed status. I doubt she would miss you."

He shook his head, but I held the knife firm, the droplet spilling onto his tunic.

"What say you, Tom?" I asked. "Shall we find out if this man's wife would miss him?"

"Begging your pardon, madam," the man said.

"Leave us," I said. "Crawl back to the hovel from whence you came."

He lumbered off, doubtless on his way to accost

another unsuspecting female.

"We should retire, Tom," I said. "I'm anxious not to attract any more attention."

****

The following morning Tom insisted I stay in our room while he made enquiries for someone willing to complete my journey to the convent. He had offered to take me himself but I didn't want to place him in any danger in case I was being watched, particularly after the attention we had drawn the previous evening.

A few hours later Tom's voice signaled his return, and I placed Geoffrey on the bed before calling out in response.

He entered the room, smiling broadly, a man following him. The man nodded at me and coughed loudly.

"I have found someone willing to take you further," Tom said. "He…"

Another man appeared and a knife flashed briefly in the sunlight before he drew the blade across Tom's throat. Crimson liquid pulsed down the young man's chest, and he fell soundlessly forward, not even a look of surprise in his eyes, so swiftly did he meet his death.

The two men advanced toward the bed.

"We've been looking for you."

"You have the wrong room," I cried, painfully aware of how close they were to Geoffrey, wriggling on the bed beside me. "You've killed an innocent man— my brother!"

I drew breath to scream but they were too quick. The man with the knife picked up Geoffrey, and held the blade against my son's body while his companion took my arm.

"I'd advise you to be silent. You are coming with us and we'd prefer it if you—and the brat—were alive."

"Please, let my son go," I sobbed, "I care not who you are—I'll say nothing, do nothing if you leave now. I tell you, you have the wrong room!"

"I'm afraid we cannot do that. We are in the right room, are we not, Lady Mortlock?"

Mon Dieu—I had been discovered.

He nodded to his companion. "Bring the brat."

"No!" I cried.

"Be quiet!" He twisted my arm behind me and took my throat with his free hand. "Dead or alive you shall be the means of my reward. Your life and that of the little bastard depends on your following orders. Play the devoted wife, and I may be more kindly disposed toward you."

He led me out of the room, crudely fondling my body as we walked through the tavern. A third man waited outside next to a cart laden with sacks. Before I knew what was happening, pain exploded in the back of my head. The last thing I remembered was Geoffrey's cries as I sank into the dark pit of despair. Yet another innocent life had been taken because of me, and I had failed utterly to protect my son.

Chapter 21

When I woke, my head hammered as if assaulted by a blacksmith. I was lying on my back on an enormous bed. A canopy, embroidered with an exotic pattern in reds and golds, hung above me. Sitting up, I rubbed the back of my neck. An old woman sat by the door watching me, but before I could speak she left the room.

Someone had changed my clothes; the peasant's garb replaced with a purple gown of soft silk embroidered with flowers. Once again I was Lady Mortlock. I had been discovered, but by whom? Where was I?

The door opened to reveal my captor.

"What a pleasure to see you again, my dear."

His handsome features glowed in the candlelight. Had I not known him I would have thought him a thing of beauty. But he was rotten inside, rotten to the core.

Wulfric, Baron de Tourrard. Lord Mortlock's cousin.

My throat constricted at the memory of his fingers crushing my windpipe at Mortlock Fort. He'd said then he would bide his time and now, here I was. By leaving the man I loved, I found myself at the mercy of the man I hated.

"Come to me."

I shook my head, and he moved with the speed of a

striking snake, coiling his fingers around my wrist.

"I would advise you to be friendly toward me, Lisetta." His voice was mild but the undercurrent of menace matched the malevolence in his eyes. "After all, I'm taking such care of the little brat."

"Leave my son alone!" I cried.

"I have plans for him, my love. He's the heir my foolish cousin always wanted, no? I am equally happy to name him my heir, to overlook the fact you had to be rutted by every man at Mortlock in order to beget him."

I tried to pull free, but his grip was too firm.

"My fool of a cousin thought his weak plot against Henry would work. The king is so grateful to me for betraying Mortlock, he thinks me a most loyal subject. And now I can claim you as my own. I know exactly how to satisfy a woman and to teach her to pleasure me. My cousin did not value your charms, Lisetta, but as my wife you'll want for nothing and neither will I. You are clearly fertile."

He clutched my belly, and I shuddered with revulsion.

"I'm married, Wulfric," I said, "Whatever you force me to do, it will not be legal in the eyes of the church."

"Ah yes, the bastard," he chuckled. "Is he the one whose seed took root? No matter; he'll be disposed of soon enough. Surely the title of Baroness de Tourrard and mistress of Malford Hall is better than being a filthy peasant's wife.

How did De Tourrard know I had married Vane?

"Come, my dear; before we eat there is something we must discuss—the whereabouts of the whoreson you married."

219

He led me down several flights of stairs. Before long, the smell of damp and decay thickened the air. He was taking me to the dungeons.

He opened a door at the bottom of the stairwell and bowed with mock courtesy, leading me through. I found myself in a dark passage with torches placed at intervals along one side. On the other side a row of doors, each with a small barred window, disappeared into the darkness. Coughing and groaning echoed around the chamber. What poor souls resided behind those doors?

I could sense de Tourrard's pleasure at my fear.

"Am I to be confined here?"

"Not yet. I have something else in mind for you first."

Taking my hand as if I were a bride crossing the threshold, he led me through the first door into a large cell. A number of shapes adorned the room; chains attached to the walls and benches supporting metal devices. A tall, thin man sat beside one of the benches. De Tourrard gestured toward him.

"My surgeon, Blanchard. He's been waiting for you."

I stepped back but de Tourrard gripped my arms and held me firm. The devices in the room cast twisted shadows on the floor. Those I recognized struck fear into my heart: a rack for stretching the limbs until the body was distorted beyond recognition; knives and needles designed to flay the skin off and extract confessions as the victims were manacled to the wall or strapped to the benches. The odor of pain and death hung like a thick fog. Dark stains, which could never be cleaned, clung to the benches and the floor. I heard echoes of the screams of the men who'd been brought here over the years. Soon my own screams would join them to haunt de Tourrard's future victims.

He placed a light kiss on the back of my head and pushed me forward.

"Let us begin with a simple question to whet the appetite." His voice was a soft caress against my ear. "No need to be hasty, aye?"

"A man who acts in haste is a fool," I said, my throat dry. He laughed at my attempts at bravery.

"As is a woman, my dear. Now, tonight you only need answer one simple question. Where is Vane Sawford?"

"How would I know?" I replied, "I have not seen him since I left Mortlock."

"Lying bitch," he snarled, "is he not your husband? You cannot prevent the inevitable. Sawford will die, though not before he resides in this room. Blanchard can keep a man alive and in agony for several days. He considers it an art form and it gives me great pleasure to watch."

The image of Vane writhing in pain while de Tourrard looked on was too real. Whatever became of me, I would never betray him.

"You evil bastard," I cried, "I will tell you nothing!"

"As you wish."

He twisted my arm, too quickly for me to pull away, and I heard a sickening crack before a white-hot flame of agony ran through me. I fell to the floor, moaning in pain.

"Perhaps by tomorrow your tongue will have loosened. See to her, Blanchard."

De Tourrard bowed before leaving me alone in the torture chamber with the surgeon.

Blanchard knelt beside me and inspected my arm. He bandaged it in silence then hauled me to my feet and led me out of the chamber and deeper into the dungeon. The wailing grew louder, the occupants in the cells sensing the approach of their torturer. Blanchard stopped by an open door near the end of the passage and pushed me through.

I sank to the floor and vomited, barely registering the key jangling in the lock, and the footsteps receding into the distance.

Not long after, the torches went out, plunging the cell into darkness. But the nightmares would not invade me tonight. What I was living here and now, what awaited me tomorrow, was far worse. I would have to be strong, stronger even than Maman, for Vane and for Geoffrey. I prayed for her spirit to give me strength and hugged myself to keep warm as I listened to the wails of the tortured souls which surrounded me.

Chapter 22

The tormented moans from my fellow prisoners faded into silence, penetrated by an occasional cough or a cry. The middle of the night had arrived—that eerie hush a few hours before the dawn which children believed to be filled with monsters. Mothers and nursemaids always said no such things existed, but I knew different.

I must have slept for Percy visited me, his empty eye sockets staring at me reproachfully, telling me I'd betrayed him and would soon betray another. I cried at him to leave me alone and the inmates' voices joined in until one began to cackle with laughter and sing coarsely. How long before I joined them in madness?

As patches of gray signaled the dawn I heard footsteps. The voices of those around me howled as our host approached. My door opened and I tried to stand, but a sharp pain shot through my arm, and I fell back as de Tourrard entered the cell.

"Good morning, Lisetta. I trust you slept comfortably."

"Where is my son?"

"My heir." His teeth gleamed as he grinned. "My *current* heir is safe. I'll reunite you soon, but first we must resume our conversation. 'Twas most ungallant of me to stop you when you were being so—talkative."

Blanchard awaited us in the torture chamber, the

tools of his trade set out before him. A fire burned in a brazier, the smell of oil catching the back of my throat. De Tourrard held me against his body, and I shuddered in revulsion as his manhood grew hard against my buttocks.

"Come, come Lisetta—I promise to satisfy you more than my cousin did." He forced my head back and covered my mouth with his, plunging his tongue inside, so deep I fought for breath. I gagged at the obscene taste of him, but he only held me firmer, crushing my arm in his grip until it felt on fire. I bit down, and he let go, snarling with anger, and backhanded me across the face.

"Blanchard!"

The surgeon approached holding something aloft; an iron poker, its tip glowing. He spat on the end, grinning as I jumped at the angry hiss.

"Careful, my dear. If you don't remain still you could harm yourself more than Blanchard intends. We wouldn't wish you to lose *too* much of your beauty."

With his free hand, the surgeon grasped the front of my gown and tore at the material, exposing my breasts. He studied them with a cool disinterest more terrifying than the lust I had anticipated.

De Tourrard laughed.

"You see, my dear, I trust Blanchard completely. He cannot be swayed by a whore's tactics." He tightened his grip. "Don't fight it, Lisetta. This will happen whether you wish it or no. Better for you if you remain talkative, but first you need a lesson in courtesy."

He nodded to the surgeon and all sensation gave way to an intense burning as the tip of the poker touched my shoulder. The pain was unbearable. I clenched my teeth and tasted blood. The odor of burning flesh accompanied the hiss of hot metal against melting skin. My lungs burned as I screamed until my mind collapsed into blessed darkness.

When I regained consciousness, I was lying on my back. I prayed this was just another nightmare, that I was back at Jack and Lily's home. But the smell of burning flesh—my flesh—told me otherwise. I tried to move but metal restraints held me down. Blanchard had chained me to a bench. God help me, I was going to die here.

De Tourrard's face appeared above me.

"Blanchard, she's ready for you again. I trust, my dear, you now appreciate the benefit of conversation. Now, tell us where you have been living with your lover."

"My *husband*," I spat back, "and you're a fool to think I would betray him."

The door creaked open.

"Ah, how timely," de Tourrard said. "The family reunited. I believe you already know my whore."

His body blocked my line of sight but when he moved I saw a woman in the doorway. She held something in her arms, and it gave a small squeal which pierced my heart.

"Geoffrey," I croaked. "No! Don't let him see this! Woman—take him out!"

She shook her head. "I'll take no orders from you."

I recognized her voice.

"Celia."

"Aye, 'tis me," she replied, "nursemaid to a whore's bastard."

"Do not speak of whores, woman." De Tourrard struck Celia across the face. She staggered under the blow and cowered, her face taut with fear. Once again I found myself pitying her, though she loathed me.

De Tourrard motioned to Blanchard who pulled the poker out of the brazier and handed it to him. He held it in front of my face, and the heat burned against my skin.

"I believe we were discussing the preservation of your beauty, Lisetta. It will break my heart to see it destroyed." He sighed wistfully. "Do you know what I deem to be your most beautiful feature?"

I shook my head, unwilling to give him the satisfaction of a response.

"No matter, I shall tell you anyway. It's your eyes. They are gray as a storm cloud. How it will break my heart to harm them! My consolation is that you have two. One beautiful eye will remain after today."

Celia gave a muffled cry.

"Silence, whore!" de Tourrard barked.

He fisted my hair and yanked my head up, holding the poker close. The heat stung my eyes, but I kept them open. If this was to be the last time I looked upon de Tourrard, I wanted him to see the hatred I bore him.

"We both know you will betray him eventually," he said. "Why not save yourself—and me—the sorrow of seeing your eyes turn to dust?"

I smiled, putting on the mask I had worn for his cousin, and spoke coldly and clearly. "Then turn them to dust, for I will never betray the man I love. I would join you in hell first."

He edged the poker closer and a searing pain speared through my head. I closed my eyes, waiting for the agony. Never before had Maman's advice been so beneficial. I began to count, slowly, in my mind. By the time I counted to ten it would all be over.

Before I reached five, hands fumbled at my restraints. De Tourrard sat me up and returned the poker to the surgeon. Celia watched me but her expression no longer showed contempt. I almost thought I saw admiration in her eyes, replaced by fear as Blanchard moved toward her.

"You see, Celia," de Tourrard said, "Though she may be a fool, Lisetta is more of a lady than you could ever aspire to be. You squealed like an old sow to betray her while you spread your thighs for me."

He turned to me. "You have passed a test, my love."

"Am I free to go?"

"No, my dear," he laughed, "if the love you bear the bastard you married will not loosen your tongue, I'll wager the love you bear his brat will."

"What do you mean?" I whispered, fear solidifying in the pit of my stomach.

"I mean your son has his mother's eyes."

"No!" I cried. "God, no, Wulfric! Have mercy— you said he was to be your heir!"

"You little fool!" de Tourrard snarled. "He's as disposable as that whore who holds him. If you refuse to talk you will live the rest of your life knowing what your lack of co-operation did to him. Or, you can see him grow to be a fine man—a de Tourrard. But I swear to you, Lisetta; only death will separate that child from me."

"You're insane," I cried, "leave him alone!"

"Are you willing to talk?"

Geoffrey's little hand poked out from the blanket, and he squirmed in Celia's arms, seemingly aware of the danger. Blanchard clasped my son's wrist and raised the poker.

"Stop!" I screamed, "I'll tell you what you want."

"All I need is the name of the village, my dear."

"First, give me my son."

"You are in no position to bargain."

De Tourrard had won. He had given me an impossible choice—to risk the life of my husband, whom I loved, or to destroy my innocent son, who was my world. The choice was simple. Vane could fight. He had a chance if I betrayed him; Geoffrey had none.

"Balsdean," I whispered, my voice thick with defeat.

De Tourrard's countenance changed almost immediately, becoming the charming, handsome courtier I had met as a child. Even then I had not trusted the dead expression in his eyes. He took my arm, praising my loyalty, and bade Celia follow us, chatting as if we had been on a pleasant excursion.

He returned me to the bedchamber.

"Give me my son." I hissed, gritting my teeth in pain, my shoulder pulsing with a raging fire.

"Later, my love," he purred. "First someone must tend to your shoulder for you have had an unfortunate accident. As soon as you are recovered you will ride with me to Balsdean so the bastard can see who betrayed him. Our first outing as a family. How pleasant! Geoffrey will enjoy riding with his new papa."

Clasping the back of my neck, he drew me to him.

"My beautiful bride. I fear you would not please

me tonight, but we have the rest of our lives to relish each other."

I turned my head away in disgust as he caressed my cheek, running his fingertips across my mouth, and I tasted soot on his skin. He pushed me into the chamber.

"Come, Celia."

I gave a sob at the sight of her holding my precious child. Standing in the doorway she cradled him almost lovingly, her eyes moist with tears. She dropped a curtsey before following de Tourrard out of the chamber. The door closed behind her, and the key turned in the lock. De Tourrard thought to imprison me but he would never understand the love a mother has for her child. Though I longed for freedom I could not leave while he had my son.

Chapter 23

The next morning a maidservant entered with a tray of food and wine, with instructions from de Tourrard that I eat and drink everything or Geoffrey would suffer. I had to be strong for my son so I complied, sipping the wine even though I knew it was drugged, while she looked on. I sat passively while she treated my wounds until the drug took effect, and I sank into a stupor.

That evening Celia entered the chamber holding a pile of clothes. Her face bore a fresh bruise and dark finger marks circled the base of her neck. She limped across the room, her expression showing nothing but pain and shame.

"Where's my son?"

"With the wet-nurse, lady. He is safe."

"He's not safe!" I cried. "You think any of us are safe here?"

A tear slid down her cheek, and I felt nothing but compassion for her. I remembered my encounter with de Tourrard at Mortlock, the relish in his eyes as he held my throat. Like his cousin he took an unnatural pleasure in inflicting pain.

"Did he hurt you?" I whispered.

She nodded and I took her hand. "Can't you leave? Is there nowhere you can go?"

She shook her head.

"Celia—you cannot let him treat you like this! Now he has me I might be able to persuade him to release you."

She fell to her knees and began to cry, her shoulders shaking as she covered her face.

"Shhh—someone will hear."

"Forgive me!" she sobbed, "I cannot bear your kindness after how I treated you. I hated you so much I let de Tourrard pay me to spy on you at Mortlock. He promised I would be his mistress, and he would treat me as a lady; but he has beaten me almost every day since I came here. I am nothing but his whore now."

"Then you must get away."

"What of you, lady; what of Geoffrey?" she wept, "I cannot leave you—I must atone for what I did to you."

I took her in my arms while she cried, before she pulled away in panic.

"We must hurry! He sent me to bring you to the dining hall. He'll come looking if you don't join him soon."

"Then I must dress—quickly!"

She helped me into the clothes, a pale gold surcoat over a white gown.

"Lady," she hesitated, "did you always love Monsieur Sawford?"

I stiffened on hearing his name, and she sighed.

"That's why I hated you. I wanted Sawford for myself. But he only wanted you. From the day you arrived at Mortlock he had eyes for none other."

"Celia, he did not want—"

"Aye, he did. I knew of Lord Mortlock's plan to whore you out. De Tourrard paid me to listen to everything. With Mortlock's previous wives Sawford always found others to do the deed, but you were different."

She placed a hand on my shoulder. "I was jealous. I thought you were yet another noblewoman to look down on us and care only for yourself. But last night, de Tourrard tortured you, yet you refused to betray Sawford. I have never loved anyone enough to be ready to die for them."

"I did betray him," I said.

"For the sake of your son," she replied. "You made a wise choice. Sawford can protect himself—and as he's not here to protect you, I will do the best I can."

Before we approached the dining hall, I took Celia's arm and whispered urgently in her ear. Celia had to treat me with the same dislike she had always shown. De Tourrard must not suspect we had become allies.

The dining hall was larger than those at Mortlock. Long tables filled the room at which over forty men sat. De Tourrard overlooked the company from a high table at the far end of the hall, beyond a huge stone fireplace. He beckoned to me. To reach him I had to pass the fireplace. Several dogs lay at the hearth and some lifted their heads to watch me. They were vicious looking brutes, and I took care to make no sudden movements. Every nerve in my body screamed to run, but de Tourrard would take pleasure in setting the dogs on me if I did.

I kept my expression neutral as he sat me on a chair at his right hand side. The cloak of dignity slipped on as easily as it had when his vile cousin had committed unspeakable acts at Mortlock. If de Tourrard wanted to break me he would be disappointed.

He poured two goblets of wine and handed one to me. To the casual observer we might have been a betrothed couple in love, not tormentor and prisoner. He asked me about the gown I had worn when I wed Mortlock, and I played along with the charade, describing it in detail. He spoke of our wedding and how much finer my gown would be the day I became Baroness de Tourrard. It was as if last night had never happened.

Finally he gave me a cruel smile.

"Of course, my dear, you will need to bathe before tonight."

"Bathe?"

"Aye. I cannot be expected to bed you while you reek like a peasant's whore."

My hand shook as I lifted the goblet to my lips.

"Ah—not the stone-hearted bitch your outward appearance would suggest, but a warm-blooded whore," he said. "After your flesh has been cleansed of his filth I shall show you what it is to have a real man between your legs."

I swallowed the wine and set the goblet down.

"I hear my cousin served your lover's head on a platter—Percy was it not? I hope soon to repeat the favor—Sawford's heart would be a delicacy. I hear a heart can still beat several times after being removed from the body."

I turned my head to see him smiling at me. He reached out in front of him to a plate of honeyed figs, which I'd not noticed before. Picking one up, he held it to my lips.

"I understand you have a particular fondness for

these?"

I slapped his hand away, sending the fig flying. The next moment his fist met my jaw, and I fell to the floor, my head ringing. De Tourrard stood over me, his face dark with anger.

"Guy!" he roared.

"My lord?"

"Return this bitch to her chamber and lock her in. Stand by the door and do not move until we're ready to leave."

He grasped a handful of my hair and jerked my head up.

"You'll learn to show proper respect or that brat of yours will pay the price."

He crushed his mouth against mine, biting my lip savagely. But I refused to cry out. He broke the kiss and helped me up with an air of gallantry.

"My poor dear, you seem to have fallen. Come, Guy will escort you to your chamber. You need your rest for we ride at dawn."

The man on de Tourrard's left rose, a cruel smile on his face. De Tourrard handed me to him, and he took my upper arm, gripping it firmly as he led me back to the bedchamber. He pulled me close, lips parted, mouth hungry. I drew my free hand back before delivering a slap on his face.

"How dare you!" I cried.

Rubbing his cheek, he laughed. "You may think you're too high and mighty for me now, whore, but when my master tires of you I will have you. We share similar tastes—in particular, I do relish a struggle."

He pushed me into the chamber and blew me a kiss.

"Until later, whore."

The door slammed behind him and the key turned in the lock once more.

****

Almost a sennight later we arrived on the outskirts of Balsdean village. De Tourrard had brought along twenty of his men. During the day, I rode beside him while Celia travelled in a cart behind us with Geoffrey and the wet-nurse. At night, after setting up camp, he made me lie beside him, my hands bound, breasts swollen and sore. My heart ached each time I heard Geoffrey crying, knowing I could not nurse him.

Though outwardly hostile toward me, Celia would squeeze my hand comfortingly when unnoticed. Before we set out on our journey to Balsdean she'd handed me my most treasured possessions—my last letter from Tarvin together with my response—the one he had never received. She had stolen them from me when I'd arrived at de Tourrard's castle, originally intending to use them against me. They were the proof of adultery that could sentence me to death. But she had returned them to me; an act of kindness to seal our new friendship.

De Tourrard's men struck camp in the woods outside the village. He believed my story that Sawford and I had stayed in the tavern. I hoped this would give Vane a chance to escape but de Tourrard placed men on the road at either end of the village, to watch the comings and goings.

The camp consisted of a number of tents. I shared the smallest with Celia and Geoffrey. De Tourrard told me if I escaped he would devote his life to hunting me down and ensuring Geoffrey suffered for my disloyalty.

Convinced Celia hated me, he took delight in insisting she care for Geoffrey in front of me. But when Celia and I were alone in our tent she handed my son over, keeping watch while I held him in my arms and took comfort in nursing him.

The first night de Tourrard went to the village to search the tavern. I lay awake trembling with fear that he would find and kill Vane, but he did not. He returned and flew into a rage. Nobody in the village had heard the name Sawford. Celia suffered from his anger, returning from a summons to his tent with fresh cuts on her face, one eye already swelling.

"You must leave," she pleaded, "before he turns his attentions to you."

"I cannot. He'll track me down and Geoffrey will suffer. I must think of my son."

"Your son will suffer at his hands no matter what you do. For his sake, you must get away. But not to the village—de Tourrard spoke of a sickness which has taken many children's lives. The churchyard is piled with their bodies. He intends to burn the village at first light tomorrow."

The sickness.

Churchyard piled with bodies.

Only death will separate Geoffrey from me.

Only death…

Geoffrey would be safe in death.

"I cannot leave," I said, "but I have a plan if you'll help me."

****

As night fell, I approached the village via the river, avoiding de Tourrard's watchmen. By the time I found the house I sought, my legs, wet from the river, were ice cold. The house looked the same as when I'd first seen it, the same stack of barrels beside the door.

Thankfully, the moonlight shone bright enough to guide me to Jack's house. Sickened by what I had done in the graveyard, I lifted my hand and knocked on the door.

Before I lost my nerve and ran, I heard shuffling footsteps and the door opened a little way. "Who is it?"

"'Tis me—Lisetta."

The door opened more fully. Jack stood before me, his expression hard.

"What do you want?"

"To warn you. You must leave. They are looking for Vane."

"I already know that, woman," he snarled. "They were looking for him in the tavern, declaring him a traitor to the crown. But none betrayed him. You betrayed him though, did you not? Just as you betrayed young Tom."

"Tom? How do you know he's dead?"

"He was discovered a few days ago at Midford tavern—his throat slit. How could you? We brought you into our home! Get out of my sight before I do the same to you."

"Please, Jack," I cried but he slammed the door in my face. I pounded on the door, not caring that my fists began to bleed.

It opened again to reveal both Jack and Lily.

"Leave us alone, bitch!" Lily cried. "Have you come to betray us too?"

"No!" I pleaded, "I have come to give you your nephew. *Please*! His best chance is with you." Only then did they notice my basket. It contained two bundles. One wriggled and squawked in protest, the other lay horribly still. Setting it down I picked Geoffrey up.

"Please take him." I held my son out to Lily, my heart breaking at the thought of giving him up. "Then you must leave. De Tourrard will burn the village at first light. His men have surrounded the village but if you leave by the river you'll pass unnoticed.

Lily ignored the child in my arms.

"Do you deny you brought them here?"

I shook my head. "Forgive me. All I can do now is ask you to leave and give my son a good life."

"No," Lily said, "we cannot take him. How do we know he's Valentine's child? My brother may be many things but he is too fine a man to cuckold another."

"A child's place is with his mother," Jack insisted. "Are you so unfit that you seek to give him away?"

"Aye!" I cried, desperation straining my voice. "He is Vane's child. Lily, I seduced him because I needed to give my husband a son. I did it to secure my position."

My ploy worked. Lily drew back her arm and struck me with full force across the face. I took the blow without flinching.

"I always knew you were nothing but a devious whore," she said. "You entrapped him to save your own worthless skin—used him for your own ends."

"Aye, I am as you say," I said, my cheek burning, "but Geoffrey is Vane's child. He deserves to be brought up with his family, free from de Tourrard. My son is innocent even if I am not."

Lily glared at me, her eyes full of loathing.

"Please, Lily!" I implored her. "I do not ask for myself, but for my son—and for Vane. You will never see me again. Tell Geoffrey nothing about his mother. It would be as if I did not exist."

"Surely de Tourrard will come looking for him—and you?" Jack asked, his gaze penetrating.

I shook my head, "I return to de Tourrard tonight and will tell him Geoffrey is dead."

"Will he believe you?"

I nodded toward the basket at my feet. "I visited the churchyard before I came here. This child will pass as my son. He was of a similar age."

"My God—you are an evil witch!" Lily cried. "You would rob a churchyard, desecrate a child's grave? You'll burn in hell for what you have done!"

"Mayhap," I said quietly, "but I would gladly burn for the sake of my son."

"How can we be sure you don't have de Tourrard's men with you now? That you're not using your son to entrap us?"

Lily truly believed me evil to think I'd use Geoffrey as bait. But I needed her to hate me to ensure she would take him. I reached into the basket and pulled out a packet, handing it to Jack. He took it, unfolding it to reveal two pieces of parchment and a ring set with a large ruby.

"The ring was a gift from Mortlock and will pay for Geoffrey's keep. I would give you others but cannot risk de Tourrard noticing their absence."

"And the papers?" Jack raised an eyebrow.

"They once meant a great deal to me. They are love letters; two of them. One was from someone who befriended me before he died. He taught me how to love though we never met. The other is my response which was never delivered. Mortlock discovered it and murdered my maidservant for it. He only spared me because I was with child—but if de Tourrard read it he could use it as evidence of adultery, and I would suffer my mother's fate. Though not much, 'tis the only offering of faith I can give."

"What happened to your mother?"

"She was burned at the stake. Papa made me watch as a lesson in how to be a dutiful wife."

Jack muttered a curse though Lily's face remained impassive.

"I'll never know if Tarvin really loved me or if he was a spy to entrap me," I said, "but I fell in love with the words he wrote. That letter is the only genuine thing I have ever said or written in my life. I have always had to hide my feelings to protect myself and others. It's all I have to give you—that, and my son."

Jack's eyes widened, and he leaned forward.

"Tarvin? Was that his name?"

"Aye. Tarvin de Fowensal."

His face paled, and I held out Geoffrey again.

"Lily, take the child," Jack said, "if you are sure—sister?"

I nodded, tears pooling in my eyes, my arms shaking as Lily approached. "Take him quickly before I lose my resolve. I must return before I am missed."

Lily took Geoffrey who settled into her embrace as if he had always been there.

"He already knows a good woman from an evil one," she said, holding him close as if she had delivered him from the jaws of hell.

"Go inside, Lily." Jack's voice was angry, and she glared at him before turning on me.

"May you burn in hell."

I watched her back as she disappeared into the house, carrying Geoffrey in her arms. I clenched my fists, the nails biting into my palms. The effort to stay still was almost unendurable—the separation was as if my limbs had been torn from me. A light hand touched my arm and I looked up into Jack's eyes, kind and soft.

"May God go with you, Lisetta."

I shook my head miserably, fighting the pain in my heart on hearing Geoffrey's plaintive cries from within the house.

"He abandoned me a long time ago, but I pray he will look over all of you."

He lifted his hand to my shoulder, and I flinched when he touched the tender spot where de Tourrard had burned me. He pulled down my sleeve to reveal the reddened, puckered flesh.

"You did not betray us willingly, did you?"

I shook my head. "I must go. There's nothing you can do for me."

He placed his lips on my forehead in a chaste kiss. I gripped his shoulders and tipped my face up to whisper in his ear.

"Is he well, Jack? Is he safe?"

His body stiffened. God had truly abandoned me if even this kind man—once my friend—had forsaken me.

"Do not tell me where he is, Jack. That would put him in danger. I know I am going to my death and don't have the courage to withstand de Tourrard's…questions. But I will find solace in purgatory if I know he is safe."

He lowered his voice to a whisper, his breath tickling my ear.

"Aye, he is well."

I took a deep breath and my stomach lurched. I felt as if my legs had melted, and I staggered back. Jack held me to prevent my fall and a sob escaped my lips as I buried my head in his chest and choked out the words.

"Please—all of you—leave the village as soon as you can. Remember—by the river."

I clung to him, my knuckles glowing white where I gripped his tunic, until Lily's sharp voice from inside broke the silence. I steadied myself and pushed him away, wiping my face.

"Thank you," I said, and I picked up the basket and fled.

I didn't make it far—barely twenty paces before I doubled up and dropped the basket with its horrific occupant. I fell to my knees and my stomach expelled its contents, the acid taste in my mouth only serving to make me retch even more violently. Long after I had emptied my stomach the spasms continued until my head burst with pain.

I crawled toward a puddle in the road. Dipping my hand in, I tried to rinse the taste from my mouth. After taking several deep breaths, the shaking subsided, and I picked up the basket before heading to the river to return to the camp.

Before I left, I took one last look at the house that had been my home, where I had caught a brief glimpse of the happy family life I craved.

I saw a silhouette in the upstairs window and smiled, my objective achieved. Geoffrey might never know his mother but at least he had a chance at life. There was nothing for me now but to face my death with as much dignity and courage as Maman. If God were as merciful as she believed then perhaps my poor condemned soul would find peace.

Chapter 24

I managed to return to the camp unobserved, though at one point the hairs prickled at the back of my neck, my instincts telling me I was being followed. But I heard nothing except the wind rushing through the trees and the water flowing in the river. With every step, I tried not to think of the little body in the basket I carried.

A sentry sat at the entrance to my tent, snoring. It would be too dangerous to walk past him so I crawled under the side of the tent at the back, dragging the basket with me. Celia helped me out of my wet things and held me in her arms while I cried for the poor little soul in the basket, and for the son I had given away. She sang softly as sleep overtook me.

Once more the smell of burning and crackle of flames woke me later in the night, the hiss of the fire turning into pitiful mewling wails.

Geoffrey!

Percy sat before me, holding Geoffrey in his arms.

"You abandoned your son," he said, "abandoned him to his fate."

Percy, he is safe, can you not see?

"He'll never be safe and will never see you again, for he now has my eyes."

He moved closer until Geoffrey's face came into view, his eyes no longer blue, but black—charred pits to match Percy's. I opened my mouth and screamed.

"Lady!" Celia's voice cut through the nightmare, and the images of Percy and Geoffrey dissolved into the darkness.

"I saw Geoffrey!" I sobbed. "Dear God, what have I done?"

"Shhh, I beg you," she warned, but it was too late.

The entrance to the tent was flung back and a tall dark shape strode in. De Tourrard.

"Can't you keep her quiet, wench?" He addressed Celia.

He touched my shoulder, and I flinched.

"Tsk, tsk, my love; I trust you'll be more amenable when we are married. Where is my son?"

He picked up the little bundle and cursed, before turning to Celia, murder in his eyes.

"What in the name of the devil is this?" he roared. "This child is dead—you've killed him, you slut!"

"Wulfric, no!" she cried. De Tourrard threw the body to the ground and wrapped his hands around her throat, choking the life out of her.

"Leave her alone!" I pulled his arms but he was too strong and continued to squeeze. Celia's face turned red and tears burst from her eyes as she clawed at his fingers and screamed for air. Her jerking movements grew weaker until a sickening crack silenced her, and her head lolled sideways. De Tourrard dropped her body beside that of the child. He had broken her neck.

"Celia!" I fell to my knees and shook her, though I knew she was dead.

"Guy!" de Tourrard roared.

"My lord?" Guy's head appeared at the entrance. De Tourrard prodded the bodies with his toe.

"Bury them in the forest."

"No!" I cried. "Have you no respect for the dead?"

De Tourrard continued as if I had not spoken.

"Find some rope and secure the lady. Then send someone to *care* for her in our absence. Rouse the rest. We ride to the village immediately."

"Aye my lord."

"Wulfric, let me go," I pleaded, "I have no value to you now."

He pulled me to my feet by my broken arm, sending a sharp needle of pain through my bones. Turning me to face him he crushed his lips against mine, pushing my mouth open in a forceful, brutal kiss.

"On the contrary my love—we can work on another heir."

"You'll have to kill me first, before I let you touch me." I struggled in his grasp, but he merely laughed, slipping a hand into my gown and squeezing my breast with his fingers.

"In time, you will learn to enjoy my touch."

He released me as Guy returned with a length of rope.

"Until later, my love. I trust you'll be more amiable when I return with your betrothal gift."

He bowed courteously, pressing his fingers lightly over his heart. Though he smiled, his eyes remained hard.

Guy began to bind my hands. I bit my lip, maintaining the emotionless expression I had worn so effectively at Mortlock. My instincts screamed at me to plead for the life of the man I loved, but my rational mind knew they would show no mercy. De Tourrard would relish my fear as salaciously as his foul cousin had thrived on my revulsion.

When he finished, Guy ran a light finger along my arm, then rubbed his knuckles against the front of my bodice where my breast still throbbed from de Tourrard's touch.

"I'll enjoy you yet, wench."

"I am no wench," I replied. "De Tourrard would not take kindly to you molesting his betrothed."

"Twice married, mother to a bastard!" he scoffed. "Do you think my master would object to my sampling the stew which has already been ladled out to so many?"

"He would have your bowels, and you know it," I snarled. "He wants a son. The mother of that son is worth more to him than a mere stew. Find yourself a whore—if one can stomach the prospect of lying with you."

He gripped the front of my gown, and his face darkened with a mixture of lust and anger. Before he could do anything de Tourrard's voice roared from outside.

Guy sneered. "Until later, my lady."

"You can depend on it," I challenged, determined not to be cowed. His eyes narrowed, but he left, his fear of de Tourrard overshadowing his lust for me.

The wait for de Tourrard's return was agonizing, knowing he raided the village searching for the man I loved and would likely burn it to the ground. My son was in danger again. My only hope was that Jack and Lily had heeded my warning and left by the river with Geoffrey. Would Vane be with them?

Vane.

At the mere thought of him my skin tightened as if

he were near. I almost expected him to be in the tent with me, knowing how quiet his movements always were. The man guarding me smiled coarsely, exposing a row of rotting teeth, and I closed my eyes.

Lisetta!

My eyes snapped open. I could have sworn I heard his voice.

"My love," I whispered.

"What is it?" My companion shifted to his feet, his clumsy motion so unlike Vane's smooth, quiet movements.

"Nothing," I said. "Stay where you are."

He came closer. My nostrils twitched at the smell of stale sweat, and I cringed inwardly as he reached out to touch me.

Before I felt his hands on my skin, a shout came from outside. He drew his sword and almost tripped on his way out. Heavy footsteps accompanied voices which faded into the distance, replaced by silence.

Now was my chance. I lifted my hands to my mouth and pulled at the knot with my teeth. It started to work loose but before I could free my hands, he returned, panting.

"What's happening?" I asked. He shook his head, but I persisted."I insist upon you telling me if my life is in danger."

Oh, the irony! I was in more danger in de Tourrard's care than I could ever be at the hands of whoever, or whatever, had caused the disturbance outside.

"A man was spotted on the edge of the forest. We suspect one of de Beauvane's men."

I stiffened with hope but he read my thoughts. "He

fled when he saw he was outnumbered. He won't be back."

For much of the night I heard the men calling to one another, their voices circling my tent, moving back and forth as they patrolled the area. Who—or what—had approached the camp had awakened their senses. I would not be able to escape unnoticed.

Eventually, heavier footfalls heralded de Tourrard's return. He strode into the tent, covered in blood and smelling of smoke, a smile of triumph on his face, Guy beside him.

De Tourrard nodded in my direction. "Get her on a horse. We ride immediately."

Guy led me toward his horse then lifted me up and mounted behind me. Almost at once, we set off at a hard pace.

We rode for the rest of the night and most of the following day until it grew dark again. When we finally stopped the horses were exhausted, their eyes wide and bloodshot, their breath coming in heavy rasps, sending visible puffs of air into the cold evening. My limbs ached, and I was desperate to remove myself from Guy's presence, from the torrid whispers in my ear and the sweaty, aroused body against me.

De Tourrard helped me down from the horse and led me toward the camp where his men had already started a fire.

"I need a moment of privacy," I demanded.

"Guy will attend to you."

"No, I need a lady's privacy."

"Nonsense, my dear." De Tourrard's voice was quiet, but had a harsh edge to it. "I would not forgive myself if you became—hmm—*lost* in the woods. Guy will protect you."

I sighed in defeat. Guy followed me to a bush, thick enough to conceal me from his direct gaze but close enough to the camp to be within calling distance. As much as I loathed de Tourrard, it was his authority and possessiveness that protected me from Guy's attentions.

After I finished, I pulled my skirts back down and looked out beyond the bush into the darkness. It reminded me of the moment after the fire at Mortlock when I'd had my chance to flee. Little had I realized then where the real danger lay.

I had done all I could to ensure Geoffrey's safety. Now I had only myself to be concerned with. Guy was nowhere to be seen. I could sprint into the forest and be gone. De Tourrard no longer had a hold over me. Standing up I stepped out of the bush, taking care where I placed my feet to ensure I made no sound. Voices rumbled in the distance, de Tourrard issuing orders to his men. I took another step, picking my way over the ground. Two more steps and I would break into a run.

A twig snapped and I turned to see Guy leering over me. He had been watching me all along. He licked his lips and smiled.

"Did you like what you saw?" I challenged.

He nodded. "Aye, I did. I will enjoy you when my time comes."

****

The fire was blazing when we returned to the camp, the men busy cooking something on a spit. I sighed at the memory of skewering the rabbit for Vane, wishing I could return to that night and tell him I loved him. How different might things have been! The role of indifference I'd used to protect myself had merely prevented me from finding true happiness with the man I loved.

"Lisetta." The voice of the man I hated returned me to the present. De Tourrard waved Guy away and led me to a blanket set apart from the men, pulling me down to sit with him. He lifted my hand and kissed my knuckles, dipping his tongue between my fingers.

"I have a betrothal gift for you."

"I've already told you, Wulfric, I am married, but I would refuse you even if I were not," I said. "You disgust me."

He let out a short derisive laugh. "I find a little unwillingness quite desirable, Lisetta. I abhor passivity in a woman."

He pulled something out of a bag, an object the size of a man's fist, wrapped in a dark cloth.

"Here, my dear. Perhaps this will help you reach the right decision with regards to matters of the *heart*."

"My heart belongs to another, Wulfric."

De Tourrard smiled and began unwrapping the cloth. The material was not dark, but a white muslin covered in stains. Only when he finished unwrapping, did it become clear what the stains were. He held his hand out until his gift was merely inches from my face.

I let out an involuntary moan. Were I not already sitting, I would have collapsed onto the ground. My throat constricted, and I struggled to breathe, suppressing a scream at what I saw before me.

In his hand, de Tourrard held a human heart.

"Who…?"

"Your late husband," de Tourrard said, his tone

that of a man sharing pleasantries. "I find it ironic that you claim your heart belongs to him. Now, his belongs to you. I hear it is a delicacy and you must be hungry after such a long ride."

"You truly are evil," I sobbed.

"Not at all, my dear. I merely removed an obstacle, a man unworthy of you. He squealed like a stuck pig when I ran him through and pleaded like a baby before I tore his heart from his chest."

Vane.

I thought I'd heard him whispering my name in my head last night. Perhaps that was the moment he had died.

Oh Vane.

"Oh Vane, indeed," de Tourrard mocked.

I thought of Geoffrey, of Jack and Lily. Had de Tourrard murdered them all?

"Was he alone when you killed him?"

"No." De Tourrard laughed. "You poor little fool. I caught him rutting in the yard on top of a whore like a dog on a bitch. His body lies in the dirt with his breeches round his ankles for all to see what he was, a filthy peasant who sought to play the spy against his betters.

"You think you are any better?" I cried. "You are sick, twisted, and evil. I will not stain myself with your touch—I would die first!"

"You have no choice," he snarled. "The time will come when you'll appreciate my attentions. My cousin was only too swift to give you to his men rather than touch you himself, and the servant you fancied yourself in love with would rather spend his time rutting in the dirt. Come, let us seal our betrothal with a kiss."

"Never!" I cried, but he was too strong and forced me back, covering my body with his. He forced his mouth over mine, violating it with his thick, savage tongue. With his free hand he grasped the front of my gown and tore at the material.

A cheer rang out, and he rolled off me, catching my wrists before I could strike him again.

"I will have you," he rasped, "but for my own sport, not the entertainment of my men on the forest floor."

"Never!" I cried.

"You will learn to appreciate me, my love," he said, "and when I tire of you, my men will have their turn. Guy in particular has no qualms about enjoying my leavings."

I could not sleep at all that night. My stomach growled in protest, but I refused to eat, instead watching as he nibbled at a piece of meat while looking meaningfully at me. At length, he settled down beside me, and his breathing fell into a steady rhythm as he fell asleep. Though thankful that he left me alone, I knew it would not be long before he claimed me as his.

****

Almost a sennight later we arrived at our destination. The terrain had begun to look familiar; forests and paths I had explored during my childhood, in happier times with Maman.

Shoreton, my childhood home.

The day we arrived, I was riding with de Tourrard on his horse. We crossed the drawbridge in single file and the main doors opened to reveal my father, accompanied by one of his men-at-arms.

"Papa." I clung to the hope he would take me into

his arms, but he ignored me.

"So, you have returned, de Tourrard."

"Aye, Shoreton. Our plans are well advanced. We have much to discuss."

"Of course." Papa gave me a cursory glance before turning to the man next to him.

"Take her to her chamber and make her presentable."

"Papa, please!" I cried.

"You disappoint me, Lisetta," he said. "But no more. Be thankful de Tourrard still wants you after your whoring, if only to inherit Shoreton. You deserve your mother's fate, not the honor of being a baroness."

De Tourrard stroked my hair. "Do not be so harsh on her, Shoreton. I will temper her behavior and ensure you have a daughter to be proud of."

He dismounted and pulled me down beside him.

"Join us for dinner, my dear." He planted a kiss on my forehead.

De Tourrard handed me to Papa's man who led me through the courtyard. A thick post stood in the center, still charred from the day Maman was taken from me. I had returned to my home, the place where I had experienced such joy as a child when she was alive. But I was no longer that child. The experiences of the past year had shed the cloak of childhood and removed the blindfold to reveal the true nature of the world around me.

He led me to my old bedchamber and locked me inside.

I wanted to escape, but where would I go? De Tourrard would hunt me down. Not even the walls of the convent would keep him out. A traitor to the king, he hungered for power and would stop at nothing to seize it. But the king would not give me sanctuary: by association I would be branded a traitor also.

"Oh, Vane—Geoffrey!"

Sinking onto the bed, I let the tears flow while my body shook with grief. I had given up my son with no certainty he was alive; the man I loved had been murdered, his body desecrated by the monster to whom I now belonged. Vane had been found with a whore—proof, if I even needed it, of his indifference toward me. Yet still I loved him. Tarvin gave me written words of love, but Vane had given me life. He'd delivered me from Mortlock, shown me a respectable, honest life. Most of all, he had given me Geoffrey.

But now, everyone I loved had gone. It would be better to join them in death than to live a life with de Tourrard.

He could not watch me forever. Eventually he would drop his guard. I knew enough of herbs and plants to brew a poison that would deliver me. The battlements were high enough for my body to be crushed beyond recognition from a fall. All I had left was my life. De Tourrard would not take that from me. My life was mine to end when I chose.

I was ready to die.

Chapter 25

The next day de Tourrard took me by force. At first light, he led me to the chapel where a priest conducted the betrothal ceremony. He silenced my protests with a blow to the face while Papa looked on, his face impassive.

Afterward he took me to the solar. Though I struggled and pleaded for mercy, I found none. Resistance only increased his relish. I saw Maman, telling me to be strong, but when I reached out to her she disappeared, and blackness overcame me.

When I regained consciousness I was still in the solar. My throat burned as if I had consumed liquid fire. I crawled toward the door, my body aching, and fumbled for the handle, but it was locked.

De Tourrard found me curled on the floor.

"'Tis not a seemly place for my lady wife to be, groveling in the dirt like a common peasant."

He carried me to the bed and pulled at the front of my dress, torn from his earlier exertions. Frustration flashed in his eyes as I stared back, not reacting to his touch.

"Lie with me again; I have much to teach you."

I lay still, closed my eyes, and began to count slowly, detaching myself from the weight of his body.

At length I heard him sigh in frustration, but I did not open my eyes until he left the solar. A woman screamed from outside the door, followed by de Tourrard's voice, raised at first in anger, before turning to lust.

His entire family was perverted and depraved. Mortlock had taken his pleasure at his own hand while leering at my naked body; his cousin de Tourrard took pleasure in inflicting pain on a struggling, unwilling woman.

****

I lost count of the days. They were all the same. De Tourrard kept me confined in the solar, spending the night beside me in the bed, after binding my wrists to prevent my attacking him in his sleep.

I now understood what my life would have been like at Mortlock Fort had Sawford handed me to others rather than take me for himself. My unwilling body had responded to Sawford's ministrations but with de Tourrard I felt nothing but revulsion. However, other than the violation itself he did not physically hurt me. My passivity was my salvation. But the echoes of women crying in the passageway reminded me my salvation came at a price.

What made me different from a whore? A whore sold her body for her own purpose, usually a coin to feed hungry mouths. I had sold my body to de Tourrard for relief from the pain he inflicted on other women. It was not my own hand striking them, but it may as well have been. Due to my own cowardice, I had turned his perversions on others.

I was worse than a whore.

I was followed everywhere, more closely than at Mortlock. Every door, every archway was guarded by either one of Papa's men or de Tourrard's. But even if I could escape, where would I go? I would be hunted down like the stags in the forests at Mortlock and with as much relish. But another means of release existed— to join Maman in death. At Shoreton I felt close to her again, could almost hear her calling to me. She was the only person who had truly loved me, and I would gladly suffer pain if it would reunite us.

****

About a month after we arrived at Shoreton, de Tourrard announced he was leaving. Guy intercepted me in the garden to take me to Papa's study. De Tourrard had begun to trust me enough to let me walk freely within the bailey walls, provided I was within earshot of his men.

In the gardens I had found a plant I recalled from my childhood—a plant Maman had warned me never to touch, identifiable by small purple flowers and dark berries from which an infusion would produce a deadly poison. I had begun to collect them and conceal them within Maman's room, careful to only touch them through a piece of muslin rather than with my fingers.

Guy knocked on the study door and announced my presence. De Tourrard sat at Papa's desk. Papa stood behind his left shoulder.

"Sit down, Lisetta."

A maidservant approached with a flagon of wine and I waved her away. She flinched at the movement, and I pressed my lips together, trying to ignore her bruised face. One eye was so swollen it was almost closed. De Tourrard may have dealt the blows but the burden of responsibility lay on my shoulders.

I turned to de Tourrard, my voice toneless. "What does my lord wish of me?"

He smiled, and addressed my father. "You see, Shoreton, with the right care and attention your daughter has greatly improved."

Papa nodded. The deference he accorded de Tourrard confirmed who the real leader was behind the plots to overthrow the king.

"I leave at sundown, my dear, and will be away for several days. I trust you'll continue to show good behavior for your father's sake.

"Of course," I replied. "Might I enquire as to where my lord is going?"

He could not resist the temptation to impress.

"To France, to overthrow that whoreson Henry and replace him with Stephen's rightful heir."

"And that is?"

"William de Blois."

I had heard of William; the old King Stephen's third son. Rumors existed of his involvement in a previous plot on Henry's life. He was a similar age to me—old enough to lead a country. But he was not a warrior. With him on the throne, the real ruler would be de Tourrard.

"Is it wise to divulge—" Papa spoke, but de Tourrard silenced him by raising his hand.

"Of course, Shoreton. I should wait until we have accomplished our victory."

He continued to instruct me on my behavior. Most of his men, including Guy, were leaving with him. I was to be confined indoors and assigned one of Papa's men-at-arms for my protection. Finally he stood and told Guy to escort me to the solar where he would 'take his leave' of me. Lowering my eyes in shame at his words, I ignored Guy's lewd gaze as he accompanied me. He said nothing, and I shut the door on him to wait for de Tourrard to violate me once more.

****

During de Tourrard's absence Papa kept himself in his study, sending and receiving messages. For the first few days my escort remained constantly by my side, but eventually he grew weary of wasting his time with a woman and sent one of the maidservants to remain with me while he visited the privy. I recognized the maidservant, Elspeth, from my childhood. She had often slipped me a sweetmeat when she'd found me hiding in the kitchen listening to servants' gossip, returning me to Harwyn before Papa discovered me.

With Elspeth's help I used those precious minutes in Maman's old treatment room to begin work on the poison, crushing the berries into a small pot and letting it simmer over the fire. So as not to arouse suspicion we brewed other herbal infusions as well, genuine healing lotions to administer to members of the household who needed it. The poison I kept for myself, for when all hope was completely extinguished.

Soon after de Tourrard left, I dreamed of Vane, of his touch. It was so realistic. His soft fingertips caressed my skin, making my body tighten with need. He brushed his mouth lightly against my own. I opened my lips with a sigh of longing and his tongue sought entrance, teasing, probing, and sending a pulse of heat through my body. I shifted position on the bed and felt his hands and lips on my ankles, his touch so gentle, leading a trail of warmth between my legs until he reached my thighs. I parted them willingly, my breath catching in my throat as I waited for him to free me, to give me the pleasure which only he could give. He whispered my name, the heat of his voice rumbling against my core until I could bear it no longer.

Vane!

I drew my hands into fists, grasping the sheets tightly and pushed my hips up toward his voice, my body open and ready, pleading for him to take that which I gladly offered. I cared not that I begged him. Neither did I care he might reject me, so overcome was I by the need to have him inside me, to have him purge all trace of de Tourrard from my body.

A loud crash made me sit up with a scream. My heart thumped so loudly the rest of the castle must be able to hear it. The pounding turned into a loud hammering at the door.

Bang, bang, bang.

"Lady!"

"What is it?" I called out, my voice shaking.

The door opened, and one of Papa's men walked in, holding a candle. I blinked at the light, shielding my eyes.

"You cried out. Are you well?"

"Aye," I whispered. "It was just a bad dream."

He nodded and closed the door, turning the lock.

The image of Vane's vividly blue eyes was so strong I looked about, hoping he was with me, but I was alone in the room. It had been a dream. I sank back, defeated. Vane may be dead but my love for him had only strengthened.

He visited me in my dreams several times after that, each more vivid than the last, my need for him increasing. Each time I woke, the bed was empty, and I rolled onto my side, my body shaking as I cried in silence.

I had no hope. The man I loved was dead, and I was a traitor's whore. If de Tourrard was successful in his campaign I would remain his whore until he tired of me and threw me to Guy. Were he to fail, I would be branded a traitor to be publicly condemned by the king and executed—or worse. Henry was not known for an even temper, neither was he known for his fidelity. He, too, might use me as his whore or hand me over to his men to be torn apart.

****

I first realized something was wrong when I heard rumors of defeat from the servants. I waited for Papa to tell me what had happened. But to him, I was merely a tool to be used to ally himself with others. He had no use for me other than to keep me alive for de Tourrard. The atmosphere turned into one of panic but the men refused to speak to me of it.

As word of de Tourrard's return reached my ears, the rumors intensified. He had failed in his attempt to overthrow Henry. William de Blois had betrayed him and even now, Henry's men were on their way to seize Shoreton. One of the men mentioned a name I had heard before—de Beauvane.

I heard de Tourrard's voice long before I saw him. His angry words echoed around the bailey, ordering the men to turn the villagers out of the grounds then secure the drawbridge and prepare for a siege. Shortly after, the door to the solar flew open. Covered in grime and sweat, body taut with rage, he advanced toward me.

"So you have failed." I spoke quietly.

Had he shown outward signs of emotion I would have feared him less, but even in the throes of limitless anger he remained controlled, each movement deliberate, serving a specific purpose. He reached toward me and caressed my collarbone before securing his fingers around my neck.

"I. Will. Not. Fail."

"We cannot withstand a siege," I said. "We're not prepared. The foodstores…"

"…have enough to keep my men and I alive for a month. We will hold out."

"But the servants, the villagers. What of them?"

"They are expendable."

"No—" I cried but was silenced as he drew his hand back from my throat and backhanded me so forcefully across the face that I fell across the bed. Pain exploded in my head, and I reached up to find my nose sticky with blood.

"Do not question me."

"In the name of God, Wulfric, give up," I pleaded. "Henry is the rightful king. Surrender to him and he may show leniency. Continue with this folly and every soul at Shoreton will die."

"I said, do not question me!"

My scalp felt as if it had burst into flame as he grasped my hair with his fist and dragged me off the bed.

"You continue to be in need of instruction with regards to your behavior." His voice was so calm I did not anticipate the next blow. His boot connected with my arm, and I heard a crack as the bone fractured. A fire burned in my belly; my body ripped apart from the inside, and I heard a woman screaming while he chided me for disobedience. I tried to crawl away but my limbs would not respond, as if stone blocks weighted me to the ground. I pushed against the floor, sending a bolt of fire down my arm until a final blow to my head silenced the screaming, ended the pain, and brought forth peace.

I was drowning in the dark. My other senses were invaded, overloaded. Fire was all over my body. Pain, always the pain, then warmth and the aroma of lavender, which grew stronger as I pulled my mind from oblivion.

"Lady!" A woman's voice. I opened my eyes but saw only blurred images, ominous gray swirls. Memories of Maman and Percy floated above me—they had visited me again while I burned in the fire. Something touched my arm, and I moaned in pain. The gray faded to black.

****

The next time I opened my eyes I saw color—soft brown shapes. They moved in front of my eyes until they sharpened into the form of a woman.

"Elspeth?"

"Lady! Thank the Lord!"

I sat up, slowly, ignoring my aching body. I waved away her protests and motioned to her to help me into a chair by the fireplace. I hated the bed—the bed I shared with de Tourrard.

"What happened, Elspeth?"

"My lord said you suffered a fall. We thought you'd never wake up. I have been tending you for four days. You took a fever after you lost—after you fell. He was so angry with us for using the water to bathe you…"

She hesitated, her voice trailing away.

"Has something else happened?" I asked. She gave a low cry and knelt at my feet.

"You lost the babe."

"The babe?"

"Forgive me lady. You were already bleeding when we found you."

Lord save me, I had been carrying de Tourrard's child.

"Does he know?"

"Aye," she whispered. "He is to join you when you have woken. You're to be confined here until then."

I felt numb. Numb with shock at the prospect of having de Tourrard's seed take root in my body and numb with the pain of losing another child. I would have to summon all my courage to face him again.

I took her hand and kissed it.

"Thank you for taking care of me, Elspeth."

She nodded, fear still in her eyes.

"Something else is wrong is it not?" I asked her. "Why would he be angry about the water?"

"We are under siege. The well is nearly empty."

"Siege!"

"Aye," she sobbed. "Shoreton has been surrounded for four days; they came almost as soon as de Tourrard returned. The men say the castle will fall soon. There is food aplenty without the villagers here but the water... I don't know what we will do if my lord does not yield."

"We will burn," I whispered, remembering Mortlock. Burning might be the kinder death. With the well running dry, disease would spread more quickly than a flame. Death would be slower, the agony more prolonged.

De Tourrard would never surrender. Shoreton would be destroyed along with the people within its walls. I could only hope that Henry's men would let the servants go free. But for me, there was only one way out.

"Elspeth," I said urgently, "there is one thing you can do for me."

"Anything, my lady."

"You must dress me first. I want to be ready for my lord when he comes."

As the sun began to set on my last day in this world, a servant brought a tray of bread and wine to the solar and told me de Tourrard would attend me shortly. I tasted the wine. As I suspected, the better quality wine had all gone, the remainder having to be spiced to mask its sourness. I took out the phial Elspeth had brought and emptied the contents into one of the goblets before filling it to the brim with more wine. The honey and ginger in the wine would disguise the sweet taste of the poison. I prayed to God that instead of condemning me to hell for taking my own life, He would reunite me with those I loved.

Closing my eyes, I lifted the goblet to my lips.

Chapter 26

De Tourrard burst through the door in full battle armor, his handsome face grim, and his body reeking of oil, smoke, and tar. I tipped my head back to drink but he snatched the goblet from my hands.

"You should be serving me, wench, rather than partaking of the wine in my absence."

"No…" I protested, but he drained the goblet then held it out to me.

"Refill it."

With trembling hands, I poured more wine into the goblet.

"That bastard whoreson Henry will not yield," he cursed. I said nothing and watched him drink again.

He sat, motioning to me to serve him. I cut pieces of dried meat and cheese and jumped as he closed his hand around my wrist. He caressed my hand with his thumb before he spoke, his soft voice almost disguising the soullessness within him.

"I hear you killed my child."

His grip tightened and his thumbnail scored my flesh.

"Wulfric…"

"You will give me another."

He gripped the back of my neck with his free hand and forced his mouth over mine. He was stronger than I but my hatred of him was too powerful. I struggled and broke free. The tray crashed to the floor. De Tourrard clutched the table with one hand and his throat with the other, his face purple with rage. His eyes bulged red, and he mouthed curses, sending spittle and pieces of meat and bread flying from his mouth.

"You—witch! What have you done?"

He lurched forward, tipped the table over, and fell onto it with a splintering crash. I jumped back to avoid his flailing hands. He tried to grasp the hem of my gown, but I stood still, knowing he would never reach me again. He crawled on his belly toward me, his body jerking and spasming in a macabre dance.

An airless scream hissed out of his lips, and his face contorted as the poison overcame him. His head lolled back and he drew one last, rattling breath before he slumped forward and lay static except for his hands and feet which twitched slightly.

I touched one of his hands with my toe. His fingers flexed and curled into a claw.

"I have only done to you that which I would do to myself," I said quietly. But I did not expect a response. De Tourrard was dead.

Lady, adulteress, peasant, whore. Now I was also a murderess.

I left the solar, closing the door for the last time before making my way to Maman's room. I heard footsteps and Elspeth intercepted me.

"They've broken through the bailey, my lady. Come and look!"

I followed her outside to the ramparts and a scream caught in my throat. The walls had crumbled and men were fighting in the bailey; the sounds of steel on steel echoed around the courtyard. Beyond the bailey the village of Shoreton burned. Plumes of smoke billowed up from every cottage. De Tourrard had turned the villagers out from the safety of Shoreton's walls, and the king's men had burned their homes. I did not know which man I loathed the most.

The smoke swirled around three huge wooden devices which stood like giant sentinels among the burning buildings: trebuchets—enormous siege engines—machines that could break down a castle's defenses. The walls never stood a chance. Men worked tirelessly on the machines, and a sharp cry rang out before the trebuchet's arm swung up in a fluid movement and let loose its burden.

"Lady!" I ignored Elspeth's scream. Rooted to the spot I watched, transfixed, as the stone hurtled through the air. It soared in a smooth arc toward me until it dipped down in its trajectory to strike the center of the wall. The ground shuddered under my feet, followed by the screams of men killed or injured by falling masonry.

The fighting in the courtyard continued, and I recognized one figure. Though clad in armor and wearing a helmet, Papa wore a tabard bearing the Shoreton coat of arms which also flashed in the sunlight on his shield as he wielded it in defense against the man he fought.

His opponent was taller, leaner, and the better fighter. But a man with nothing left to lose fights as if the devil's hounds snap at his heels. Papa parried a blow and struck a glancing blow on the other man's arm. I let out a cry and Papa's opponent lifted his head toward me.

Papa swung his sword at the man's legs, just missing his target. The two men continued to fight, as if engaged in a dance, each attack met by a counterattack. But it was clear who the victor would be. Papa slashed wildly at his opponent, his mind focused on attack and ignoring his defenses. He lifted his shield arm too high, exposing his body. His opponent saw the mistake and drove his sword forward, burying it into Papa's chest. Papa dropped his sword, crumpled to his knees, and fell back.

The other man was clearly injured. He dropped his shield arm to his side where it hung awkwardly, and he staggered forward. He looked back toward the village before turning to face the castle wall. Lifting his head he raised his sword in salute. I shuddered, sensing his eyes upon me. Would I be his next victim? Elspeth tugged at my sleeve but I ignored her.

His voice rang out among the sounds of screaming and fighting.

"Get thee back!"

I had no time to wonder at his meaning. Elspeth pulled at my arm again.

"Lady, please!" she cried.

I looked up and screamed. Another giant stone flew toward me. I leapt back as it struck the battlements, disintegrating the wall where I had been standing just moments before. Elspeth helped me to my feet.

"Shoreton is lost," I said. "We are dead."

"What can we do, lady?"

I led her to Maman's room, where I'd sent her only that morning. I had another phial of the poison and intended to use it. De Tourrard's death had been an unpleasant sight, but it would be a better fate than whatever the king had in store for me.

We reached Maman's room and footsteps followed

us—too heavy and too many to be servants. We didn't have much time. I pulled the door open, ignoring the searing pain in my arm and lifted the lid of the chest where I'd hidden the phial.

"Elspeth, this will give me the release of a quick death. I cannot say what they will do to you but they will show me no mercy. I'll leave some for you to give you a choice."

A deep male voice spoke behind me, "Neither of you has a choice. You are now the property of the king. Take them!"

A pair of strong arms took hold of me, and I dropped the phial. A second man took hold of Elspeth.

"No!" I cried, but my captor held me firm. My body still ached from de Tourrard's beating, and each time I struggled the man tightened his hold.

Their leader picked up the phial.

"Woman, what is this?"

"A tonic," I replied quickly before Elspeth could speak.

"I think not," he replied. "Garret!"

The man holding Elspeth twisted her arm behind her back, and she howled in pain.

"Please, stop! It has nothing to do with her," I pleaded, but he continued and Elspeth's screams only grew louder.

"All right!" I cried. "It's poison."

"I thought so." He dropped the phial on the floor and smashed it with his foot, grinding it into the stones.

"Garret, Edric—take them away. The rest of you, search the building. I want every traitor found."

"Where are you taking us?" I asked.

"To London," he said, his voice grim, "where you

will be tried and executed."

****

After a long, slow journey from Shoreton I found myself alone in a cell in the Tower of London on the eve of my execution. At Shoreton they'd separated me from Elspeth, and I had not seen her since. I had been bound and secured to a small cart along with a handful of Papa's and de Tourrard's men, including Guy. Most of the men had been killed either during de Tourrard's campaign in France or in the siege at Shoreton. Those too injured to be moved were left to rot.

The reality of war was such that no matter which side came out on top, the outcome was always the same. Those unfortunate to be on the losing side were tortured and subjected to agonizing deaths. There was neither good nor evil—only pain and suffering. There would always be someone eager to seize the king's position from him; the balance of power would continue to shift back and forth. Today's victor would be tomorrow's defeated and the cycle would continue. I did not wish to live in such a world.

Save a few hateful remarks from Guy, silenced by a cuff from Garret, I had largely been ignored until we arrived at London. As we passed through the streets, the jeers of the gathering crowds grew louder. We were traitors headed for a public trial and execution. With Papa and de Tourrard dead, I was the only family member alive for them to direct their hatred toward. A stone had flown past me, narrowly missing my head; catcalls and insults hurled in my direction.

It was a relief to find peace in the cell. The trial had been a mere formality. It had come as no surprise that as Baron Shoreton's daughter, Mortlock's widow, and de Tourrard's whore, I was declared a traitor by association. Standing between two liveried men-at-arms as the sentence was passed, I had only been vaguely aware of the king. He sat in silence, seemingly bored by the whole charade. I'd offered no defense. Traitors were treated harshly and a woman's word counted for nothing. The less I said, the sooner it would all be over.

My only companions were the vermin who visited the cells at night. The squeals of the rats fighting kept me awake. They fought over scraps of food; the mold-ridden bread my jailer threw into the cell each day, which I was too sick to eat. Other, unseen visitors came in the dark. At night, my whole body itched. Scratching my skin brought temporary respite, but each morning huge welts covered my body, pulsing an angry red, their perpetrators having disappeared by dawn, waiting in the cracks in the walls to crawl over my body when night fell once more.

My cell had a small window but it was too high for me to look out. Sounds drifted in from outside, voices of the executioners readying themselves. That morning I heard Guy crying, pleading for mercy. The man who'd bullied and terrorized me had been reduced to a sniveling wreck, his pleas cut short with a thud, followed by cheering. The next time I saw daylight it would be my turn to entertain the crowd. I was the only one left.

The door rattled open. Had my execution been brought forward? A man entered, wearing a hooded cloak and holding a candle. He nodded to someone at the door who closed it again. He placed the candle on the floor and removed his cloak to reveal a cleric's robes.

"Father!"

I'd asked for a priest to hear my confession but had not expected my last request to be honored.

"My child," he said, his light voice indicating his youth. "I have come to give you absolution."

I knelt at his feet. "Thank you Father. I will find much solace in the confession of my sins."

He placed a gentle hand on my head before uttering a prayer for my soul and the souls of the people of Shoreton.

"Father," I whispered, "do you know what became of the servants at Shoreton—the villagers?"

"They have been found new homes, my child. The king was merciful."

"Elspeth…"

"She is well, lady." He said, before resuming his prayer, the soft Latin words giving me little comfort.

"I am ready to confess my sins," I said. He nodded and waited.

"I killed a man."

He started a little before responding. "Who?"

"Wulfric de Tourrard," I said. "I intended to take the poison myself, but he took it instead, and I could not stop him."

"The lord will forgive—" he began but I interrupted him.

"I seek no forgiveness, for I am glad he is dead. I will confess my sin but to face God in truth I cannot tell you I regret his death."

"Why, my child?"

"He killed the only man I have ever loved," I whispered. "He tore out his heart and handed it to me on a platter. He made me whore myself by lying with

274

him, and I was too weak to fight him, for I knew he would take me by force whether I resisted or not."

"Who was the man he killed?" the priest asked.

"His name was Sawford. A servant; the bastard son of a cooper," I said. Hysteria bubbled up inside me. I wanted to expel the sins from my body by relaying all the sordid details to the priest.

"I committed adultery with him, though at the time I thought I loved another man who was also not my husband. I hated my husband."

"My child…"

"…and I hated my father. It gladdened my heart to see him killed. I care for no one, and I only look forward to joining my Maman in death. She was a whore and an adulteress as well, branded a sinner in this world yet she was the kindest person I have ever known and I loved her."

"What of your son?" he asked.

"How do you know about my son?" I said, my voice breaking. "He is gone."

"Is he?"

"Yes!" I cried. "Do not speak of him. He is—was—innocent."

The priest remained silent.

"Please!" I begged, "Do not speak of my son."

He nodded. "Of course, my lady. What passes here today will remain between you and me and him who loves you."

"Who do you mean?"

"Why, God of course."

He called out to the sentries, and left as swiftly as he came.

The next morning, they took me to the courtyard. A

platform had been erected in the center. The gathering crowd began to murmur excitedly as I was brought forward. The pyre on the platform told me I would not share the manner of Guy's execution. The best entertainment had been set for last.

Faces watched eagerly as I was brought to the stake and my hands secured behind it. Men chatted animatedly in small groups. Families stood together; husbands embracing their wives, children staring, wide-eyed in fascination at the subject of the lecture their parents would have given them about the evils of sinful behavior.

The king sat on another platform, his red hair shining in the sunlight. In my position I faced him directly. The executioner offered a blindfold but I shook my head. The crowd muttered at my reaction. I had no wish to entertain them with a weak woman's crying. At the moment of death I wanted to look into the eyes of the man who had condemned me. King Henry was my distant relation, the man Maman had supported. This would be my final act of courage, the one thing I had the power to do. I would face Death and welcome my departure from a world of cowards and voyeurs.

The executioner stood beside me, holding a burning torch aloft. The smell of the oil that doused the woodpile beneath my feet grew stronger.

"Do you wish to say anything?" he asked.

"No," I replied, "I know you are carrying out your duty as a loyal subject to the king. I pray that unlike many here you have not brought your family to witness this."

"Nay, lady," he replied, "I would not bring my

children here."

"You are wise," I said. "Be kind to them." My voice shook as fear began to choke me.

"Please, sir, administer your task quickly. My courage will desert me if you tarry."

"God bless you," he said and lowered the torch to the woodpile.

I held my head up, breathing in the smell of oil and smoke. King Henry's eyes were upon me, and I met his gaze. The wood burst into flames, and I groaned at the intense heat burning my legs. The crowd had been eerily silent but among the hungry snapping sound of the fire I heard a woman sobbing. Another joined her and the sobs turned into a roar. Smoke stung my eyes, and I closed them to blink away the tears. The pain was agonizing. I gritted my teeth to suppress the scream threatening to burst from my chest. A hissing noise surrounded my ears. Adulteress, murderess, there was no place in heaven for me. The serpents of Hell were calling to me.

I could contain it no more. I opened my mouth, drawing in gulps of air that burned my lungs, and I let out one final scream for the man I would soon join in death.

"Vane!"

Chapter 27

The hissing increased as I felt a cold shock on my skin, and I opened my eyes. The lower half of my gown was dripping wet, the fire almost out. The crowd had fallen silent. A deep, stentorian voice echoed around the courtyard.

"Stop this! Douse the fire again. Quickly!"

The king had risen to his feet. A party of about ten men on horseback wearing identical livery stood in the yard. The man who had spoken sat astride an enormous black destrier. Two men in the same livery stood beside me, holding empty buckets. A third ran toward the platform with a bucket full of water which he poured onto the wood at my feet, extinguishing what remained of the fire.

"Release her."

The executioner untied my wrists and helped me down. I moaned in pain—my feet and the lower part of my legs were badly blistered.

The king's voice rang out across the yard. "Hold her!"

He spoke to the man on the horse. "What is the meaning of this, de Beauvane?"

So, this was de Beauvane. About two score years with dark hair graying at the temples, he had an imposing face, a strong brow, straight nose and a large, square jaw. He looked at me with a hard expression in his eyes.

"This woman is innocent."

The king's face reddened with anger. "To interrupt the execution of a traitor is a punishable offence. Explain yourself."

"I can vouch for her personally, my liege. She is not a traitor."

"Then what is she?"

"My mistress."

The king nodded toward me. "Is that true?"

I shook my head but de Beauvane continued. "Whatever she says, she is my mistress. Only her modesty prevents her from admitting it."

"My patience wears thin, woman. Are you Sir Roger's mistress?"

"Aye she is," de Beauvane interrupted. "She has borne me a son."

"I have not..." I stuttered but de Beauvane continued, his eyes staring right at me.

"His name is Geoffrey Valentine."

I gave out a low moan of shock.

"Geoffrey..."

"Tell him," de Beauvane ordered harshly. "Tell him who you are."

De Beauvane dismounted and strode toward me.

I nodded, afraid to move. "I am as he says."

De Beauvane curled his gloved hand around my bandaged arm.

"Why did you say nothing of this?" the king demanded. "Why should I not still have you executed for treachery?"

"If I may speak," de Beauvane said, "I'll assume responsibility for her. She has given me no occasion to

doubt her loyalty to me—or to you. She has always
supported your mother's claim to the throne. I took her
under my protection when Lord Mortlock was killed.
She was foolish enough to venture out unaccompanied
and de Tourrard took her, for which I will punish her.
You may doubt her loyalty, but do not doubt mine. Be
assured I will treat her harshly and deliver her unto you
if she gives me the slightest cause."

"You have still not answered my question,
woman," Henry said. "I would have you explain
yourself."

De Beauvane's grip on my arm tightened.

"Forgive me," I said, my voice hoarse from the
smoke in my lungs. "I—I had no wish to bring disgrace
on my—my lover."

"Mayhap I will release you," Henry said casually,
"though I am minded to continue, to ensure England is
purged of traitors."

De Beauvane wrapped his arms around me. "I
would beg you to be merciful. Grant your loyal servant
this one wish." He dipped his head as if to brush a kiss
on my neck and whispered harshly in my ear.

"Madam, you must play the part of the loving
mistress lest Henry change his mind. With the throne he
inherited a legacy of treachery. He's not known for a
forgiving nature, or a gentle disposition. Do as I say or
you'll never leave this place alive."

"But…" His grip increased, and I groaned in pain.

"Your arm hurts does it not?"

I shivered at the coldness in his voice, the iron
strength of his hold on me. No wonder Papa and de
Tourrard had been afraid of him.

"Obey me," he said, "or I'll abandon you to your

fate here. I pray to God you are worth the risk I take today. I dislike the notion of wagering the lives of good men to save that of a treacherous whore."

"I am no—" I began indignantly, but he silenced me with an angry word.

"Having trouble disciplining your mistress, Sir Roger?" The king chuckled.

The man who believed himself my savior, but who I only saw as my new tormentor, replied with equal amusement.

"Of course not."

"If she's worth your trouble, I may keep her for myself. Would you give her to me?"

"If my lord wishes."

The two men exchanged more words, their discussion growing more cordial until de Beauvane let out a shout of laughter. I hated them for bartering over me as if I were a vat of wine to be consumed casually as they saw fit. Eventually, the king relented.

"Very well," he sighed, "she's not particularly pleasing on the eye, so you may keep her. Take her away."

"Put your arms around my neck," de Beauvane ordered. He lifted me effortlessly, carrying me to his horse before handing me to one of his men while he mounted. At his nod, I was lifted like a sack of grain onto the saddle in front of him.

"To me!" he cried to his men, then he bowed to the king, and rode out of the courtyard.

Yet another man had claimed me as his property for a reason I did not know.

After riding several miles, de Beauvane ordered the party to stop. He motioned to one of his men who drew his horse alongside us. De Beauvane handed me over to him. The man's horse was smaller than de Beauvane's, and he took my arms to prevent me from falling.

"Have a care of her arm, Oliver, 'tis broken."

"Aye my lord."

Oliver smiled, and I recognized him.

"Father!"

"I'm afraid not, my lady," he said. "Forgive my deception."

We resumed our journey, de Beauvane leading the party.

"Who is de Beauvane?" I asked.

"One of King Henry's most trusted warlords," Oliver replied, pride in his voice.

"You admire him."

"How could I not? He is renowned for his loyalty, having never changed his allegiance. He fought for Matilda under Stephen's reign. Since Henry came to the throne, de Beauvane has thwarted several plots against him, infiltrating traitors with his network of spies. He's a great warrior and a brilliant strategist."

"Did he know of de Tourrard's plot?"

"He suspected it," Oliver said. "He never trusted de Tourrard's betrayal of Lord Mortlock, believing it a ploy to divert the king's attention; and he was proven right. He masterminded the siege at Shoreton. Henry's enemies will be reluctant to conspire against him now. De Beauvane's reputation for destroying traitors is unmatched."

"If he's a destroyer of traitors what does he want with me?"

Before Oliver could reply, de Beauvane cut him short.

"Woman, you will hear nothing until we reach our destination," he barked. "Do as you are bid and be silent."

"Why?" I asked. "I know nothing of you. You have deferred my death but will life in your custody be any better?"

"I would ask you to trust me." The anger in his voice had lessened but still he spoke gruffly.

"How can I—a condemned traitor; and a woman with no power over my fate? You would have my gratitude if you could spare a few words to assure me I'm safer in your hands than I was in de Tourrard's."

His expression softened, and he reached out a gloved hand to my face where de Tourrard had broken my nose, his eyes narrowing as I flinched.

"Wise words," he said. "I assure you I am nothing like de Tourrard, but I can understand your mistrust. Perhaps the name Tarvin de Fowensal would make a difference?"

"Tarvin?"

He nodded. "Aye, Tarvin. I will explain once we arrive at my home. I am anxious to reach there lest the king change his mind. Until then I would ask you to do as you are bid and only speak when spoken to."

"Am I to be your mistress?"

"Perhaps. Perhaps not. In due course I shall decide what is to be done with you."

For the remainder of the journey, I did as he asked and remained silent. The men ignored me with the exception of de Beauvane, who occasionally enquired after my health, and Oliver, who he had assigned to me. The young knight took care of me, tightening the bandage on my arm when it worked loose during the ride. The first time we stopped, he bound my feet, which were becoming increasingly painful from the burns. He assured me we'd arrive at Beauvane Castle soon, where I would be tended to properly.

At night I would wake, crying with pain, to find myself in Oliver's arms. He shushed me to sleep, silencing the protests from the men I had woken. The injuries from de Tourrard's beating were healing but the burns to my legs penetrated my dreams. About halfway to our destination. I woke, screaming from a nightmare, crying out for Percy. Thinking he stood before me, my eyes cleared then I recognized Oliver, his expression laced with concern.

"Hush lady, you are safe."

"Percy…"

"No, lady. 'Tis Oliver. Who is Percy?"

"A young man unfortunate enough to have secured my friendship," I sighed. "Mortlock had him executed. He put his head on a pike for all to see and made me take my meal sitting next to the poor man's severed head. The world is full of evil, Oliver."

"Aye, my lady, there is great evil in the world, but also great good. Do not fear de Beauvane. Your fortunes changed for the better the day he took you into his care."

When we reached our destination the sun was low in the sky, casting long shadows across the road. A soft pink glow illuminated the stones of a huge building which stood on a raised area of land, surrounded by a high bailey wall. Built after Duke William's invasion, the castle had been constructed from a combination of English stones and lighter colored stones brought over from France, giving it a banded appearance. A wide moat surrounded the castle. The horses' hooves clattered against the wooden drawbridge as we crossed it.

The castle courtyard was full of people; villagers and servants alike. They greeted their lord enthusiastically, welcoming him home. De Beauvane clearly commanded great love and loyalty among his people, ruling them with respect rather than the fear I had grown up with. Who was this man? What did he want with me?

The party dismounted, handing the horses to the grooms and squires who had come running as soon as our arrival had been announced. A tall, slender woman stood at the main doorway. She was elegantly dressed in a purple surcoat over a gown of blue silk, her graying hair almost completely covered by her wimple.

"Husband."

De Beauvane clasped her hands and kissed her full on the mouth before taking her in his arms. I stood back, reluctant to intrude on their reunion. Their love was obvious. How different might my life have been had Papa married me to such a man!

De Beauvane released his wife and beckoned to me. With Oliver's support I limped toward her.

"Adelia, I present to you my mistress."

I hung my head in shame, but she looked at me kindly and took my hands.

"Nay, I cannot do this." I drew away, but she pulled me back and embraced me.

"Come, child, you are my guest and are most welcome. I have a chamber ready for you. You must be exhausted, you poor dear, and I can see you're hurt."

"How can you be so kind to me?" I asked.

"Because you have nothing to be ashamed of. And please call me Adelia, if I may be permitted to call you Lisetta?"

I nodded, and she smiled again. Her soft, caring manner reminded me of Maman.

"Oliver, help Lisetta to her chamber."

"Aye, my lady." Oliver lifted me in his arms. Kindness shone in his soft brown eyes. He reminded me so much of poor Percy, and I rejoiced in his fortune at having a kinder lord than Percy's. He followed Adelia into the building where she led us to a bedchamber.

The chamber was warm and welcoming, a fire blazing in the hearth. Tapestries lined the walls to keep out the draughts. A solid oak bed covered with thick furs dominated the room. At a word from Adelia, Oliver placed me on the bed. We had been followed by two maidservants. Adelia instructed one woman to undress me and nodded to the other who held out a goblet, full of some liquid. I pushed the goblet away.

"Lady Adelia, your husband said he would explain all when we arrived here."

"Drink first," she insisted. "You're in no state to discuss anything".

I took the draught and almost immediately a warm sensation overtook me. Reason told me that de Beauvane would hardly risk the king's wrath to prevent my execution then carry me halfway across England, only to poison me as soon as I reached his home. But I dropped the goblet and tried to stand. Adelia pushed me back.

"Shhh, rest now. You are under our protection and will not be harmed. We can discuss matters when you are well."

A warm blanket of sleep overtook me and my eyes lost focus. The patterns on the tapestries morphed into dancing whorls of blue and gray, slowly spinning to an inaudible rhythm.

In the distance Adelia's musical voice spoke while her gentle fingers caressed my forehead.

"Nay, she is not well, but she will recover. Trust us. She is in good hands."

A low murmur joined her voice. I struggled to hear the words but my body sank under the bed furs. The last thing I saw before I finally closed my eyes, were the whorls of blue which spiraled together, forming two intense pools before darkness claimed me once again. If this was death at de Beauvane's hands, it was far gentler than the death I had been expecting.

Chapter 28

For the next five days and nights I remained in the chamber and received greater care and attention from Lady Adelia and her maidservants than I had experienced since Maman's death. I found myself almost completely unable to move or speak. Initially I was afraid I had been poisoned, but Adelia explained my body had merely yielded to the exertions and horrors of the past months. Unable to sit unaided or move without pain, I had no choice but to trust her.

The first time I woke after a drug-induced, but peaceful sleep, my senses came to life at the aroma of herbs and spices and the sound of splashing water. Adelia bathed me personally. She rinsed and combed my matted, lice-ridden hair which someone had hacked short while I had lain unconscious. Though the lady of the estate would often bathe her male guests, women were not usually afforded such honor. She silenced my thanks with a smile and a gentle hand on my forehead, issuing instructions to her maidservants in a low voice while she dressed my wounds.

My worst injuries were the burns on my legs and feet, which she treated with an ointment not unlike the calendula salve I had made at Mortlock. My arm, though sore, was healing well. The swelling around my broken nose subsided, and I could breathe freely again. The marks from de Tourrard's beating were fading, but the maidservants could not contain their cries at the bruises and welts on my body when they first undressed me to lower me into the bathtub.

Adelia fed me personally, offering up a light broth, spoon by spoon, while I lay, exhausted, on the bed. She had a natural maternal instinct and knew even before I did when I'd eaten enough for my weakened stomach to handle. She gave me a little more each day as my appetite increased.

On the morning of the sixth day I woke feeling much stronger. With Adelia's help I climbed out of the bed and sat at a table in the chamber to break my fast. She had brought a more substantial meal and smiled with encouragement at my efforts to eat unaided.

"You are recovering well, child. My husband is most anxious to see you better."

I thanked her and took another bite of the stew. She watched me closely until I finished eating.

She placed a hand on my bandaged arm. "How did you come by such extensive injuries? I have never seen my maidservants so distressed. I understand the burns, but not the other injuries, the broken bones and the bruises. What happened to you?"

Unwilling to trust anyone, I remained silent, but she persisted.

"Rest assured you are safe here, my dear. It must be difficult for you to place your trust in others, but we mean you no harm. You committed no sin that I know of."

I shook my head. "You're mistaken. I have committed adultery and murder."

"Tell me about the man you killed."

I told her about de Tourrard, and the poison I had

made for myself. I expected her to recoil in horror but she did not.

"What of the adultery?" she asked. "How did you fall into de Tourrard's hands?"

"I had no choice," I sighed. "I could not help what happened to me, nor the direction in which my heart travelled."

"Tell me, my dear. Tell me all that you have done and all that has happened to you."

I shook my head. "I cannot."

She sighed and her voice grew stern. "You must understand, Lisetta. The daughter, widow, and—betrothed—of three renowned traitors, will not be judged with friendly eyes or ears by those loyal to the king. My husband risks much in giving you his protection. He asks for nothing in return but your honesty."

I bit my lip, knowing I could not escape the truth. Eventually I would have to relate my history, either to Adelia or to her husband. Rather than subject me to his form of interrogation, De Beauvane must have decided that a siege at softer hands would breach my defenses more readily. I flinched, recalling his iron grip on me. My resolve crumbled at the memory of his strong voice, his hard eyes and stern demeanor. He may not be an evil man like de Tourrard, yet I still feared him. My fate lay in his hands.

With nothing left to lose, I told Adelia my story, beginning with the day I arrived at Mortlock, a hopeful young bride, to the day I was brought to execution, an adulteress and murderess, twice widowed, who had given away one child and miscarried another.

I kept my eyes cast down as I spoke, afraid her

silence indicated revulsion and hatred. When finished, I clasped my hands, trembling with the effort to maintain an even voice. My body shook to suppress the sobs when I spoke of Vane and Geoffrey. She pulled my hands apart, tutting at the imprints of my fingernails on my palms. I bit my lip, focusing on the sharp pain, seeking comfort in it while I waited for her judgement and condemnation.

I flinched at a movement near my face but felt nothing except a light caress as if a feather brushed my cheek. Adelia ran a light finger down my face, following the line of the tears I had not realized I was shedding.

My calm demeanor shattered as soft, loving arms enveloped me. Once again, the wall I had built up against my emotions was destroyed by kindness. I reached out to the woman holding me in her arms and let out an inhuman wail. My heart burst with desolation at what I'd endured and all I had lost. I cried for Maman while she rocked me back and forth, singing softly to me as if I were a fevered child.

"Shhh, ma petite, *Maman est avec vous.*"

She held me as I grew quiet, comforting me like her own daughter, until three loud knocks on the door made us both jump.

Adelia smoothed my hair with her hands and whispered, "Courage, child," before calling out. The door opened and de Beauvane entered.

An imposing figure in a chain mail *hauberk,* he was even more intimidating dressed in finery—soft calfskin boots, a tunic of dark blue velvet, embroidered in gold. His broad shoulders all but filled the doorway. When I lifted my eyes to his face, he was looking directly at me. His arm muscles rippled as he beckoned to his wife, never once taking his unsmiling eyes off me.

"Leave us, wife." His voice, though quiet, carried across the room and Adelia immediately stood. Afraid, I reached out to her, and she took my hand.

"Now, Adelia. I will not ask again."

She released my hand as if it burned her, dropping a curtsey to her husband. As she passed him, she whispered into his ear, and his lips curled into a slight smile before he turned his stern gaze upon me once again.

"May I sit?"

I nodded, gesturing to a chair.

Sitting down, he stretched his long legs and looked me up and down. I waited for him to break the silence but he did not. Eventually he leaned back. Though his body appeared relaxed, his eyes told me he was anything but. Observant and insightful, he could penetrate my thoughts from a mere glance, let alone such careful scrutiny.

I almost burst with the need to speak, to ask him what he wanted with me. But I was determined not to show weakness. I lifted my head, forcing myself to maintain eye contact.

"I trust you are recovered."

It was a statement, not a question. I nodded.

"...and Adelia has not failed in her duties to be hospitable?"

"No!" I burst out, unwilling for him to find fault with his wife. "She has been most attentive. She could not have been kinder—"

I broke off, smoothing my face back into its

emotionless mask.

The ghost of a smile played on his lips, and he leaned forward.

"I must decide what is to be done with you."

"With me?"

"Aye. If you're able to convince me of your loyalty to King Henry, you are free to remain a member of my household."

"I have explained to Adelia…"

"I would have you explain to *me*."

"Your preventing my execution would imply you need no explanation."

"I was persuaded by another to stop the execution. But *you* must still convince me of your worth."

Wearied by the continual accusations of treachery, I could barely control my anger.

"What can any woman say or do to convince a man of anything? I've been branded a traitor merely by association with the men who held power over me. A woman's worth is measured only in relation to the men who control her. I have no desire to be subjected to that again."

"God's bones, woman, have you no sense?" he said, his calm demeanor dissolving. "Have you no interest in knowing who spoke to me on your behalf— or why I risked my men and my reputation to drag you from the pyre?"

"Forgive me if I seem ungrateful, my lord, but I had accepted my fate. I was ready to welcome the death you prevented."

"Would you not wish for the protection and respectability a husband can give you?"

I shook my head. "I have no wish to marry again.

I'd rather enter a convent."

"I am not minded to procure the funds to secure a place for you. Even if I was, no convent would accept you."

I bit my lip at the insult but said nothing. Why should I not be surprised he thought me a whore?

He sighed. "You are young and healthy. One of my knights has requested an audience with you. If, as you say, the world judges you by the men in whose power you place yourself, then as his wife you would be free from any suspicion."

I gritted my teeth in frustration. Once again I would be given to a man against my will. I closed my eyes and rubbed my aching forehead.

"Have you nothing to say, madam?"

"Nay."

"Very well," he said. "I will not press the matter now. But we must discuss your future soon. Marriage is the only option to assure the king of your loyalty. He released you into my care. As your overlord I am expected to find a suitable husband for you. My knights do as they're bid and marry at my direction. Their wives enjoy comfort and status."

"I care nothing for rank or nobility."

"Perhaps you'd be more easily persuaded if you understood it's not just *your* future at stake."

Standing, he opened the door and called out. After a short while a young woman entered, holding a bundle wrapped in a blanket. I heard a mewling cry which tugged sharply on my instincts, calling to me on a primal level. Without thinking I rushed over to her. I pulled back the blanket and cried out on recognizing the babe in her arms.

Geoffrey.

Silently, she held him out to me, and I clutched him to my breast and fell to my knees. Huge sobs tore from my throat as I rocked him back and forth.

"Geoffrey! Oh, my son, my beloved son...*mon petit fils*...I thought I'd never see you again..."

My child had grown while we had been apart. I pressed my face against him and drank in his beautiful baby smell. Cradling him in my arms, I ran a fingertip down his sweet face, marveling at the smooth, fair skin. His little pink fist uncurled as I ran my finger across his palm, then curled again as he clasped my finger. He gurgled with pleasure, his face lighting up with joy. Through the tears I let out a laugh.

"Yes, my sweet one, Maman is here, and she will never leave you again."

A hand touched my shoulder. De Beauvane had knelt beside me.

"Sir Roger"—I choked—"I cannot thank you enough."

"My dear, nothing has given me greater pleasure. I wonder, however, at your gratitude, when you show me none for sparing your life."

"I'm grateful for that too, my lord; for you have reunited me with my son. I am in your debt. I know you don't need my approval or permission to be my overlord, but I gladly give it."

"Perhaps I have misjudged you," he said, "I can now see the quality in you that *he* has done."

"Who?"

"Why my knight, of course. He saw you on the battlements during the siege at Shoreton, and persuaded me to spare your execution."

Mon Dieu. The man who fought—and killed—Papa, who warned me about the trebuchet's missile. Was it he who argued for my release? Who was he to base such actions on a mere glance from a distance?

"Who is he?"

"He goes by the name of Tarvin de Fowensal."

His words extinguished the small ray of hope in my heart. Tarvin, who I had thought was dead, was alive. But it was not his resurrection I hoped and prayed for.

"I believe you knew him?" de Beauvane asked softly, "you loved him?"

"I had thought I loved him," I said, sadly. "His letters were a great comfort when I was alone and friendless. He made me realize it was possible to experience love. But I grew to love another. Part of me will always care for Tarvin, but I cannot marry him. I would not make him happy. The man I love is dead."

"You love that man still?"

"I always will." I blinked back tears. "Tarvin deserves better than I. You said yourself I was known to be a whore. I am also a murderess. I could not let him bear the shame of it."

"Ah, yes, I have spoken with Oliver. It seems de Tourrard took his own life, mistaken or no. All the king would have to be angry for is how you denied him the pleasure of executing a traitor. Tarvin would be proud to be married to the woman who rid the world of such a man."

I shook my head. "My lord, he does not deserve a woman who will spend the rest of her days loving a dead man."

"In time you will come to love another."

"Perhaps, but I cannot risk the heart or happiness

of a good man by marrying in haste."

He studied me for a moment then smiled. "You are an unusual woman, Lisetta. You're not afraid to speak your mind. Few men dare be so bold with me."

"What would the purpose be in deception?" I asked. "If you meant me harm, my boldness would not change that."

To my surprise he laughed. "I can see the attraction. 'Tis no disrespect to my beautiful Adelia to say I'm glad I am not twenty summers younger. I will not force you to marry, but there are few alternatives. You could remain here as my mistress..." he raised a hand to stop my protest "...in name only, my dear. You would be left chaste but your position would ensure your protection."

"Could I not be given a position as a servant? As chatelaine, or lady in waiting to Adelia?"

"You would rather be a servant than the wife of a knight?"

"The life of a lady has brought me no joy, Sir Roger. I had a brief moment of happiness when I lived as a peasant, when I loved—and lived—humbly but honestly."

De Beauvane looked at me, curiosity in his expression, and a smile played on his lips.

"The position of a servant is, of course, out of the question," he said, "but we will speak no more of it today; you need to rest. Let Lena take your son. She'll take good care of him and will continue to do so as long as you require."

As much as I wanted to argue, I let the maidservant take Geoffrey. Sir Roger was right; I could barely keep my eyes open. So many questions swirled in my mind.

Who was Tarvin? How did he escape Mortlock alive? How did de Beauvane find Geoffrey? What had happened to Jack and Lily? My head ached with it all, but I clung to what was real. Geoffrey was alive, and I would never willingly be parted from my son again.

"Join us in the main hall tomorrow night," de Beauvane said. "We'll decide your future then— whether you are to marry or become my mistress."

He held out his hand and as I took it, he bowed and kissed my fingers.

"Until tomorrow."

Shortly after he left, another maidservant entered the room and helped me back into the bed. Adelia visited me later.

"You have nothing to fear, child," she said. "My husband believes and trusts you. Both you and your son will be taken care of."

"How did Geoffrey come to be here?" I asked. "I understand nothing of what happened, or Sir Roger's role in it."

"I know," Adelia said. "My husband will grant you an audience before we dine tomorrow, and you will understand then."

She insisted I take another sleeping draught, and I did not resist. She covered me with the bed fur and held my hand until sleep overcame me once more.

****

The next evening I waited in my chamber for Sir Roger's summons. Adelia had given me one of her gowns. She was taller than I and I'd lost weight in the past months, so the gown hung loosely on my frame. Her maidservants treated me like a delicate piece of parchment ready to crumble to dust at the slightest

298

touch. They dressed me with gentle hands, taking care with my bandaged arm as they fitted the undergown and surcoat. There was little they could do with my hair which barely touched my shoulders, but a veil disguised the short locks. Adelia declared that despite the fading bruises on my face, I was unrecognizable from the filthy, battered creature her husband had brought into her home.

Adelia understood my distress. I had no wish to disgrace her in a position as her husband's mistress but she reassured me there was no shame in it. Most noblemen had mistresses, many enjoying a position of rank almost equal to that of a wife. De Beauvane, though faithful to Adelia, would maintain a façade for my protection and to provide a future for Geoffrey. They had one child—a son who had been fostered at a young age and now served the king. But they had not been blessed with others. They had room for Geoffrey in their heart and household, and as Sir Roger's mistress I would remain with him.

At a summons from one of Sir Roger's men, Adelia led me to a chamber beside the main hall. The chamber was lit by a single candle on the desk at which Sir Roger sat. A small chair had been placed before the desk, and he gestured to me to sit while he dismissed his wife.

The murmur of voices could be heard from the dining hall, and I began to tremble. Tonight my fate would be decided and declared publicly before the entire household.

Sir Roger glanced over his shoulder into the darkness behind him. Leaning forward he placed his elbows on the table, the movement bringing his face into the candlelight. A faint trace of amusement danced in his eyes.

"So, Lisetta. Marriage or mistress?"

"I am not willing to marry, my lord."

"Tell me why."

"I have already done so."

"Indulge me by telling me again."

"Because I love another."

"Tell me about him."

"My lord, I see no benefit in doing so. He is dead and it pains me to think of it."

"Nevertheless, I insist."

"Very well," I said. "The only man I have ever loved was a servant. A peasant. Bastard born."

I had expected Sir Roger to react but he merely smiled.

"Did he love you in return?"

"Nay, he did not," I said, wiping my eyes. "I saw the love he had for others, yet he only ever looked at me with indifference. He left me to go whoring, thinking me a whore myself, while I gave birth to our son, and it broke my heart."

My voice cracked. "Please, don't make me marry again. I have no wish to experience another marriage without love or to break the heart of a good, honest man. I have known the pain of loving so deeply and not having that love returned. I will not inflict that pain on another."

De Beauvane let out a sigh. "Tarvin would understand, child, and he is not a man to judge. He would be willing to risk a little heartbreak. Men are different than women, my dear. Our hearts are a little sturdier. At least let him speak with you before you make your final decision. You owe him—and me— that."

"Very well," I said, "but not today, I beg you. I feel nothing but shame for the words I wrote to him, knowing I cannot love him."

Ignoring me, he looked over his shoulder.

"I believe you have heard enough. You can show yourself now and claim your wife."

A shape moved in the dark behind Sir Roger. I had been tricked.

"Nay!" I cried, rising from my chair. Ignoring Sir Roger's order to stop, I ran toward the door. I heard a crash as the desk was swept aside. Sir Roger was on me before I reached the handle. He took hold of my arm.

"Be still, madam," he ordered. "Remember you're under my authority." He turned me to face the man who had been concealed in the dark.

"Step forward."

The man moved toward us, making no sound. He closed the distance until I could feel the heat radiating from his body.

He was tall—he even dwarfed Sir Roger—but where Sir Roger's frame was broad, the man before me was lean yet muscular. Thick hair fell to his shoulders in waves. His brow creased into a frown and his nostrils flared. His jaw was set hard and his mouth firm—the full lips unsmiling. I followed the line of a scar, its redness indicating the wound was recent, which curled up the side of his face. When I finally summoned the strength to meet his gaze, strong blue eyes, dark with anger, bore into me.

My throat constricted as I tried to breathe and my legs felt as if they had turned to liquid. Sir Roger's arms tightened around my waist to prevent me from falling. He lifted my arm and guided my hand toward the man standing in front of me until he took it. The shock of recognition tightened my skin as his flesh touched mine. My body silently called out and was rewarded with a response as long, lean fingers curled around my wrist in a possessive grip.

"*Mon Dieu*," I whispered. Despite all my prayers, never did I think I would see a man return from the dead.

The living, breathing man standing before me was Vane Sawford.

Chapter 29

I stared at my husband, oblivious of Sir Roger's presence until he released my arm, took his leave, and closed the door behind him. Vane continued to focus his eyes on me, the anger in their expression only intensifying.

"You're dead!" I cried. "De Tourrard told me he tore out your heart. He showed it to me!"

"He lied."

"But you let me believe it! You heard me pour my heart out to another while you hid like a coward in the dark. Did what I say give you satisfaction?"

He shook his head, his eyes blazing.

"What right have you to be angry with me?" I screamed. Drawing my free hand into a fist, I pummeled him on the chest. He stood still as stone, weathering the blows. Finally I relented, sobbing in frustration at his lack of reaction, and he drew me to him.

"I am not angry with you *cherie*," he said quietly.

"You deceived me."

"I had to convince my overlord you were a worthy choice and not a traitor; that you do not seek to secure your position by manipulating yourself into his household. In marrying you without his permission, I did him a grave insult."

"'Twas your choice, not mine! Or does your

memory serve you so poorly you forget you took me unwilling? Is de Beauvane's opinion of women even lower than yours, or merely his opinion of me?"

I struggled against his arms, but he only tightened his hold.

"I freely admit my opinion of women. They are impelled by a desire to further themselves in the world by seduction and betrayal. Too often have I seen it. But you, *sweetling*, are different. Your actions are driven by love, as mine have been."

I shook my head, "Nay."

He cupped my chin in his hand. "Aye, Lisetta. I heard your words to my brother that night, the admission of sins you had not committed. You condemned yourself as an unfit mother so Lily would take your child, and you risked your life to warn us. Was that not an act of love?"

"Mayhap," I said bitterly, "but as for your actions—is not one whore easily replaced by another? Did you not say those very same words to Celia, before taking me for yourself?"

He loosened his hold and pushed me away. I could almost hear my heart rip in two. I turned my back, reached for the door, and pressed my forehead against the wood. He remained silent, and I turned the handle, wanting nothing but to leave with the pieces of my shattered soul.

"Stay, damn you!"

The angry demand only served to fragment my heart further.

"Why?" I turned to face him, my voice cold. The mask slipped into place once more—my only defense against him.

304

He placed a hand on the door either side of me, imprisoning me with his arms.

"Because you pledged to obey me."

"Aye, I did," I snarled. "Your whores may do as they please, but your wife is bound to you by law and by the church."

The door jerked as he smashed his fist against it. He brought his face close to mine, the intensity of the anger and pain in his eyes rendering me immobile.

"Satan's bones, woman!" he said through gritted teeth, "do you want me to beg? Will that give *you* satisfaction?"

I shook my head, unwilling to trust myself to speak, blinking away the moisture in my eyes.

"Nevertheless, I will."

He took my hands in his own, tenderly caressing my palms with his thumbs. My body tightened with a mixture of fear and yearning at the feel of his skin against mine. His gentle touch destroyed my defenses, releasing the tears which rolled unchecked down my face until I tasted salt and desolation on my lips.

Slowly, he lowered himself onto his knees, his eyes never leaving mine. He circled his arms around my waist and drew me to him.

"Lisetta, do not leave me. I cannot live without you. Forgive me, my love. Forgive my deception. I wanted you to love me, but I was willing to remain dead in your eyes so you could be free to find love with another. That is why I remained hidden."

"Vane—"

"No, let me tell all. From the moment I saw you I wanted you, but only when you cried out in the dark that night I first took you did I understand the depth of my desire. I knew then I could love you. Every action I undertook since, was to ensure your protection."

"But you treated me…"

"…so cruelly, *sweetling*, I know. I bear great shame for my actions toward you, but I was so proud of your strength. You carried yourself with dignity and bore your burden at Mortlock more bravely than any man. I only saw glimpses of your inner feelings when we were alone at night, or during the day when others showed you compassion. Percy and Harwyn—you suffered for the kindness they showed you."

I flinched at the memory of their deaths. Vane looked up at me, his eyes laden with vulnerability and, unmistakably, for the first time, love.

"Tell me honestly, my love—had I been openly kind to you, had you known the depth of my love, would you have had the resolve to withstand Mortlock's treatment and conceal your feelings? Had you acted inappropriately he would have had you killed. I did what was necessary to prevent it."

"But you treated me like a whore!"

"Believe me, I had no wish to. Your fate was sealed the day you married Mortlock. You were to be given to any number of men of my choice, to be mounted like a mare in heat, then discarded after you served your purpose. I could not bear to give you to others so I took you for myself. I wish I could have treated you more kindly. You may have suffered at my hands but the alternatives were not to be borne."

"You were so cold," I whispered.

"We both had a role to play," he said. "De Beauvane had secured my position to gain Mortlock's trust. It gave me no pleasure to meet Celia in your chamber while she tended to you but it was the only way to be near you, to watch over you without arousing suspicion. As for lying with you shortly afterward—*cherie*, you must forgive the needs and weaknesses of a mortal man. I wanted you. I still do. Devil take me, woman, I crave you so much I could die from it."

"But 'twas not merely the needs of the flesh that drew me to you, my love. I saw and understood your courage. I had no wish for you to be entirely friendless. As Tarvin I could give you hope, the ability to nourish the strength from within you to endure the events to come."

"Why did you never tell me you were Tarvin?" I cried. "Why did you let me think he had died, that I had lost a friend?"

"Lisetta, you loved him and hated me. You cried *his* name when I took you. To reveal that the man who gave you such hope was an illusion created by a man you hated—I couldn't do that to you. And yet, even though you hated me, you tended to my wound with such care. Woman, you even saved my life. To see you in that forest, soaked to the skin, heavy with child, brandishing your knife, prepared to defend me against another! Your eyes were full of courage—how I loved you at that moment! I began to hope you might grow to love me."

"I did grow to love you, Vane," I whispered, "though it brought me no joy. Outside the confines of Mortlock I saw something of the man behind the mask, how you treated Jack and Lily with love. Yet you turned unfriendly eyes toward me. You believed me a whore—a seducer of your brother, though it was you who went out whoring."

"Was that why you left me?"

His accusation stung.

"Could you blame me? I could bear it no longer. I wanted my son to be like you, but I did not want him to be brought up to despise me as you did. Selfish I may have been, Vane, but if I could not have your love, then by leaving you I could ensure I would have Geoffrey's."

"Yet you risked your life to return."

"Only to ensure Geoffrey's safety. When I realized I would never be free of de Tourrard, all I had left in my power to do was ensure Geoffrey would not have to endure him."

Vane sighed, "'Tis as Jack thought. He said I was a fool to let you go. He persuaded me to look for you after he saw your letter to Tarvin. It was a name I often adopted when spying for de Beauvane—a silly made up name from our childhood—a play on the letters of my own name. Valentine Sawford became Tarvin de Fowensal. I was angry and jealous, seeing the easy friendship between you and Jack. Lily told me you had claimed the babe you carried was another's. I thought you had spoken out of hatred for me."

I shook my head, "Nay, Vane. I spoke out of love. Lily loved you as a sister. She had great faith in your goodness. I could not shatter that faith. I handed Geoffrey to them because I wanted him to grow up in a loving family. After Maman died there was no love in my life. I grew cold and unloving in order to survive. I wanted no such life for our son."

"Oh, Lisetta!" Vane's voice wavered with emotion. "You are neither cold nor unloving. I know what you have suffered in the name of love. The lady Adelia has shown me. I have seen with my own eyes what you endured on my behalf and to protect our son. My greatest wish is that you had not killed de Tourrard yourself. As your husband, lover, and protector, it was *my* duty."

He drew me down to kneel with him and took my face in his hands.

"I tried to find you, Lisetta. I bitterly regret what I said to you. I visited no whores, my love. I wanted to hurt you, to make you as jealous as I was. But it did not ease my pain, for I only succeeded in losing you. After you had gone, I told Jack and Lily to leave with Geoffrey, but I stayed behind to look for you. I found where they held you but they spotted me. I tried again when Shoreton was besieged. I was among the first who broke into the bailey, but I couldn't fight through. A man stopped me. Forgive me, Lisetta for not being able to free you."

A man stopped me. "Papa—that was *you* at Shoreton—you who killed him?"

"Aye. Forgive me."

I shook my head. "You need no forgiveness. 'Tis a sin to say, but you delivered his due reward for what he did to Maman. But he injured your arm. I saw you fall."

"It heals," he said, a smile forming on his lips, "but your concern pleases me."

He leaned forward to brush his lips against mine but before I could kiss him back, he pulled away. I frowned at the sense of loss.

"Vane…"

"Hush, *sweetling*, I must first ask you something." He caressed my cheeks with his thumbs and brought his face close until I could see nothing but his beautiful eyes. That vivid blue had comforted me during my nightmares. It had not been Maman's ghost watching over me in the darkness, but someone living, someone who loved me just as much.

"I would ask you to be my wife."

"I am already."

"Aye, but now I ask you openly, as I dreamed of doing when first I looked into your eyes, kneeling before you as a man in love."

I hesitated, and he drew me to him, kissing me on the lips. "Do not fear love, *ma cherie*, it can bring you joy if you let it. My heart is yours—yours alone, and forever."

My heart burst with love and I lifted my hands to his, smiling through the tears.

"Ah, my love," he said gently, "'tis the first time I have seen you smile for *me*, and I would not have your beauty marred by tears."

"They are tears of joy, husband."

"Then you will have me?"

"I will gladly give myself to you."

He kissed me again and I melted into his embrace. I offered him my lips and sighed into his mouth as his tongue begged entrance. I replied with my own tongue, drawing him into a slow, sensual dance. I gloried in the taste of him, the taste of wine, spices and man, a heady cocktail that obliterated my senses. I was completely at his mercy, but I willingly yielded to him. After a long journey I had finally reached my home.

Chapter 30

A knock on the door shattered the moment, and we jerked apart. Frustration scorched across Vane's face, and he called out in a pained voice. Sir Roger answered, instructing us to attend the feast without delay, adding that now he could no longer hear fighting, he trusted we were both still alive.

"We'll be there directly." Vane spoke through gritted teeth, and we heard a low laugh from the other side of the door.

"God damn the man!" Vane swore.

"'Tis but an interruption."

"Aye," he said crossly, "but my body has been in need of you these past months. I'm in agony with it and now I will not find the release inside you that I crave." He stood up as if in pain before pulling me up against him. The source of his agony pulsed hotly against my thigh.

"Come, let us dine, husband. I promise I'll ease your pain later should you still need it."

Sir Roger and Lady Adelia waited for us at the entrance to the hall. Together we filed in amid murmurs from the assembled company. Oliver sat at one of the tables. As I passed him he stood and bowed.

"'Tis good to see you restored to full health, my lady."

Before I could thank him, a firm hand pressed

possessively against the base of my spine. With a low growl, Vane ordered Oliver to sit before he propelled me forward. I glanced back at Oliver's shocked face, but a sharp tug on my arm kept me moving.

We sat down and the hall fell silent. After a moment, Sir Roger stood and cleared his throat.

"Friends, we are gathered here tonight to celebrate our victory over those who would destroy England's stability and Henry's reign."

A thundering noise reverberated around the hall as the company thumped the tables with their fists in approval. Sir Roger held up his hands for silence.

"We're also here to welcome a young woman into our household, reunited with her husband. Until now we have been unable to celebrate their marriage, but tonight we do so. Company, I give you Sir Valentine and Lady Sawford!"

Adelia nodded to me, and I stood, together with Vane, who took my hand and raised it in salute. The company cheered in response. The only face I recognized was Oliver's. He raised his goblet, a shy smile on his face.

Sir Roger nodded toward the door, and a line of servants entered, carrying huge platters of food which they distributed among the tables, serving the high table first. Vane ladled potage onto the trencher we shared—a large hunk of stale bread which would be given to the poor of the village once the meal was finished.

He fed me morsel after morsel, alternating between holding a piece to my lips and taking a bite himself. His face was stern, his body tense. Ignoring him, I sipped my wine and spoke to Adelia who sat on my left.

"What is that young man to you?" a gruff voice

made me turn back to him.

"Oliver?"

"A mere boy, I know not his name." His dismissive tone could not completely disguise his jealousy, and I smiled to myself.

"Oliver first visited me in the guise of a priest and heard my confession. He was enquiring after my health tonight, nothing more."

"Nothing more!" Vane grumbled as he continued to chew, his eyes staring at a fixed point in front of him.

"He heard my full and frank confession," I said, "an account of my sins and of my heart. Given that, do you think him foolish enough to speak to me on any terms other than a casual acquaintance? Unless, of course, he lacks all wit and is unaware that *you* are Vane Sawford."

His jaw showed a slight tic, but he continued to stare straight ahead.

"Husband, why should the company of a *mere boy* interest me over that of a man?"

He continued eating, his expression dark.

"Lord have mercy on you, you fool!" I hissed. "Do you wish me to speak plainer and say I love none but you? Please tell me how often I need to repeat it, or are you only convinced when you skulk in the dark and eavesdrop on private conversations?"

Not answering, he lifted his wine goblet and took a sip.

"Have a care, husband, or I will forget my promise to ease your pain—the agony you spoke of that can only be soothed by—"

"Be silent, wench!" He slammed the goblet onto the table, spilling the contents. A servant hurried over, thinking it a request for more wine.

"Thank you," I said brightly, "my husband is somewhat thirsty tonight."

Adelia made a small sound, not unlike a suppressed giggle. Vane's jaw was set hard but the corners of his mouth were beginning to curl into a smile.

"Witch! You torment me."

"Is that a request, husband?"

I was surprising myself by my boldness, but Adelia smiled encouragement. For the first time in my life I felt relaxed and happy.

Before the servants cleared away the meat dishes, Vane asked if we could be excused. Adelia nodded, a sly smile on her lips, before suggesting he escort me to my chamber.

"But the meal is not finished," I protested. "I have no wish to dishonor Sir Roger by taking my leave so early."

"My dear child," Adelia laughed, "did you not hear my husband? We celebrate your marriage tonight and thus you are expected to take your leave and consummate your union."

Vane pulled me to my feet and a cheer rose. I blushed at the bawdy remarks and gestures the men aimed at Vane as we crossed the floor. Approaching Oliver's seat, Vane glared and curled an arm round my waist, challenging him to speak. The young man blushed and cast his eyes down.

"Lovesick colt," Vane growled under his breath, "I've a good mind to geld him."

"Jealous, love?" I laughed.

The breath was forced from my lungs as Vane squeezed my body and tipped me back. He fondled my buttocks, tightening his hold, before sending a trail of kisses along my neck, until he reached my ear. He drew my earlobe into his mouth and nipped it sharply, the message clear though the words remained unspoken.

Mine.

"I believe only one stallion can satisfy this mare," he declared before swinging me up over his shoulder. A rowdy cheer erupted.

"Let me down!" I struggled in his grip, but a sharp smack on my buttocks told me he had no intention of doing so. The cheering increased, and I surrendered, letting him carry me out amid the joyous cacophony of thumping and laughter.

Vane kicked my chamber door open, letting it crash against the wall before setting me back on my feet and slamming the door behind us. I backed away. A platter had been placed on the table and a pile of honeyed figs glistened in the candlelight, together with a flagon and two goblets. Instinctively I reached for a fig.

"Do not touch them." Vane advanced toward me, his tall frame dominating the room, the suppressed strength in his muscles rippling underneath his tunic. His eyes were dark, almost black, their expression ravenous.

"Wife, remove your clothes."

A shiver of fear rose inside me until his mouth lifted into a broad smile. His eyes danced with merriment.

"As my husband wishes." Moving toward the bed, I unlaced my gown and stepped out of my slippers before pulling off the surcoat and undergown. I lifted my thin chemise over my head to reveal my naked body.

A low growl made me look up. Vane stood before me in all his naked glory, his hard muscular body tense. His shoulders sloped downward, and I followed a line with my gaze down his throat, drinking in the sight of him; the hard planes of his chest covered with a light dusting of black hair, the muscles of his stomach, which dipped into a v shape above his groin. Nestling amid a mass of black curls, his beautiful manhood jutted out, thick and firm, beckoning to me.

My skin tightened with need, and my breasts ached, the nipples puckering from the heat of Vane's smoldering gaze. A fire radiated from my core, which began to pulse faintly. Embarrassed, I lifted my hands to cover myself, but he shook his head, his voice a low rumble.

"Lie back on the bed."

I reached behind me until I felt the edge of the bed. Not taking my eyes off him I lay back and waited.

"Close your eyes."

"Vane…"

"Do as you are bid."

Closing my eyes heightened my other senses and my heart throbbed with anticipation. I heard movement but not knowing what he was doing only increased my need for him.

I sensed, rather than knew, he was close, when something brushed against my lips.

"Open your mouth."

I parted my lips, and a rush of sweetness burst on my tongue. Something grazed against my teeth. I took a bite, moaning with pleasure at the soft, rich flesh of the fig and the sweet, lush taste as the smooth liquid ran into my mouth. I leaned forward to finish it but was rewarded with a devilish chuckle.

"You must learn to share, wife."

He brushed his lips against mine. A moment later I felt another fig against my lips, and I opened my mouth to take it, but he moved it away, running it lightly across my chin and down my throat, leaving a trail of sticky honey. He kissed me again before following the line of honey with his lips. His hot tongue lapped up the sweetness, sending bursts of flame through my senses. Though lying on the bed, I felt as if I was falling, and I clutched the bed furs to steady myself.

A light swirling sensation caressed my skin. Vane brushed another fig across my throat, circling lower until it dipped into the valley between my breasts. He circled one breast, spiraling in until he reached the center. The cold sensation of honey was replaced by burning heat as he took my breast into his mouth. I cried out as he suckled, nipping it with his teeth before drawing his tongue across to soothe the sensitive little bud.

He kissed me again, and I drew his tongue into my mouth, tasting honey. Fisting my hands in his hair, I pulled him to me and drank from him, plundering his mouth mercilessly, wanting to devour him as he devoured me.

The bed moved with his weight, and he nudged my thighs apart. I could bear it no longer and opened my eyes. Two sapphires, darkened with passion, stared back into me, penetrating my soul. A glorious agony burned from within, and my body ached with a hunger which only he could satisfy.

"Vane…"

"Not yet, my love."

"Please, Vane—I need you."

He pushed my thighs farther apart and settled himself on top of me. His rigid manhood pulsed against my leg, and he kissed me again, pillaging my mouth as the tip of him begged entrance to my body. I stiffened with an involuntary surge of fear and squeezed my eyes shut, whimpering at the memory of the last man to take me.

"Shhh, *sweetling*, he is gone forever. Let me purge his memory from you and then we shall look only forward, to our future. Tonight I claim you as mine."

With these words, he sheathed himself into me with a single thrust, silencing my cry with his mouth. I opened my eyes in a brief moment of panic but saw nothing but intense blue—the blue that had comforted me in my darkest moments; which now radiated strength and love. He stilled his body and ran his lips over my face, kissing away the tears until I relaxed, letting my body stretch to accommodate him.

Vane pressed his forehead against mine and moved, easing himself out of me, before entering me again with a deep sigh as our bodies molded together. With each movement he increased the pace and a low sound rumbled in his throat, morphing into a moan of anguish.

"Is all well, my love?" I whispered.

He closed his eyes and leaned forward, burying his head in my shoulder. I reached up, holding him close, caressing his thick dark locks and gripping his hair as I lifted my hips to meet each thrust.

A sweet ache began to build where our bodies met, igniting into a scorching agony, begging to be eased, soaring and intensifying until I clawed at Vane, pleading for release. He placed his hands on the bed and lifted himself up, his muscles bulging and trembling with the strain. He threw his head back as if to face the stars, groaning as he continued to pound into me. The ache within me peaked until my body burst as if on fire, rippling with wave after wave, splintering my soul. He entered me with a final punishing thrust, and I screamed out his name while he roared into the night until his voice broke. He collapsed on top of me and rolled onto his side, still inside me. Holding me close, he whispered my name over and over.

We lay with our bodies fused together, unable to move or speak. His chest rose and fell against mine, sticky with sweat. I opened my eyes to see the love I bore him mirrored in the deep blue. His eyes crinkled into a smile and a single tear spilled over the brim. I lifted my hand to brush the tear away and stroked his forehead with my fingertips.

"Tonight I claim you as mine, my love," I whispered, smiling before I nestled into his embrace, where I belonged.

He smiled back, our hearts slowing to a soft rhythm in unison, until I drifted into sleep, safe in his arms, knowing I would never again be plagued by nightmares.

Epilogue

Five years later

"Maman, Maman!"

I lay still, not wishing to move, listening to the sound of the wind in the trees above me and the faint musical melody of the nearby stream.

"Maman!" The voice drew closer.

Summer was over but the heat of the sun bathed my face. The bright sunlight penetrated my eyelids, giving a sense of being enveloped in a warm, red blanket.

"Maman, they are coming! Sir Roger is on a big black horse!"

I rolled to one side, opening my eyes to look across the field. The roof of the hall was barely visible between tall pointed tufts which gently moved from side to side in the breeze. The wheat was growing, and I smiled at the prospect of a good harvest.

A strong arm pulled me back and a hand coiled around my waist and settled over my belly where the swelling was beginning to show. I covered the hand with my own, interlocking with the long, slim fingers.

Hurried footsteps approached and the voice called out again. A soft kiss landed on my forehead, and I looked up into a blue more brilliant than the sky overhead.

320

"Geoffrey grows impatient, *cherie.*" His deep voice reverberated through his body where I lay with my head in his lap, and I sighed.

"'Tis as if he wants to leave me."

Vane drew me to him and placed a kiss on my lips before helping me to my feet. We heard squeals of delight as our son caught sight of us. Cradling my face in his hands, Vane wiped away the tear that had begun to form before I had even realized it. My husband knew me better than I knew myself. He always would.

"'Tis a great honor for him, Lisetta, and he's not going far. Beauvane Castle is barely two days' ride away."

Geoffrey was to be fostered as a page to de Beauvane, the first step on his path to manhood and eventually knighthood. Sir Roger and Lady Adelia were to stay with us for a sennight before taking him back to Kent.

Shortly after Vane and I were reunited, Sir Roger granted Vane an estate situated between Beauvane Castle and London; a fertile plot of land with a hall and various outbuildings. The hall itself was considerably smaller than Shoreton and Mortlock, but it was warm and comfortable, and I had never been happier. The village and farm which served us had grown and prospered since we arrived. Sir Roger had established many of the villagers and servants from Shoreton, including Elspeth who kept house for us and looked after our children. Our servants even included some of the children from Mortlock. The night Vane had left me alone at the smith's hut, he'd returned to Mortlock in search of survivors, delivering them into de Beauvane's care, and including Cedric, who was now our head groom.

Jack and Lily visited us regularly, having settled nearby. Lily had been staying with us to spend time with Geoffrey before he left. I waved at her as I spotted Geoffrey pulling her behind him. My son adored his aunt. She would miss him almost as much as I.

As he reached us, Geoffrey threw his arms around my waist. At five summers he already reached my chest in height; he would likely grow to be taller even than his father. He chattered animatedly.

"*Tante* Lily was helping Elspeth in the kitchens when Cedric told us he saw them coming. Sir Roger has brought the big horse he said he will let me ride one day. He…"

My son's joy for life was infectious, but when I saw Lily her eyes were wet with tears which mirrored my own. She opened her arms, and we embraced while Vane lifted Geoffrey into the air, swinging him round as he screamed with laughter.

"Again, Papa, again!"

"No more, young sir, or I'll be unable to greet Sir Roger properly." My husband's voice was stern but his eyes sparkled with mirth. He set Geoffrey down and my son gave me another quick hug before he took Lily's hand and ran back to the hall, insisting that as the eldest son, the right and duty to lead the welcome party belonged to him.

Vane took my hand and gave it a reassuring squeeze.

"Lisetta my love, do not worry. Geoffrey will be in good hands. I know you'll miss him, but rejoice in his future; he'll grow up to be a knight like his father—as will little Henri."

"I could wish for nothing more for either of our sons than to be like you, Vane. For you are the best of men."

He pulled me close, turning me around so my back was against his chest, and he wrapped his arms around my front, caressing my belly. Our child responded to his touch, and he murmured with delight at the flutter of movement. He dipped his head and nipped my ear, his hot breath fanning my neck. "Perhaps after two sons you might bless me with a daughter to cherish."

I leaned into his warm body.

"She's considerably more restless than her brothers were. This past fortnight I have slept poorly."

He chuckled softly, molding his body against mine where his rigid manhood pulsed against my lower back.

"If I recall, wife, it's your husband who has been restless this past fortnight. He is in pain now, and I would have you soothe him."

"But Sir Roger, Lady Adelia…"

"…will be greeted by Geoffrey and will think no less of us for being otherwise occupied. Come, wife, I expect you to honor your vows and be obedient."

He was not in a mood to be denied, and he pulled me back down onto the blanket on which we had been lying.

"I. Love. You. Wife," he said, kissing me between each word on the forehead, nose, cheeks, before finally claiming my lips. I reached up, gladly opening myself to him. We made love in the field under the warmth of the evening sun before returning to our home, hand in hand as any young couple in love, to greet our overlord and dine with him before retiring to our chamber to share a plate of honeyed figs.

A word about the author…

Emily Royal grew up in Sussex, England and has always loved medieval knights, Highland heroes and Regency rogues. She began devouring romantic novels almost as soon as she was old enough to read. To indulge her passion for dark, sexy heroes, she began writing after moving to rural Scotland where she now lives with her family and menagerie of exotic pets including a boa constrictor called Twinkle.

Living a stone's throw away from a medieval palace, Emily finds inspiration each time she looks out of the window. When not writing, she enjoys target sports, for which she spent a brief period on the British team, as well as hill walking in the Scottish Highlands and painting.

Lightning Source UK Ltd.
Milton Keynes UK
UKHW020742140922
408851UK00009B/863